CONTENTS

CONTENTS

1. The Dancer

Don't be fooled by the sunshine in their faces. They are a sad people inside, tormented by the knowledge that one day the great mist will rise and suffocate them all to death. And no one can do anything about it. The mist has a mind of its own. It does what it wants to do when it wants to do it. No one can stop it. Even those who have the gift of controlling lightning and of sending it to destroy their enemies are powerless against the mist.

Yet they conduct their lives in song and laughter, as if their world will live for ever. In the evenings you can hear the girls singing the songs of the pumpkin. In the olden days these songs were heard only at harvest time. But nowadays the girls – sometimes joined by the lonely young women whose husbands are toiling in the mines a world away – sing them all year round. Even in the middle of winter, when the whole land hibernates under thick layers of snow, they sing and dance to the songs of the pumpkin. The white slush swallows their stamping feet right up to the calves, and then spits them out again in a frenzy. The maidens dance round in circles, to the sucking rhythms of their feet making vengeful love to the holes they have made in the snow.

They sing of lost loves and unfulfilled desires. Of husbands who have been devoured by the city of gold, never to return to their families again. Of young men who have become too big for their gumboots since graduating from looking after cattle at the cattle-posts to ferreting in the bowels of the earth for gold that will never be theirs. A maiden steps into the arena, kicking the mud-soiled snow, and laments in a voice that borrows from the men:

> If I were ruling and were in command,
> I would instruct that all the mines be closed.
> Be closed for all these haughty boys.
> They bother the girls with love proposals:
> You'll hear them say, 'Nywe, nywe, I love you.'
> Come my husband!

As she rhythmically recites her lament, the others clap their hands and punctuate each line with a chanted response. At the end they all shout, 'Come my wife!' and fall into each other's arms laughing, obviously proud of their performance.

They will sing and dance until night falls. Only darkness, and the fear of the things of the night will drive them home. If the moon is full they will carry on as if their sole responsibility in this world is to sing the songs of the pumpkin, until their angry mothers call for them, 'Hey you, lazy girl, who do you think will cook for the family while you are busy kicking your thin legs in the snow?' Indeed, for a reason no one understands, the village of Ha Samane has taken to cooking the evening meal late at night, instead of just before sunset like other villages throughout the land.

Dikosha threw her feet into the dying embers right under the three-legged pot. They were as hard as rock, almost frozen from all that stamping in the snow. Her mother merely glanced at her, and continued to stir the pot of papa, the famous staple of maize meal cooked in boiling water to form hard porridge. She had long given up hoping that Dikosha would one day participate in preparing the family meals. She would rather be out there singing and dancing. She danced so well too, this Dikosha. She moved her emaciated body with a grace that transformed her ragged dress into sheer elegance. And she was beautiful. Yet her beauty was not noisy at all, it did not call attention to itself. It was the grace of her movement that drew everyone's eyes. But as her mother always said, 'No one has ever eaten a dance.'

Her quiet beauty was in keeping with her own silence. She never spoke with anyone, not even with her mother or the girls with whom she sang and danced. They heard her voice only when she sang. She broke her silence only when her twin brother, Radisene, visited from the lowlands. Then she would actually talk, and giggle happily, and ask him all sorts of funny questions about life in the lowland towns where he attended the high school. Since he only came once or twice a year, Dikosha had long periods of silence, broken now and then by outbursts of song.

Radisene and Dikosha were not really twins in the true sense of the word. The people of Ha Samane called them twins because they had been born in the same year, eighteen years before. Radisene had been born first, a bouncy baby boy who was the envy of all the neigbours. When he was only four weeks old his mother left him with his grandmother and went to a night dance. It was at this dance that Dikosha was conceived. After she was born, her mother could be seen with two babies on her back, as though they were twins. The people of the village called her Mother-of-Twins in derision. That became the name that even members of her own family used.

As Dikosha baked her feet, songs were ringing in her head. Songs always rang in her head. Perhaps that is why she did not want to speak, for speaking would interfere with the flow of the songs. Mother-of-Twins dished out papa and boiled cabbage. They ate in silence, rolling the stiff porridge into small balls in their palms, and then scooping up cabbage and shoving it all into their mouths with their fingers.

Dikosha gave the empty plate back to her mother. Then she stood up and walked into the single rondavel that was her home. She selected her blankets from a pile and rolled herself on the floor. Soon she was fast asleep.

In her dreams she saw the new dance steps that she was going to teach the girls the next day. Even when she taught the girls she never spoke: she just danced the new steps and the others followed suit. Her dreams were always rich with new songs and new dances. Her worst nightmare was that some evil people would steal her dreams, and take her dances and her songs away, leaving her as empty as a hollow shell. She feared this as much as she feared the mist.

The next day was quite warm and the snow was melting very fast, turning into slush on the ground. Dikosha sat on the stoep of the rondavel, basking in the sun. From a distance she could hear the songs of girls who were going to draw water from the well or to wash clothes in the icy water of the Black River. These were joyous songs. But she did not want to feel joyous. She held on tightly to the sorrow that was being wrenched away from her by the songs, and nurtured it, and let it grow, until it overwhelmed her. Then she was weighed down by this mammoth grief, and she heaved a heavy sigh, and moaned softly. Passersby stopped to look at her closely, and uttered words of sympathy among themselves, 'Poor Dikosha, it is because she was conceived at a night dance.'

Dikosha's loneliness was self-imposed, for people of the village lived in what appeared to be happy communion. She was happiest in the world of sadness she had created for herself. She felt that if there was neither song nor dance, there was no need to be bothered with people.

She walked among the aloes on the hillside, turning over boulders and rolling them down in search of snakes. She loved snakes and was not afraid of them. She believed that no one had any right to be afraid of beautiful things. So she played with them, she mesmerized them with her dance. She could handle even the most poisonous snakes, like marabe and masumu, although she did not care much for the marabe adder with its dull grey colours. She preferred brightly coloured snakes, the ones of green, and yellow, and blue. She laughed at the hopeless wrath of the masumu cobra.

When she was tired of playing with the snakes she drained the venom out of their long-suffering bodies, skinned them, dug a hole in an anthill and made fire in the hole. Then she roasted the meat in the anthill oven. The wind savoured the aroma and threw it in different directions. The herdboys on distant parts of the hillside or on the veld sniffed, and knew immediately that the girl who never talked was somewhere near. The wind, whining as it pushed its way among the bushes, led them to the girl. They crowded around her, leaving the animals unattended. The girl who never talked shared the meat with them. Sometimes the herdboys would come with potatoes that they had stolen from the fields, and would roast them in the anthill oven together with the meat.

People of the village referred to Dikosha as a lefetwa, a girl who had long passed the age of marriage. After all, she was eighteen years old, and at that age women of the village were either married or at high school somewhere in the lowlands. Even those who were at high school, when they came home during holidays and behaved in the uppity manner of the lowland people, were called spinsters by people of the village. It was supposed to be the worst insult that could be hurled in the direction of any woman.

Yet Dikosha did not mind such labels. She was determined to live her life in her own way. And her way did not include marriage. Boyfriends and courting did not feature in her world. Boys were the mindless creatures with whom she shared snake-meat, and nothing more. They also did not think of her as anything more than the girl who could dance and kill the most dangerous of snakes. Even those who had long since reached puberty, and were already experimenting with sex on goats in the veld and at the cattle-posts, did not have any dirty thoughts about her. She would be alone with them out there on the hillsides, far away from the village, and they would think only of the pleasures of the juicy snake-meat.

Dikosha could have been one of the high-school girls, but after she had completed Standard Seven with a first-class pass her mother was unable to pay the fees. Her twin brother was lucky though, for the Holy Fathers of the church took him under their wings and paid his fees at a Catholic high school in the lowland town of Mafeteng, even though he had received only a third-class pass in Standard Seven. After all Dikosha was a woman, they argued, and bound to find a good man of the church and settle down in blissful matrimony. Radisene, on the other hand, even though he had received an unimpressive pass, showed promise as somebody who could be prepared for the work of the Lord. He was a man.

For a long time Dikosha was angry with the Good Fathers, with her mother, with her twin brother, with herself, with everybody. But many years passed, and she resigned herself to the fact that she would never go to school. She still had fond memories of her schooling. She used to absorb everything the teacher said. It stuck in her mind for ever, and she never had the need to study. When others were swotting for exams, she was playing diketo with a handful of little pebbles. Sometimes the other children joined her for a game of dibeke, which was like rounders, and if someone had a skipping-rope they played kgati. At the end of the year those who had been foolish enough to play with her failed, while she passed with flying colours. Even then she was not much of a talker, but it was obvious that she was happiest at school. Her only regret was that she had never fainted in class, like other children. Almost every day someone would faint at school. No one knew exactly why. Some blamed the sun. But the sun knew otherwise.

At midday Dikosha was still basking herself in the sun, and wrestling with the sorrow that was eager to be dragged away from her by the distant song of the village girls. She was startled by the thunder of an aeroplane flying over her hut. The little children were jumping up and down in all the village compounds, and shouting to the plane, 'U ntlele le dipompong! Please bring me sweets!'

It was Wednesday. Every Wednesday the plane came to Ha Samane from the capital city of Maseru in the lowlands. In the two hours that it took on that route, it flew over great mountain ranges that were capped with snow for the greater part of the year. It flew over rivers and over gorges. Through the windows of the ten-seater Cessna, passengers from time to time saw small villages nestling in the valleys, surrounded on all sides by high mountains. Those were villages that had never seen a car in their lives and could be reached only on horseback. The passengers could see herds of cattle, sheep and goats grazing at the cattle-posts, miles and miles away from the nearest village. All these were the size of ants. The mountains were cheerless and naked, and patches of green were rarely visible in a waste of dull grey and brown.

The excitement caused by the plane did not move Dikosha. It was the same every Wednesday. The plane landed at the airfield, and passengers from the lowlands alighted with their rich baggage.

Most of these were the moneyed people – businessmen returning from negotiating deals with wholesalers, nurses coming from complaining in Maseru about the lack of medical supplies at a village clinic, farmers who had recently been paid for the wool of their sheep, extension workers of various government departments. Once in a while there would be a migrant worker from the mines of South Africa who was too impatient to wait for the four-wheel drive vans and trucks that ferried passengers from the lowlands to mountain villages such as Ha Samane. Such vehicles took many days to reach their destinations because the roads were bad. At some places there were no roads at all and the trucks had to negotiate their way on pony-tracks. But even though it took so many days, it was fortunate that the trucks could reach Ha Samane at all. Some villages were completely cut off to vehicles.

Hlong, the club-footed old man who was the manager and the sole employee of the airfield, inspected the tickets of the five new passengers, and then allowed them onto the plane. He pushed a trolley of their baggage and loaded it into the belly of the plane. Soon the propellers were whirling and the plane was speeding along the runway. Hlong watched until it disappeared into the sky. Then he went into the one-roomed building which served as his office, bedroom and kitchen, to chat with some of the passengers who were waiting for their relatives to come and meet them with donkeys to carry their baggage home.

'Ntate Hlong, may I leave this bag of cabbages here? I'll come back with a donkey to fetch it.'

'And who are you? Ah, don't tell me now. You are Radisene, child of Mother-of-Twins. You children stay in the lowlands for such a long time that we tend to forget you. Of course you can leave your bag here.'

Hlong thought that educated young men were really spoilt. He could not understand why this young upstart could not carry a small bag like that on his shoulders, especially since his home was not that far from the airfield. That was the problem with sending children to imbibe dangerous customs in the lowlands.

Radisene walked out into the village. Already a great number of saddled horses were tied to the stumps and poles outside the post office. It was the same every Wednesday. As soon as the plane arrived, people from Ha Samane and from neighbouring villages such as Ha Sache rode their horses to the post office to see if they had received any letters from their husbands, sons, fathers and brothers who worked in the mines. They waited outside while the postmaster and his assistant quickly sorted the letters. Then the assistant would stand at the door of the small building and read out the names on the envelopes or the registered slips. The lucky ones who had received postal orders jumped with joy, while others went home disappointed. But they would be back the next week. Some wives and parents had been coming to the post office every Wednesday for years on end. Their husbands and sons had long been swallowed by the city of gold, and had established new families there. Perhaps the table had fallen on some of them, which meant that they had died underground. Yet their relatives never lost hope. They came every Wednesday.

Dikosha saw a knock-kneed and lanky figure approaching. She knew immediately that it was her twin brother, Radisene. She could never mistake his gait. When they were young she used to tease him that he was a kiss-madolo scarecrow, a reference to the fact that his knees kissed each other when he walked. The figure that was approaching now could not by any stretch of the imagination be called a scarecrow. He looked quite handsome, in a new grey suit. She ran to him and threw herself into his arms.

'You're only carrying a paper bag.'

'Because I'm only staying until the weekend, that's why. The bag contains something for you. I bought you a nice red dress.'

'With what? You are only a student.'

'I finished school last December. I'm a teacher now. Been a teacher for the last six months. I teach at a night school which holds its classes at the high school where I was a student.'

'We don't know anything about that because you never write. It's June now and we haven't seen you since … long before

Christmas.'

'I am here now, am I not? And I brought you a whole bag of cabbage.'

Mother-of-Twins was also very happy to see her son, after almost a year. She was particularly happy about the bag of cabbage. She was going to share it with her friend and neighbour, Mother-of-the-Daughters, and would be stingy to those who had made snide remarks about her and her children behind her back. Cabbage was quite precious at Ha Samane, and indeed in all the villages throughout the land. Together with other vegetables such as spinach, beetroot and carrots, it could only be bought from the lowland towns, which in turn imported it from South Africa. And cabbage was a staple! Yet no one had ever been struck by the bright idea that it was possible to cultivate this vegetable ... to grow it in the very village soil. People of the village grew maize, beans, peas, sorghum, wheat and even potatoes. But never cabbage.

2. The Twins

Dikosha stood in the centre of the room and Radisene sat on a bench near the pile of bedding. She wanted to change into the red dress, but her brother was refusing to go out of the room. 'What have you got that I haven't seen before?' he asked, with a naughty grin on his face. 'Ha, you think I am afraid of you,' said Dikosha, stripping her ragged dress off. She wore no petticoat, and stood naked as a snake in front of him. Only a strip of beaded thethana covered her femaleness. She giggled and shook her waist in a subtle tease, her small breasts firmly pointing out, and quickly put on the red dress. She felt very good as she had not had a new dress for years. She strutted to the bench, pecked her brother on the cheek, and thanked him for the gift.

'It's going to last me for ever.'

'Only if you're going to live for a few months, and then fade away and die.'

Mother-of-Twins came in, and stopped in her tracks when she saw Dikosha jauntily parading in her new dress. 'You are no better than an animal, Dikosha,' she screeched. 'Take off that dress at once! It's going to be your Sunday dress. You know that you ran out of Sunday dresses long ago.' Dikosha just looked at her and walked out of the room. Mother-of-Twins remained fuming, accusing the ancestors of cursing her with a disobedient girl like Dikosha. While Radisene was trying to play the peacemaker, assuring his mother that Dikosha was not really a bad girl but simply needed some understanding, they heard the voice of Mother-of-the-Daughters outside.

'Ko! Ko! Where are the people of this house?'

'The door is open, friend.'

'Ahe, Mother-of-Twins! We heard that our son is back from the lowlands. We said we should come and see him with this billycan of sour porridge.'

Mother-of-the-Daughters was a plump woman, whose smooth

youthful looks expertly hid the fact that she had given birth to ten daughters and was grandmother to a number of granddaughters. She was the direct opposite of her friend, Mother-of-Twins, who was quite wiry and visibly ravaged by the world. She, of course, had struggled alone to bring up two children born of pleasure, whose fathers she could not even point out; whereas Mother-of-the-Daughters had a husband who worked in the mines in his youth, bought a few sheep and cattle, inherited more from his father, and was then relatively well off. Father-of-the-Daughters spent his time attending feasts with the other horse-borne men of Ha Samane, travelling to distant mountains to inspect his animals at the cattle-posts, and participating in court cases either as a litigant or as a witness. Litigation was his favourite pastime. Mother-of-the-Daughters, on the other hand, was a homely woman who enjoyed a robust laugh with her neighbours. Even though she was better off than most of them, she did not have a proud bone in her body.

Mother-of-the-Daughters was not the only one who wanted to see Radisene. Another three grandmothers of the village followed her. He offered them a bench from the rondavel. They would have preferred to sit on the ground, as was the custom with grandmothers, but it was muddy with melt water. "Let us hope we have seen the last of snow this winter," said one of them. Another one observed that spring was still a long way off since it was only June. The snow was sure to visit them again before long. Indeed, the weather was no longer the weather they had known as young girls. Because of all the terrible things that the youths were doing in the world the weather had become so unreliable that the previous year snow was seen in December – right in the middle of summer.

After sharing a pinch of snuff among themselves, each one rolling it with her tongue between the toothless gums and the inner lips, they surveyed Radisene. He stood in front of them with a respectful smile. They marvelled at how grown-up the boy was, and how handsome. They said soon Mother-of-Twins was going to have a daughter-in-law who would relieve her of all drudgery.

Radisene was a good boy, they said, for though he had become such an important person in the lowlands, who wore a suit, a white shirt and a tie, he had not forgotten the fact that he did not spring up from a rock, but was given birth to by a woman. 'You are a fortunate woman, Mother-of-Twins. When our children leave they leave. We never see them again, we never hear from them,' one grandmother declared. The others nodded in agreement. Mother-of-the-Daughters said it was not so much a matter of luck, but that the poor woman had worked hard to bring her children up properly, and to teach them to respect their elders and to be proud of their mountain roots.

When the grandmothers were about to leave they each gave him a five-cent or ten-cent coin. He was touched by their gesture. They were poor, their dresses had patches all over and their shawls were threadbare. One even had moth-eaten lace over her shoulders. Yet they were sacrificing their last cents to welcome him home. His conscience would not allow him to take the money. Instead he gave them a ten rand note to share among themselves, and said, 'I thank you very much, my grandmothers. It is very kind of you. But I think you can use the money for yourselves. Buy snuff or sweets. I know that sweet grandmothers like you love sweet things.'

The grandmothers were offended. They went away mumbling among themselves that the child they had brought up had become too proud to accept their money. 'He is too proud to accept money from us poor people,' they said. The fact that he had given them a ten rand note did not stop the whole village from talking disgustedly the next day about the proud son of Mother-of-Twins. When he passed they pointed at him and said, 'There goes that proud boy.'

People of the village often said that Dikosha transformed herself into a person when her twin brother was around. She became lively, and showed some enthusiasm for other things in life apart from singing and dancing. Her daily routine changed somewhat. Usually she spent the greater part of the day following the sun around her mother's rondavel. She went to the hillside to mes-

merize snakes, and in the evenings she sang the songs of the pumpkin. But now she took walks with Radisene, and even visited
friends and relatives that he wanted to see.

People of the village peeped through the cracks of their doors
and saw the twins walking hand-in-hand up the path that led to the
general dealer's store. But instead of going into the store they
turned towards the airfield. Hlong was sitting outside the building
reading a book, most probably his favourite Evangelical hymnal.
They shouted their greetings at him. He greeted them back, and
asked them in English where they were going on such an unusually warm winter morning. He liked to speak in English, especially
with the lowland people, to show them that he too had some
schooling. They told him that they were just walking, with no particular destination in mind. He wished them a good day, and
resumed his reading. Under his breath he cursed the proud boy, for
he had already heard the story of Radisene's disgusting behaviour
from some passers-by, who had shared with him the latest gossip.

The twins walked through the lower part of Ha Samane where
most of the houses were decorated with colourful ditema patterns
on the walls. In this part of the village women still took pride in
painting elaborate murals. The people in the upper part of the village – that whole area on the other side of the airfield where the
twins' home was located – laughed at them, and said that painting
murals on the outside walls was old-fashioned. It was an art that
had been practised by their grandmothers who lived in darkness,
and was kept alive by people of the Free State farms, who really
knew no better since they were enslaved by Boers. People of the
upper part of Ha Samane felt that they were civilized Christians
who had turned away from this heathen practice. Their houses
were all smeared with the grey soil of the village, and had a dull
grey sameness to them.

Dikosha walked very slowly, stopping from time to time to
admire the ditema patterns. They overwhelmed her emotions in a
way that she could not explain, that left her whole body tingling.
She wished her own home, and all the other houses in her neigh-

bourhood, had ditema. Radisene patiently stood when she stood, and walked when she walked. He did not understand what was happening, nor did he see anything wonderful in the patterns that so captivated his sister. But he had learnt long ago not to question anything she did. He would get no explanation.

On the other side of the village, the twins descended on steep grasslands where cattle were grazing and herdboys filled the air with the music of the lesiba. It was Radisene's turn to walk slowly, for he was admiring the cattle. He loved cattle. He had a deep longing in his eyes, and his heart was throbbing like the wild drums of the mathuela diviners. He was filled with nostalgia for the days when he was a herdboy. Even though his own family never had any animals he had grown up with cattle. When he was four years old he was hired by Father-of-the-Daughters to look after calves. In that way he was able to earn milk and grain for his mother and sister. In a few years he graduated from calves to cattle, and a strong bond developed between himself and the animals. He never drove the cattle from behind, but led them. In the morning they followed him in one long line from Father-of-the-Daughters' kraal to the very grazing lands where he was now standing with his sister. The bells that hung on the necks of the bulls jingled with peals that resonated in his belly. It was the best, and the only music he had ever appreciated. In the evenings he led the cattle back to the kraal and milked the cows that needed milking.

'Perhaps I would be having a herd of my own by now,' he thought aloud. Father-of-the-Daughters had promised to send him to the cattle-posts to live there and take care of his larger herds that were permanently based on those distant mountains. After every year he was going to pay him with a sheep, and after every five years with a whole cow. And those cows would give birth to other cows. But before that could happen, his life took a different turn. One day he followed some of the village boys to church and found that he liked it. His mother was not a churchgoing woman, and could not be bothered about her son's new interest in religion. His church friends were pupils at the mission primary school, so he also became a pupil. At first his mother objected, for he was the only breadwinner of the family, but Father-of-the-Daughters promised to retain him as his herdboy. He could tend the cattle after school and on Saturdays. He was no longer going to be paid with animals though, since he would not be a full-time herdboy at the cattle-posts. Instead he would be given the usual grain and milk.

Dikosha insisted that she was going to school too, and there was no stopping her. In any case, Mother-of-Twins was happy to be rid of her because she never helped around the house, but spent her time moping. So the twins began Substandard A together. Since Radisene wanted to be an altar boy like his friends, the twins were baptized in the name of the Father, and of the Son, and of the Holy Ghost. Radisene was given the church name of Joseph, but Dikosha refused to be named Mary. She insisted that her name was Dikosha, and no church could change that. Radisene's church name soon fell into disuse. Even on Sundays he was called Radisene.

'Hey, dreamer, wake up! We can't stand here for the whole day'

'Don't be selfish, Dikosha. When you were looking at those heathen houses I stood with you. Anyway, what is all the hurry about?'

'If you love cattle so much you should have stayed, you know? You shouldn't have gone to the lowlands to be a teacher. You could have been a herdboy for the rest of your life, and maybe the Good Fathers would have sent me to school instead.'

'I promised them that I was going to be a Father or at least a Brother. That's why they sent me to school.'

'You never told me that!'

'They would have sent you to school too if you had promised to become a Sister.'

'Never! I don't make false promises, Radisene,' and she sang a few bars of ''Manyena', the song the village girls used to mock nuns and the way they dressed.

They walked among the cattle on the narrow footpath that led to the fields on the banks of the Black River. The herdboys were about to take exception, for girls were not allowed to walk among the cattle. But when they saw that it was the girl who never talked, and who did things her own way irrespective of what custom demanded, they let her pass. The cattle also looked at her in amazement and lowed their disapproval. But when they realized who she was, they went on with their grazing. Radisene had a searing longing to lead the cattle.

On the banks of the Black River most of the fields lay fallow. Those which belonged to the more adventurous farmers were green with winter crops such as wheat and peas. The people of Ha Samane did not care much for winter crops. Most of the farming activity happened in spring. The twins took a short cut through the fallow fields and descended to the river. The water was quite shallow, so they crossed to the other side, where there was a huge cave with its granite mouth opened on the river.

This was the Cave of Barwa, which had been home to the ancient Barwa people hundreds of years before. The Barwa, or Bushmen as the white people called them, were the original inhabitants of the land. They lived here happily for centuries, hunting animals and gathering wild fruits and roots, until the twins' ancestors came and drove them away, and killed some, and married others. They left a legacy of caves with wonderful paintings on the walls, and the Cave of Barwa was the most famous of them all. It had red and black paintings of big-buttocked people chasing deer with bows and arrows, or dancing in a trancelike state. Dikosha was spellbound by one painting especially, which showed a dancer with the body of a woman and the head of a beast. It was a fierce-looking beast that no one had ever seen before. Dikosha saw herself as the monster-woman-dancer, ready to devour all the dancers of the world, imbuing herself with their strength and stamina, and then dancing for ever and ever, until the end of time.

She was sad that people had written their names on some of the paintings with white chalk to show future generations that they had once visited the Cave of Barwa. The walls of the cave, especially towards the mouth, were scrawled with names that intruded on the entrancing life of the hunters and dancers. Only those paintings that were on the deeper walls remained untainted, but even there the names were encroaching. What angered Dikosha most was that these were the names of important people from the lowlands who came to the Cave of Barwa as tourists. Some of these destroyers were even ministers of the government, or important people whose names you heard mentioned on the radio all the time. Yet they thought nothing of scrawling their vain names over such sacredness.

The twins sat on the granite rock at the mouth of the cave. While Dikosha was entranced by the dancers on the wall, Radisene was engrossed in the dark water of the Black River as it lazily flowed past the cave. He remembered the days when the river was teeming with letshwala, as they called the catfish. He was about five then, and spent his days looking after Father-of-the-Daughters' calves. Sometimes the water came in a flood that would last for only a few minutes, and when the water receded the catfish were left stranded on the sand. Together with the older herdboys he would collect the fish and take them home to feast on with his mother and sister. Then the government people who said they were doing development came and introduced a new kind of fish called trout. They said it was going to bring in money, because the Black River passed through areas that had holiday resorts where tourists went to fish. Tourists liked to fish for trout. Since then the letshwala and other indigenous fish were no longer seen in the Black River. The elders said they had been eaten by the trout. Now feasting on the catfish only ever happened in the stories that grandmothers told their grandchildren.

Dikosha put her head in the brother's lap. He ran his fingers through her hair, entangling locks that had not seen a comb for ages. Her long legs were spread to what had once been a hearth, and her feet played with the ancient ash. Although it was centuries old, it retained its warmth as if a steaming pot had been removed only an hour ago. Dikosha knew it was the warmth of ages, a warmth that would always be there. Her brother discovered a nest of nits in a tangled lock, and crushed them with his nails.

'You are eighteen, Dikosha. You should be a lady who washes her head regularly and straightens her hair.'

'You can be a lady if you want. I want to be a monster-woman-dancer.'

'And what is that?'

She merely laughed at his gross stupidity and ignorance.

'A lady would not roll in the ashes in a new dress.'

'It is my dress, is it not?'

'You should have listened to mother when she said it must be your Sunday dress.'

'She is just jealous because you did not bring her anything.'

'But I brought her a bag of cabbages.'

'You have a lot to learn about women, elder brother. Women, even at their most whimsical, don't wear cabbage.'

'I will remember that next time. Anyway, what are you going to wear on Sunday when we go to church?'

She laughed, and told him that she never went to church. Ever since the Good Fathers had denied her the chance to go to school she saw no need to go to church. When others were singing about the grace of the Holy Ghost she went to the hillside to play with beautiful things that had glossy colours.

'You know, you worry mother so much, Dikosha!'

'Then she must go back to that night dance and unconceive me!'

Radisene ignored that remark. He had heard it before when Dikosha was angry with her mother. Instead he patiently explained that she should not bear a grudge against the Good Fathers for not sending her to school. They were under no obligation to do so. It was their money, after all, and they had the right to decide what they would do with it. Dikosha retorted that she did not care what they did with their money. They could eat it with their cronies such as Radisene until it choked them, for all she cared. What she detested was that they denied her the opportunity solely on the grounds that she was a girl, even though she was smarter than any boy in the history of that primary school. And this at a time when mountain people were selling their cattle to send their daughters to school. Radisene agreed that you could go to any high school in the country and you would find that there were more girls than boys. It was because boys looked after cattle at the cattle-posts. When they got older they went to the mines. He insisted, however, that even if the Good Fathers were wrong not to send her to school, that had been a decision made by individual human beings. It was not reasonable to turn against the church, and therefore against God, because of the mistakes made by individuals, who were not infallible even though they were Fathers in the church.

Dikosha could vouch for their fallibility. Not only had they denied her the opportunity of going to school, but they had scribbled their names on the walls of the cave too. And so had some Evangelical ministers, who did not even have the shame to use their reverend titles. They were all vandals as far as she was concerned.

Night had fallen when they walked back home. How time flew when she was with her brother, thought Dikosha. It flitted by like a Saturday afternoon dream. They had sat in the Cave of Barwa, talking about nothing in particular. There had been long moments of silence, while they listened to the deep rumble of the Black River and to the whispers of the long-departed inhabitants of the cave, carried on the wind. And of course they had talked about Misti. Radisene wanted to know where she was, and how she was doing. He was smitten with this petite girl from Ha Sache, but he was afraid to approach her. He wanted Dikosha to talk with her on his behalf. But she could not promise to do so, for she did not like to talk with anyone but her brother.

As they passed the airfield a man came staggering towards them. He was from one of the many shebeens in that area. 'Heita! Heita, Radison!' he shouted. Only a lowland person would use that kind of street-slang greeting, and would Anglicize his name.

'Who's that who knows me in the dark?'

'Your eyes don't see any more, eh Teacher? It's me, man!'

'Oho! It's Sorry My Darlie.'

It was indeed the city dandy, Sorry Mr Darlie. That was his soccer name, and everyone used it instead of his given name, or even his church name. He played for one of the first-division teams in Maseru, and was often in the newspapers and magazines. He also played for the national team, and had featured in countries as far away as Mauritius and Cameroon, representing his country. On Saturdays and Sundays people crowded around their radios throughout the land to hear sports broadcasters sing his name, 'Sorry … My … Daaaaarlie!' as he dribbled past the opposition and scored countless goals. He was a celebrity, and his home village of Ha Sache was very proud of him. They boasted about him, and said that even though Ha Samane had an airfield, a clinic, a post office and a general dealer's store, they had the star of the nation, Sorry My Darlie.

The girls were all gaga over him, but he really had no time for the village belles. Nor for the city débutantes who were always keen to be photographed with him so as to feature in the social pages of magazines. Even though he was exposed to some of the beauty queens of the world, he was in love with Dikosha, and wanted only her. But Dikosha had no time for him and was always rude and abrupt whenever he tried to make his advances. Even as they were standing there, while Radisene asked him what he was doing in the village on a weekend and Sorry My Darlie explained that since there were no soccer matches that weekend he had decided to come and see the old people, Dikosha was pulling her brother's sleeve. 'Let's go, Radisene. It is very cold and we can't just stand here for the whole night.' Indeed it was cold, and the twins were not wearing any blankets. When they had set out for the Cave of Barwa it was warm, and they had forgotten that winter sunsets brought with them winds that froze the ears. But Sorry My Darlie knew that it was not so much the cold that Dikosha was running away from, but himself.

They left him standing there, mumbling something about girls who didn't know what was good for them. One day he was going to get this Dikosha, even if he had to pursue her to the end of the earth. He would use the age-old safety pin method: if the lovelorn one stuck a safety pin on the spot where the object of his unrequited love had recently peed, she would immediately stop spurning him. In fact, she would fall head over heels in love with him, and start chasing after him. The safety pin was more potent than any love potion known to man – or woman, since women had also been known to use it to catch their men. It was even more effective than potions like zamlandela, velabahleke and bhekaminangedwa that the lovesick bought from Durban mail-order houses.

The problem was that Dikosha only relieved herself in the pit-latrine that Radisene had built for the family, instead of going behind the aloes like those who did not have toilets. He hoped to catch her one day, perhaps in the fields. There were no toilets there, and women who went to hoe or to harvest the corn squatted on the side of the paths that divided the fields to pee. But then Dikosha never went to the fields, even during letsema when people of the village formed work-parties to help one another with the hoeing or harvesting. And of course Sorry My Darlie was in the lowlands most of the time, and was therefore unable to follow Dikosha wherever she went. But he was not one to give up that easily. He showed his friends his safety pin and said, 'One day is one day.'

3. The Coup – 1970

The radio was blaring the Mahotella Queens' 'Leabua ke 'muso ngwan' aka' for the umpteenth time. Radisene cursed aloud, and switched it off. He was sick and tired of the song. Since the previous day, when the government had suspended the constitution and declared a state of emergency, the radio had played nothing but this song, which defiantly proclaimed that whether one liked it or not Leabua was the government.

At first nobody believed that the government could be so crazy as to declare a state of emergency. The ruling National Party had lost the elections to the opposition Congress Party. But instead of handing over power, the National Party had instructed the Police Mobile Unit to round up the Congress Party leaders and lock them up at the maximum security prison in Maseru. They nullified the elections and continued to rule by decree. People thought the whole thing was a big joke. It wouldn't last, they said, for the masses would rise and overthrow the undemocratic National Party. Everyone knew that the coup was led by two white officers, Roach and Hindmarsh, who had been seconded to the government by Western powers. These men advised Prime Minister Leabua not to hand over power to what they termed 'a communist opposition'. People were glued to their radios hoping to hear that the coup had failed and that opposition leaders had taken their rightful place as the new government of the country. But all they heard was the same old song by the Mahotella Queens, and periodic announcements by Prime Minister Leabua that a state of emergency, or qomatsi, was in force and that there was a curfew from six in the evening to six in the morning.

What a stupid thing to try to do, imprisoning people in their own houses, Radisene thought. He was frantically searching for his books in his cluttered one-roomed flat. He lifted the blankets on the bed and found one of the books hiding between the sheets. He must have fallen asleep while he was reading it the previous night.

The bed was never made, so it was not unusual for various items to take refuge among the blankets, only to be discovered weeks later. He found the second book on the small table between the Primus stove and some dirty dishes. There were always dirty dishes on the table. He cleaned each plate only when it was needed for use. It was the life of a bachelor, and he was proud of it.

But he took particular care of his personal looks, and was always well groomed. Although he did not have many clothes, the few that he had were always clean and well pressed. The pride of his wardrobe was the grey suit that was hanging on a nail on the wall. He had bought it on terms from Sales House – six months to pay. That was two years ago, when he last visited his family in the mountains. Yet he had not finished paying for it, and had ignored numerous Final Notices. Then there were the black bell-bottom pants he was wearing, with a crease so sharp it could cut a fly in two. He was also wearing his dark brown platform shoes, a black wash-and-wear shirt and a colourful lumber-jacket. The shoes had a shine that reflected his image. That also was the life of a bachelor, and he was proud of it.

In the White Café, which was next to the line of flats where he was renting his room, Radisene bought two sticks of Rothmans Kingsize. With the measly wages he was earning at the night school he could not afford a whole packet of cigarettes. And unlike Lexington or Gold Dollar which came in packets of ten, Rothmans only came in twenties. As it was, his grocery account at the White Café was getting to be unmanageable. His lifestyle was nothing to sing about, yet he was living beyond his means.

Leaving the café, he crossed the road into the precinct of the Catholic mission. At the gate a group of women dressed in the black and purple uniform of the Mothers' Union were discussing the emergency. Radisene knew that the church supported the defeated government's decision not to hand over power to the 'Godless communists'. Even the priests preached about it in their churches throughout the land. However, he had no view of his own on the matter, one way or the other. All he wanted was to teach his students in peace, and maybe get a better paying job soon. He greeted the women, and walked past the church to a block of classrooms in the rear. Most of his students were there, and as it was already five thirty he began his lesson. He talked about main clauses and subordinate clauses.

At seven thirty the class was over and he climbed the hillock behind the school to Ha Romokhele – the liveliest of the townships of Mafeteng. Even though it was long after six, people were walking up and down the muddy streets, carrying on with their lives as if nothing had happened. They had no intention of observing the curfew. Radisene walked past shebeens where men were drinking beer and playing dice on the stoep. The air was filled with the stench of urine, home-brewed beer and boiled sheep's head and trotters. Drunken women, who took pride in calling themselves matekatse, or whores, the devourers of men, whistled at him and in their musical voices invited him to rub his lanky figure against their hungry bodies. They crowned their invitation with graphic descriptions of the things they would do to parts of his anatomy if he were to walk into their secret chambers, and boasted that he would not survive the ordeal. He ignored them and walked into Mr and Mrs Qobokwane's shebeen, popularly known as Red House.

This was a better class of shebeen, for it sold only European liquor rather than the home-brewed stuff of the neighbouring shebeens. The owners of the little red-brick house, both husband and wife, were teachers at the Catholic mission. They were also the proprietors of the night school where Radisene taught. When Mr Qobokwane saw the plight of students who had failed their Junior Certificate and had nowhere to go, he decided to open a night school. He negotiated with the Good Fathers to give him a classroom that he could use at night for a nominal rental. Students registered to prepare for supplementary examinations in the subjects they had failed. Some adults of Mafeteng, most of them working in government offices, heard that the Catholics had opened a night school, and enrolled in great numbers. They did not know that it was Mr Qobokwane's private enterprise. And by the time they found out, it really did not matter. 'A man is gotta eat,' they said. When Radisene obtained his General Certificate of Education at the Catholic high school, Mr Qobokwane employed him to teach English Language at his night school. It did not seem to matter that English Language was one of the subjects he had failed dismally.

Radisene joined a group of regular patrons at the table, asked for a glass from Mrs Qobokwane, and poured himself a drink from a bottle of Martell VO Brandy that was on the table. That was the custom of Red House. The regulars – mostly teachers, civil servants and policemen – shared their drinks.

Roll-Away, the roly-poly Police District Commander, was the centre of attraction. He had put his sub-machine-gun on the table, and everyone was fascinated by this new toy. 'It's called an Uzi ... straight from Israel,' he boasted. He showed them how to dismantle it and put it together again, skills he had been taught that very morning. Times had changed, he told them, the police force was no longer a peaceful force that everyone took advantage of. The government had ordered them to shoot to kill anyone who tried to go against the emergency regulations.

'Things are great now,' he puffed. 'Not like before, when we could be sued even for using the smallest force on those we arrested.' The regulars laughed. They could not imagine the grandfatherly Roll-Away harming a fly. Trooper Motsohi wanted to know if they, as junior peace officers, would also be armed with such fancy machine-guns, instead of the heavy pre-war 303's that were issued to troopers of the mounted police when they went after cattle rustlers. 'Come on, Motsohi, what can you do with a machine like this? You'd pump bullets into your own foot,' said Radisene. They all laughed. Trooper Motsohi was always the butt of everyone's jokes. Not only was he believed to be the youngest of the regulars, he looked quite delicate and handsome. In fact, he was the same age as Radisene, who nevertheless looked older because of his towering height. The regulars said Trooper Motsohi was beautiful and should have been a girl. They often told him, 'You are lucky you are not in prison or in the mines. They would have made you a wife.'

Radisene ordered a bottle of Paarl Perlé wine to be put on his tab. At the end of the month Mr Qobokwane added up all the nips of brandy and bottles of Paarl Perlé he had consumed that month and deducted the amount from his salary. Most months his debt swallowed all his earnings, and he had to ask for an advance from Mr Qobokwane to pay part of his accounts at the White Café and Sales House. Mrs Qobokwane put the bottle on the table, and those regulars who had no qualms about mixing wine with brandy fell into it.

'Where is he? Where is the bastard?' enquired a raspy voice outside. Everybody in the shebeen froze. They knew that voice. They looked at Trooper Motsohi pityingly and shook their heads. The door was kicked open and Tampololo stormed in. She was Trooper Motsohi's wife, and she was menacingly huge and beautiful. She had the smooth, plump features of her mother back in the mountain village of Ha Samane, Mother-of-the-Daughters, although she was much darker in complexion.

'What do you think I am eating when you walk straight from work to waste time with these layabouts?'

'Please, sweetie, one of these layabouts is my boss. Sit down. Let's have a drink.'

'Don't you sweetie me, you fool! Your boss, your boss! Who cares? And you Roll-Away, u tsofaletse bohata … you are old for nothing. What kind of a District Commander are you to sit with this useless loafer and not tell him to go home when it's late like this?'

'Hey, Tampololo, I don't involve myself in my policemen's family affairs!'

'I'll show you what I'll do to him, then next time you will involve yourself if only to save his life.'

Tampololo leapt at Trooper Motsohi and throttled him with both hands. She threw him on the floor, sat on him, and rained fists on his face. The regulars pleaded from a distance, 'Please Tampololo, don't do this to your husband.' Trooper Motsohi was only saved by Mrs Qobokwane, who came rushing from her bedroom when she heard him screaming, with a sound like a pig being slaughtered. She gently removed Tampololo from her husband, and reprimanded her, 'One day you're going to kill this man. You'll see where you are going to get another husband.'

As he was being frogmarched home Trooper Motsohi pleaded, 'If you must beat me at all, my love, please don't do it in public. You make me the laughing stock of my friends.'

'My love?' Tampololo snapped back. 'How can I be a love of a thing like you?'

They passed throngs of people who gawked or laughed. They were used to this scene. Tampololo was known to beat up her husband every day for the flimsiest of reasons. Trooper Motsohi wondered what all these people were doing in the street after nine. Didn't they know that the curfew began at six?

The following morning Radisene was woken up by a loud knock at the door. He had a terrible headache. His head was spinning and buzzing. That was always the problem when one drank a lot of Paarl Perlé. What was worse was that he had mixed it with brandy, creating the hangover of the world.

'Who's that at this time of the morning?'

'At this time of the morning? What do you mean "at this time of the morning"? It is eleven o'clock, Radison. Come on, open up, man.'

It was Sorry My Darlie at his dandiest. They say he never bought his clothes locally. He ordered them from such famous Johannesburg mail-order houses as Kays, Manhattan and American, or from Charles Velkes in Cape Town. That morning he was wearing an eight-piece cap, a navy-blue double-slash double-breasted blazer with glittering buttons, grey bell-bottom slacks, and black Crockett and Jones shoes. His maroon cravat was stuffed inside his open-necked Terylene shirt. He walked into the room, and looked for a place to sit. It was all too cluttered, so he paced the floor.

'Hell, man Radison, you're sleeping at this time? I thought you were with somebody, man. You sleep with your own knees, man, when this town is famous for its beauties!'

'I had a late night, man. Anyway what puts you here on a week-day like this.'

'I was just taking a drive. I thought I should show you my Valaza which I have just bought.'

Radisene peeped through the curtain. And there it was, glisten-ing in the morning sun, a navy-blue Valiant. He was suddenly hit by pangs of envy. Where was justice in this world if people who slaved to pass matric could not afford a decent meal, while a num-skull who did not even pass Junior Certificate could buy a beauti-ful car like that – all because he knew how to kick an inflated pigskin! Sorry My Darlie suggested that they go for a drive, and Radisene was pleased that the people of Mafeteng would see that he too had friends who drove cars. And of course this was not just any friend. This was Sorry My Darlie!

'I hope you will tell your sister that I have a car', Sorry My Darlie said, making a show of changing the gears. He lamented the fact that he could not go to his home village in his car, since only trucks and four-wheel drive vehicles could get there. But he would send the old people photographs of the car. 'I will give you one photograph to give to Dikosha,' he pleaded.

Radisene laughed. 'You know that she doesn't care for things like that.'

'How do you know? She has never seen a car before'

'She saw it in the *Bona* magazine that I once bought her. She was not impressed. She said it was much smaller than the trucks she had seen bringing bags of food to the clinic or to the general dealer's.'

'Listen, Radison … do me a favour, man. Let me give you money to buy a ticket for her to come and visit you. Then she will see the things of the city, and will know that by city standards I am a good catch. I have a car, Radison! What more could she want?'

'I know my sister, Sorry My Darlie. She will not come to the

lowlands. Anyway, where do you get all this money to throw
around?'

Sorry My Darlie explained that ever since he'd changed teams
his finances had improved tremendously. He was then playing for
Maseru United, which was owned by a rich businessman who also
owned a hotel, a restaurant and a number of stores. Unlike the
players of other first-division teams who had to work at other jobs
to earn a living, Maseru United players were full-time profession-
als. The businessman pampered his players. They lived at his hotel
free of charge and had all their meals there. He also gave them a
stipend, and they could choose the clothes they wanted at one of
his stores. Sorry My Darlie, of course, did not get his clothes from
there since he specialized in imported 'threads'. He was able to
buy his Valaza, he said, from money he earned when his picture
appeared on billboards praising the mellow taste and the potency
of a particular kind of brandy. He also appeared in magazines
extolling the virtues of some deodorant or other. According to the
advertisement, he used this deodorant after a tough match and it
made the girls follow him. Radisene was amazed that just by
telling lies on hoardings or in magazines one could buy a whole
car. There and then he made up his mind. He was not going to be
a teacher for ever. He was not going to be poor for the rest of his
life either. He would find his niche. Somewhere there must be easy
money waiting for him.

'You know, Radison, if you invite your sister to the lowlands I
can help you get Misti. She is my homegirl, you know? I can talk
with her.'

'Misti! Where is she? You know I have not been to Ha Samane
or Ha Sache for the last two years.'

'You don't know? She is in Ireland. She went there to read to be
a medical laboratory technician. I can give you her address if you
promise you'll get Dikosha to visit you.'

'Give me the address first.'

'No, get Dikosha first.'

'No, give me the address first.'

Sorry My Darlie dropped him outside the flats and drove away to Maseru. That afternoon Radisene wrote to Misti. It was not a love letter. He could not be so presumptuous as to tell her in the very first letter he had ever written to her how he felt about her. He told her about the coup and the state of emergency. And about his great work as a teacher. He wished her well in her studies. He knew, he wrote, that she would be a great success, and when she completed her diploma she was going to be the second pride of Ha Sache, the first one being Sorry My Darlie. He ended the letter with 'Your loving friend, Radisene', and hoped that the word 'loving' would give her a hint that this was not an innocent brotherly letter. In the next letter, he promised himself, he would be more intimate.

At five thirty Radisene crossed the road to the night school as usual. But there were no students. Two other teachers – Makhele, the old man who taught Geography, and Cynthia the young woman who taught Mathematics – stood outside the classrooms, discussing the students' failure to turn up. They decided to wait for a while, hoping that some would still arrive. 'Perhaps they are on strike,' Cynthia suggested. The students were always complaining that they did not get what they called a 'proper education' even though they paid exorbitant fees. Sometimes the teachers failed to come to class, especially at the end of the month, or on Mondays when hangover bells were ringing in their heads. But that hadn't happened much lately, ever since Mr Qobokwane had threatened not to give them any more credit at his shebeen if they didn't attend to their duties. Although they felt that they were underpaid, and therefore could not muster enough commitment to the school, this threat made them toe the line. For the past few weeks they had been attending to their teaching duties regularly. The students should have no reason to strike. And they would not strike without complaining to Mr Qobokwane first. After all, most of them were responsible adults with families and would want to follow the proper channels. No, it couldn't be a strike.

By six thirty no students had arrived, and Radisene and his colleagues decided to go to Red House to discuss the matter with Mr Qobokwane. They had only just walked out of the mission precinct when they were blinded by flashlights. Makhele bolted, and a shot rang out. Radisene and Cynthia froze on the spot. Makhele carried on running. There was another shot, and he fell to the ground. Radisene tried to go to him, but a whip lashed across his back. 'Stop right there!' shouted one of the four policemen confronting them. 'You want to die like that old fool?'

'What are you doing here at this time? Don't you know there is a curfew?' growled the second policeman. They knew that voice from Red House, and were relieved to see Trooper Motsohi standing in front of them.

'Hey, it's us, man, we have just come from school,' said Radisene.

'And where is your curfew permit?'

'Curfew permit? We don't know anything about that, man. Don't you see? It's us, Motsohi man, your friends from Red House.'

'And who are you calling "man"? What gives you the right to call a peace officer of His Majesty's government "man"?'

Radisene couldn't believe his ears. Surely this was not the Motsohi of Red House! While he was pondering this question two policemen grabbed Cynthia and said, 'You are coming with us, Mistress. We need a few lessons in the privacy of our police van.' At the same time Motsohi and the fourth policeman began to lash at Radisene with their whips. He screamed and ran away. They chased him, whipping him all the while, until he got into the yard of his flat.

Radisene was seething with anger. He had weals all over his body. His shirt was stuck to his back, and when he pulled it off the weals opened up and began to bleed. He cried. Not because of the pain. He cried because of the rage that was imprisoned in his chest and wanted to burst out. He was going to get this Motsohi. He was going to report these atrocious crimes to Roll-Away. He had never imagined that any human being could be that vicious. And

Motsohi of all people! He wondered if old Makhele was dead. He couldn't bring himself to think about what had happened to Cynthia in the police van. He could not sleep. He thought of his sister. How he wished Dikosha were there. Not that there was anything she could do. But it would have been comforting to have her there. He cried the whole night.

The following morning Radisene went to the police station to lay a charge. The policewoman at the desk wanted to know what he had been doing in the street at that time. Didn't he know there was a curfew? 'I am glad you have actually brought yourself to the charge office for breaking curfew regulations,' she said slyly. 'I can throw you into a cell and forget about you for ever. But because I am a merciful woman I'll advise you to disappear from my sight before I decide to lock you up.'

Radisene rushed out, and went straight to Red House. 'I was wondering when you'd come,' said Mr Qobokwane. He told Radisene about Makhele: he had been found dead by some pupils arriving at school that morning. As for Cynthia, she had been terribly assaulted and repeatedly raped by the policemen, and then left for dead. As she was stumbling towards her home, she had come across another group of policemen from the Mobile Unit and they beat her again for breaking the curfew regulations. She was in hospital. 'The students won't come to class any more because the police beat them up,' cried Mr Qobokwane. 'We have no choice but to close the school.'

For the first time the meaning of the coup registered in Radisene's apolitical mind. His colleagues were either dead or dying, and he had lost his job. How was he going to pay his rent? His whole body felt numb, and his knees were like jelly. He buried his head in his hands.

Mrs Qobokwane gave him a bottle of Paarl Perlé and said that it was on the house. He poured himself a drink and slugged it all at once. Then another one. And another. He was becoming giddy and happy. He suddenly burst out laughing. He laughed for a long time, until tears streamed down his cheeks. They streamed on and on, until they were no longer tears of laughter, but tears of pain. At the same time he kept drinking the wine as if it was water. Then he put his head on the table and promptly began to snore.

When he opened his eyes the paraffin lamp had already been lit, and some of the regulars were drinking around the table. Roll-Away was there, and Trooper Motsohi. It was like old times. He touched his body and felt the weals. No, it was not like old times. He stood up and staggered to Roll-Away's side of the table. He pointed an accusing finger at Trooper Motsohi. 'They killed my colleague Makhele!' he shouted.

'Who are you talking about?' Roll-Away asked casually.

'Motsohi and three other policemen.'

'Can you point them out?'

'No, I didn't know them. I only knew Motsohi.'

'Who pulled the trigger? Did they all pull it at once?'

'I didn't see. It was at night.'

'Then stop making false accusations. It can be very dangerous to your health if you make wild accusations like that. Come on, drink and stop being stupid.'

Roll-Away poured Radisene a brandy. He winced and swallowed. He winced again when he heard a woman screaming outside, and the sounds of sjamboks eating into her flesh. Soon they could hear screaming from all over Ha Ramokhele. Trooper Motsohi explained with relish that the Police Mobile Unit was invading the shebeens and using whips to advise the patrons to go home to their families, since it was long after curfew time. 'Don't worry, Teacher, they won't come here because they know this is Roll-Away's joint.' For a change the joke was not on him, and he was having a great time. He poured Radisene another drink, and said, 'Drink, Teacher, and be merry, for tomorrow we die.' Radisene winced and gulped the whole glass. 'You see, it's nice to have friends who are cops because you can sit and drink in shebeens long after curfew time,' said Trooper Motsohi, bubbling over with new enthusiasm for life. Radisene felt like vomiting on him. Instead he stood up and staggered to the door. Mr Qobokwane

tried to help him. Mrs Qobokwane had long since taken refuge in
the bedroom. 'Take him home, boys. He's always been our friend,
you know that,' barked Roll-Away.

Radisene vomited at the door. Trooper Motsohi and two other
policemen dragged him outside, and bundled him into the police
van, where he passed out. They drove away at great speed. A
group of children were playing hide-and-seek in the street in front
of their home. 'What are those little devils doing out after curfew?'
asked one policeman. The van screeched to a halt and Trooper
Motsohi and his comrades-in-arms jumped out with their trusty
whips. They lashed out and the children ran helter-skelter, screaming for mercy. The policemen came back to the van laughing, and
drove Radisene home. In his room they undressed him, folded his
clothes carefully, and put them on the chair. They put him in bed
and covered him with blankets. He snored. 'I must take care of
him, you know,' joked Trooper Motsohi, 'he's Tampololo's home-
boy.' They opened the pot on the Primus stove and ate all his papa
and steak. Then they bade him good night and the sweetest of
dreams, and melted into the darkness.

The days that followed were the saddest that the people had
known in living memory. It was as though they were back in the
days of Difaqane, when cannibals like Motlejoa ruled the roost,
and neighbour cooked neighbour for dinner. As days became
weeks, and weeks became months, hope burned in their hearts that
things would improve and the beautiful carefree life would return.
But things did not improve. They became worse instead.
Something ugly had been unleashed. An ugliness that people had
never even suspected lurked inside them paraded out into the sun-
light. They amazed themselves, for they had not known this ugliness was there all the time, hiding in the recesses of their blissful-
ness, waiting to emerge at the slightest provocation. They had
woken up in the mornings, smiled at their neighbours, and greeted
them with the age-old greeting: Kgotsong ... Peace to you all,
mothers and fathers ... Peace to you my children ... Peace to you
old people ... Beautiful people ... Peace to you people of the

crocodile, and to you people of the lion ... Peace to people of the rabbit, of the cat, of the hippo, of the elephant ... And to you totems of the east, people of the big tree, and of the red ochre ... Children of Sekonyela ... Peace! Yet here they were shamelessly rendering the greeting meaningless. Sibling turned against sibling as they took different sides, some supporting the Congress Party and others the ruling National Party. Here were leaders of the Congress running away from their country of birth, into exile in the kin-country of Botswana. Even the churches of God were perceived to have taken sides in this war, with the Catholics supporting the National Party and the Protestants – especially the Evangelicals – the Congress Party.

Mafeteng was one of the worst hit of all the lowland towns. Most of its citizens were supporters of the Congress Party, so the Police Mobile Unit sent its men to discipline them. Roll-Away was deemed to be too soft. A new commander, Potiane, was sent from Maseru to take over the operations in the townships and villages of Mafeteng. He and his men razed to the ground whole villages and killed whole families suspected of supporting the Congress Party. Roll-Away joined in some of these expeditions lest he lose his pension.

The coup and its emergency endowed Trooper Motsohi with a new sense of importance and respectability. In the eyes of the populace this delicate fellow loomed over the other policemen of his rank. All of a sudden he was feared throughout Mafeteng, and he loved it. He became Potiane's favourite boy, and they would be found in shebeens competing to see who had the fastest draw. Potiane always won, of course. Then the patrons would congratulate them with beer. And those who did were protected from the whippings that befell curfew-breakers. They could drink in the shebeen until midnight if they so wished. The unemployed Radisene, who had swallowed his pride and learnt to live with the new dispensation, benefited from this generosity. He went to Red House every day and drank himself into a stupor.

Trooper Motsohi and Potiane were always together. They were

together when they doused the beard of businessman Molahlehi with petrol, and set it alight. Then they forced him to make love to his own daughter. Mr Molahlehi, who was a pillar of the community and a leading member of the Congress Party, later died of shame. His daughter surrendered herself to the world in Maseru, and became a lady of the night.

Tampololo's fists, on the other hand, continued to rain down on poor Trooper Motsohi. The more she beat him up, the more viciously he treated the curfew-breakers. When there were no curfew-breakers to be found on the streets, he invaded people in their houses and demanded that they prove that they were not curfew-breakers at heart. Then he and his colleagues sjamboked them. People pleaded with Tampololo, 'Please, Tampololo, stop beating up your husband, because now he takes it out on us.'

4. **The Silence**

After Radisene left Ha Samane and went back to his teaching job in Mafeteng, Dikosha's silence became even more intense. She did not utter a single word. She seemed to have lost interest even in the songs of the pumpkin. The other girls came to her house, stood outside the door, and pleaded with her, 'Dikosha, please come to the village playground. We miss your new songs and your dances. Please Dikosha, come and dance with us.' She did not respond. Instead she walked out of the house, passed the girls as if she did not even see them, and disappeared into the veld. She did not go to the hills to mesmerize snakes either. For a while the herdboys complained that their palates longed for the delicacy of snake-meat. But then they gave up hoping that she would ever go back to the idyllic life of hillside banquets.

When the plane that carried Radisene out of her life had disappeared, Dikosha went to the lower part of the village and spent that whole afternoon looking at ditema patterns. The people of the village saw a girl in a red dress staring at their houses, and wondered what was wrong with her. Some young women went to her and greeted her. She spoke with them – it was the last time she would speak for many years – and told them how beautiful the murals were. They expressed their pity for her because she came from that part of the village which had no sense of beauty. She told them she had always wanted to paint her home with similar patterns. They took her to quarries below the village, which had ochre of different colours. From each quarry she dug out ochre which she mixed with water from a nearby stream and rolled into a ball. When she went back home she was carrying three big balls of red, yellow and off-white ochre.

At home she mixed each ball with water and began to paint ditema patterns with her fingers. The rondavel was built of stone, so she could not paint patterns on its outside wall. It would need to be plastered with mud first, in order to cover the stones and create a smooth surface for painting on. The doors and the windows, however, were framed by wide borders of caked black mud. It was on those frames that she painted her ditema. She got some laundering blue from the house and added it to the red, yellow and white. When she finished she was quite happy with the result. Perhaps next time she would plaster the whole house and paint murals that were as beautiful as those she had seen in the lower part of the village. No, they would be even more beautiful. She would combine the ditema with paintings of the big-buttocked people of the Cave of Barwa.

When Mother-of-Twins returned from a letsema work-party late in the afternoon she was stunned to see ditema on her rondavel. She stood for a long time staring at them. Dikosha came and stood beside her, smiling proudly, waiting for praise. But Mother-of-Twins pounced on her, grabbed her ear and twisted it. 'What is this you have done to my house?' she demanded. Dikosha moaned softly in pain. 'You want to make me a laughing stock of the village!' Mother-of-Twins shrieked. 'You are not satisfied with making a fool of me by getting yourself conceived at a night dance!' She pulled Dikosha by the ear, and ordered her to get water from the well at once, and clean the frames she had messed up with heathen patterns. As Dikosha cleaned off the beautiful ditema she wailed like a banshee. Passers-by stopped and looked at her pityingly. They commented among themselves, 'Poor Dikosha! It is because she was conceived at a night dance.'

After she finished scrubbing the ditema off the frames, she wailed all the way to her grandmother's compound. She sat on the granite grinding-stone in front of the rondavel and wailed even louder. Nkgono, as grandmother was called by all and sundry, came out of the rondavel and pored over her granddaughter for some time. Then she shouted, 'What is wrong, Dikosha? What is eating you?' Dikosha did not answer. She just went on yowling. Nkgono did not have the patience to waste on spoilt brats, as she thought of her granddaughter. She had always reproached her daughter, Mother-of-Twins, for not spanking Dikosha. It was her fault that Dikosha had got out of hand. Now the old woman fumed, 'Get out of my compound, you little witch! You will call me the eyes of the people. I suspect you have fought with your mother. But why do you come to me? You only know me when you are in trouble!'

This last remark was her usual complaint to everyone who was prepared to listen. She always lamented that her grandchildren never visited her. Even the child of her own womb, Mother-of-Twins, only came to see her once in six months or so. It was as though they lived in a different village far away. 'I tell you, my people, to give birth is no longer the glory it used to be,' she would end her lament. And sometimes she would ask, 'These grandchildren, where would they be if I had not given birth to their mother? Where would the ungrateful wretches be?' The height of ungratefulness was that her grandson, Radisene, had visited Ha Samane, but did not even come to greet his own grandmother. This wound was fresh and still smarting. She had heard from people of the village that Radisene was there, that he was a teacher who wore a suit, and that he was too proud to take the gift of money from the kind-hearted village grandmothers. Instead he had given them ten rands. Nkgono had put on her clean seshweshwe dress and sat outside her rondavel waiting for her grandson. But Radisene never came. Today, she had heard, he had gone back to the lowlands. She felt very slighted. She muttered, 'He gives money to people who are not even his relatives, yet he does not come to see his own grandmother. Has giving birth turned to be such a curse?'

Dikosha did not wait for Nkgono to tell her a second time to clear herself from her compound. She knew that her grandmother was capable of seizing anything in sight and hitting her with it. Her wailing did not stop as she ran off the direction of the Cave of Barwa.

Indeed, Nkgono's fiery temper was well known throughout the village. She was always strutting around the compound, threatening to beat up somebody, to break someone's jaw, to make someone defecate. Sometimes her threats were not directed at people but at animals, especially stray pigs, or a hen followed by a brood of chickens. Once, when Dikosha was about six or seven, Nkgono became so angry with her that she grabbed a piglet that was grunting and sniffing around in the clearing in front of the rondavel and hit the girl with it. Fortunately neither the girl nor the piglet was seriously hurt. But Dikosha never forgot the incident.

There was a reason why Radisene, and even Mother-of-Twins, were wary of being seen in the company of Nkgono, even though she was their kinswoman. A terrible rumour circulated in Ha Samane that she had killed her husband. Radisene's grandfather had been a miner. Then one year he had come back from the mines paralysed from the neck down. The mine shaft had collapsed, and he was quite fortunate to escape with his life, for his companions had all died. The mine bought him a wheelchair and gave him a lump sum as compensation. After a few months the money was finished, and he had to survive on Nkgono's attempts to coax a yield from a stubborn and rocky patch of land. He felt humiliated having to depend on a woman. He thought he could assert his manhood by boasting to all who came to see him about his exploits as a lover who had had a string of women breathlessly running after him in his youthful days. He said all these things in the presence of Nkgono. When they were alone in their sleeping-room he constantly taunted her with the affairs he had had in the nineteen-forties, in the early days of their marriage. Those were affairs which had nearly broken their new marriage, but he had mended his ways and had long been forgiven. Now, in their old age, he relished hurting her with them. Finally, so the story went in the village, she could take it no more. She smashed him to death with his bedpan. No one, however, was able to explain why this instrument left no mark on the dead man's body.

Although Dikosha kept on reminding him that if it were true that Nkgono had killed Grandfather she would have been sent to jail, Radisene never really forgave his grandmother. He had loved the old man, and remembered him as a jester who was full of interesting tales. Grandfather had fought in the big war of the world, and never ran out of stories about his experiences in the land of the white people. He had been taken prisoner by the Germans, but in the camp where he was held he was used as a servant by the other white prisoners. He was eventually saved from this servitude by a senior officer who was also a prisoner. He said he would not allow Grandfather to be exploited by other prisoners since he was his personal servant. He would not share him with others. Everyone seemed to respect the officer, and so the old man – who was quite a young man then – served only him. When the war was over they were all released from the prison camp and sent back home. Like all black soldiers Grandfather was rewarded with a bicycle. In addition to that the old man was given two guns because he had been a faithful servant to the officer, who turned out to be a magistrate in one of the lowland towns. He was not given any bullets though, and was warned, 'These guns are not for shooting people. They are just for you to keep, so that you may remember that you fought bravely in the war. They are what we call "souvenirs".' The magistrate arranged that Grandfather be given a licence to show that he was a 'collector' of firearms. Nkgono always teased him that his guns were useless, since they had not shot so much as a bird.

When Dikosha left her grandmother's compound she went to the Cave of Barwa, hoping to recapture the warm moments she had spent there with her brother. And for the next four years she went there almost every day. Once a week she spent the whole night there. For some reason she seemed to be at peace with the world. Even though her silence was intense, she got on much better with Mother-of-Twins. She spent her days, and sometimes her nights, in the Cave of Barwa, while Mother-of-Twins spent hers attending one letsema work-party after another, or visiting Mother-of-the-Daughters. Lately no one cooked at home, for Mother-of-Twins ate at the places she visited. She did not care to find out where Dikosha ate. 'I am tired of cooking for a lefetwa whose twentieth birthday has come and gone. If she is hungry she will take the mealie meal and cook herself papa,' she told Mother-of-the-

Daughters, who assured her that she was doing the right thing. She said, 'I have given birth to ten daughters. I can tell you that by the time they were four years old they could prepare their own meals.' But Dikosha never prepared any meals for herself. People of the village, who made the troubles of other families their own troubles, joked that she lived on Holy Spirit.

Rounds of feasts and work-parties, on the other hand, kept Mother-of-Twins well fed. She was one of the women who always arrived at a feast three days early, and helped with the brewing and the cooking. And she left two days after the feast, for she was one of the women who washed the dishes and the big three-legged pots, and finished off whatever remained of the food so that it should not go to waste.

Feasts came in all sizes. Some were small affairs where neighbours gathered to eat a single sheep quickly and drink a few calabashes of beer. These feasts were mostly made to thank the ancestors for the gift of life. Others were mammoth affairs where people came from distant villages, even from the lowlands, to celebrate an important event. Such was the feast that took place at Ha Sache, across the Black River. It was the feast of feasts.

One of the daughters of the village, a girl called Misti, had returned from across the seas. She had gone there to suckle their knowledge, and now she had returned to spew it back on her own people. As usual Mother-of-Twins arrived three days early. This time she was joined by Mother-of-the-Daughters, who had also come to help with the preparation of food and the brewing of beer. Both these women of Ha Samane were reputed to have a beautiful hand in all matters pertaining to brewing sorghum beer. Mother-of-the-Daughters, particularly, often hosted men from Ha Sache who visited her husband solely for the purpose of tasting her beer. With her in charge of brewing, and with the assistance of another respected brewer such as Mother-of-Twins, the feast was bound to leave the revellers in a blissfully woozy state for a long time to come. In fact there was a debate in both villages as to which woman was the better brewer. Each one had her own followers, although each group grudgingly admitted that it was sometimes difficult to tell the difference between the one beer and the other. But both groups agreed that when the two women were together they brewed the beer of the world.

Revellers began to gather in the morning at the girl's home. The first to come were the local men who participated in the slaughtering of the beasts. They drank beer as they roasted those parts of meat that were reserved for men only. Later in the morning the men from Ha Samane arrived on their horses. They were led by Father-of-the-Daughters on a black horse. He was wearing his chiefly blanket, the Seana-Marena, which was red and had black designs of mealie cobs and leaves. He was followed by formations of horsemen, each wearing a yellow and black Seana-Marena. A few of the men were wearing the Lefitori blanket, named after the original colonizer of the people, Queen Victoria. The Lefitori had designs of crowns and aeroplanes on it. All the men were wearing conical grass hats.

The horses themselves were arranged according to their colours. First came the brown horses, and then the white, and at the rear of the formation the rarest ones of both brown and white. All had a sheen that spoke of excellent breeding, good feeding and expert grooming. They all moved in a rhythmical trot, keeping the same step. Sometimes they broke into a canter, all in unison, and then into a rack. As they trotted through the village, women stood outside their houses and gave piercing ululations. This inspired the poets among the men to sing the praises of their horses and the occasion. When they approached the homestead the ululants, who were busy at their pots, danced around, waving dishcloths and cooking utensils. They filled the air with ululations that could be heard even in distant villages across the Black River.

When the horses arrived at the homestead, they bent their knees to the ground so that the horsemen could dismount. This was a new trick that people had never seen before. They burst out laughing, and ululated even louder. The men were welcomed by the father of the homestead, who led them to a spot under a big tree, where they

sat on rocks and aloe stumps and were served beer. Young boys
unsaddled the horses and drove them to graze just below the village.

More men and women arrived from other villages and from Ha
Sache itself. The favourite blankets of people from Ha Sache were
the Matlama, named after one of old King Moshoeshoe the First's
regiments. These blankets were either plain brown or grey, and
edged with a delicate blue on which were ornate patterns. They
also had tassels on all four sides. Although the Matlama were very
expensive blankets, men of Ha Samane really looked down upon
them because one could buy them at any store – even at the
Fraser's general dealer's stores that dotted the mountain villages
throughout the land. The Seana-Marena, on the other hand, could
only be purchased from one store in the whole country:
Robertson's in the lowland town of Hlotse. The manager of
Robertson's, a puny white man in khaki shorts who went by the
name of Boy, had somehow acquired the world rights to sell
Seana-Marena blankets. He did not stock them all the time, but
brought in stocks only twice a year. On those occasions people
from all over the country went to Hlotse, and spent many nights
camping outside the store in a long queue. This helped to make the
blanket very uncommon and to keep the price very high.

Men and women from higher up in the mountains came
wrapped in their Qibis, named after the otter because of its thick-
ness. The Qibi, mostly light brown with white and yellow, was the
warmest of all the blankets, and was the favourite with those men
who travelled to the cattle-posts often or spent time in places that
had snow most of the year. Because of its warmth, people nicknamed the Qibi 'the thigh of a nursing mother'.

In front of one of the rondavels a big tent had been erected, and
benches were arranged inside in neat rows. Most of the benches
were borrowed from the neighbours. In fact, neighbours did not
wait to be asked. When there was a feast they brought their benches and their utensils and crockery.

The guests were called to take their places inside the tent. Then

a small group of young men and women walked out of the rondavel and sat in the front benches facing the rest of the guests.
Most of them were wearing black gowns. Over their shoulders
they had hoods of different colours and on their heads they were
wearing mortarboards. The women welcomed them with more
ululations.

Among the young women in gowns people of the village could
identify the petite Misti in her radiant yellow beauty, and Tampololo, the big-boned, dark beauty of Mother-of-the-Daughters. They
did not know the others – Misti's friends from the lowlands, so
they were told, who had come to celebrate with her. Among those
who were not wearing gowns people could only identify Sorry My
Darlie, the very son of Ha Sache. When they first saw him, they
began to shout, 'Sorry! Sorry! Sorry My Darlie!' but the uncle of
the homestead quickly called them to order. 'It is true that Sorry
My Darlie is a very important person in the country, and we are
proud that he is our honoured guest. However, this is not his feast,
but Misti's. Sorry My Darlie has come to celebrate with his homegirl. Today's accolades must go to our daughter.'

The uncle of the homestead then proceeded to make a speech.
He said that Misti had gone across the seas, to a country called
Ireland, where she studied hard and received letters that were
above any letters ever received by anyone from Ha Sache, or even
Ha Samane. 'She now works at the big hospital in Maseru where
they are able to cure even those diseases that have defeated Staff
Nurse Mary at the clinic at Ha Samane.'

A man stood up and demanded that he be given the opportunity
to ask a question. The uncle of the homestead said it was a democracy and everyone had the right to ask a question. A heckler
shouted that it was not a democracy since Leabua continued to sit
on the chair of the government by force even though he had been
voted out by the people. 'My question is this,' said the first man.
'Why is she wearing that gown? Did she join the Zionist Church
when she got to Ireland? Did she become a Mopostola? And that
child also, whom we know very well, the daughter of Father-of-

the-Daughters, did she also join the Apostolic Zionist Church?'
Those who knew what the gowns meant laughed.

'These are gowns that these children wear because they are very
educated,' explained the uncle of the homestead. 'Your question
teaches me that you do not attend our feasts. If you did, you would
have remembered that only a few years ago we were at Ha
Samane, at the homestead of Father-of-the-Daughters, where we
were celebrating Tampololo's feast after she finished at the university at Roma. All of us did not know these strange dresses then.
We asked the same question. We were told that Tampololo had
received a letter called B.A., and people with such letters wore
such gowns. You would be knowing that if you were regular in
attending people's feasts. In any case, man, you know that the
gowns of the Zionists are blue and white, or green and white, or
yellow and white. They are not black like these gowns. And you
do not see these children beating drums like Zionists, and dancing
around, and being possessed by the Holy Spirit.'

One of the important guests from the lowlands offered to
explain what it was exactly that Misti had studied in Ireland. She
was older than the rest of the gown-wearers, and her gown was
quite different. It was red, with blue decorations in front. Her cap
hung loosely and carelessly on her head, and was not flat on top
like the others. It was more like an oversized beret. This woman
explained that she was Misti's friend from Roma where she was a
teacher at the university. People of the village wanted to know why
her gown was not black like the others. She told them that she had
letters that were much higher than the rest, which she also received
across the seas. She was in fact a doctor, although not the kind that
cured people. When people reached the highest stage of learning,
she explained, they became doctors of letters. People mumbled,
'What good is a doctor if she can't cure ailments?' Others said
maybe it was because she was a woman. If she were a man with all
that learning surely she would be able to cure ailments.

The doctor explained that she had met Misti when she was in
her first year at the university. Because she was a brilliant girl with

an enquiring mind they became friends at once. After passing her first year with flying colours, she had been awarded a scholarship to complete her B.Sc. in medical laboratory technology in Ireland. 'Does that mean she is more important than Staff Nurse Mary at the clinic at Ha Samane?' the inquisitive voice demanded again. The doctor tried to be diplomatic, especially because Staff Nurse Mary was also there. 'Staff Nurse Mary is important,' she said. 'Everyone is important. Misti is very important because she is the first one in this country to get a degree in this field. She helps doctors to find out ailments of people by examining their blood or saliva or even urine, so that doctors can cure them.' People of Ha Sache concluded that Misti was more of a doctor than the red-gowned doctor who was explaining these complicated things to them.

After the speeches the dances began. The women of Ha Sache excelled in the mokgibo dance. A lone cowhide drum provided the rhythm, while the women, all wearing blue seshweshwe dresses and white shirts, moved their shoulders and their heaving chests up and down to the tempo of the drum. They wore hats made of animal skins, and had red and white sashes over their shoulders. Mokgibo was a subtly sensual dance, which the women performed kneeling on the ground, now and then sitting on their heels, and rising again to a kneeling position. The whole audience joined in by singing and clapping hands. In addition to the drum, the leader of the dancers blew a whistle, both to keep the rhythm and to tell the dancers when to start a different movement. She had a flywhisk with which she pointed in different directions in a most graceful manner.

Then it was the turn of the men to perform the mohobelo dance. While the audience members sang and clapped hands, the men gracefully moved their arms, and kicked their legs up, and then brought them slowly down to the ground again. The men from Ha Samane, led by Father-of-the-Daughters, did the slow, graceful version of mohobelo, while the men from Ha Sache, led by the father of the homestead, did the faster more agile type.

Nobody took any notice of the Dikosha, sitting alone a little distance from everyone else, watching the dances. Her emaciated frame subconsciously followed the movement of the dancers. Her whole body was aching to dance.

Between the dances food was dished out. There was a big dish of samp for the men, and another big dish of meat. There was a lot of meat because Misti's father had slaughtered three oxen and five sheep. There were big dishes of samp and meat for the women, the girls, and the boys. Each group sat with its dishes some distance from the others. The people dug into the samp with their hands and shoved it into their mouths. They attacked the meat with their teeth. Each of the guests from the lowlands, however, had his or her own plate of food because that was how they ate where they came from. They used spoons or knives and forks, and their plates also had rice, green salads and beetroot.

Dikosha sat alone and watched them eat. She was free to join in, for a feast belonged to everyone. It was unheard-of to be invited to a feast or to be invited to help yourself when the food was served. When the dishes were put on the ground everyone knew that they had the right to eat to their satisfaction. Dikosha chose not to join in the feasting. Some of the people from Ha Samane merely glanced at the thin girl in the red dress, and whispered among themselves, 'Poor Dikosha! It is because she was conceived at a night dance.'

Somebody remarked how beautiful Tampololo looked. She smiled sweetly, and continued to help Misti's mother and numerous aunts to serve the drinks. There was bottled beer and brandy for the lowland people, and the potent brew of Mother-of-Twins and Mother-of-the-Daughters for the rest of the revellers.

'Why have you not come with your husband, Tampololo?' a man wanted to know.

'He is busy at work,' she replied.

'Busy? Busy beating up people! And killing them! He is a policeman, is he not?' That was Hlong, the airfield manager.

Hlong had every reason to feel bitter towards policemen. After the state of emergency had been declared two years before, the troubles of the city had slowly crept to the mountain villages. Soon neighbour was attacking neighbour. Neighbour was burning neighbour's house. An Evangelical like Hlong was a hard-headed Congress Party member. On a number of occasions his airport dwelling had been attacked by the Peace Corps, a group of National Party members who dressed in brown overalls, and had been armed by the government and authorized to attack members of the Congress Party. What pained Hlong most was that these Peace Corps people were fellow-villagers who had lived in harmony with everyone else before the troubles that emanated from the lowlands. Despite the beatings Hlong was adamant in his support of the Congress Party. Even when he heard from air-travellers that Congress members in the lowlands were being killed by government soldiers and policemen, or were being exiled to other people's countries, he said he would rather die than change his politics.

People dismissed Hlong's comments about Tampololo's husband. It was sheer envy, they observed. They said Tampololo was quite fortunate to be married to a man who worked for the government as a policeman. Indeed she deserved it. Not only was she the most educated of Father-of-the-Daughters' children with a B.A. and all, she was also the sweetest. And her husband was very handsome too. 'Yes,' the women agreed, 'Tampololo's husband is very beautiful.' They said that it was obvious God had made a mistake. When he was moulding the parts between the legs he forgot that he had set out to make a girl. Tampololo sustained her sweet smile. She was flattered that her husband was the envy of the village women.

'But where is Radisene?' Hlong wanted to know. 'All the children of Ha Samane and Ha Sache are here to celebrate with their homegirl. Where is the son of Mother-of-Twins?'

Somebody said that perhaps since he was a teacher in the lowlands he felt that he was too important to attend other people's feasts. 'Didn't you hear what he did to those grandmothers when he was last here many years ago?'

Tampololo laughed and explained to them that Radisene was no longer a teacher. He had lost his job two years before when the state of emergency was declared. In any case he was not a real teacher, since he only had a low-pass matric and was teaching at a makeshift fly-by-night school. 'You should see him now,' enthused Tampololo. 'He is a rag who is drunk all the time. He survives on begging from people like my husband.'

Dikosha overheard all this, because Tampololo was shouting at the top of her raspy voice. She felt sick in her stomach. She was disgusted that Tampololo should talk like that about her brother. She slowly walked away to the Cave of Barwa.

As she walked through the fields and among the wild flowers she heard the songs of the mokgibo dancers reverberating on distant hills. The flowers covered the veld and the hills with splashes of purple, white, and pink. They also filled the air with scented freshness. However, the farmers thought of these flowers as a dangerous weed, and to sheep owners they were a nuisance since their spiky seed-vessels stuck on the wool and decreased its value.

When Dikosha arrived at the Cave of Barwa the setting sun was beaming its yellow rays into the dark interior. She stood at the mouth, and admired the grotesque shadow of her body that was cast on the rough walls of the cave. Then her eyes gorged themselves on the paintings. Each one was surrounded by a ring of light, which seemed to be emitted by the painting itself. There were red paintings of men and women with protruding buttocks. Some were pointing fingers at animals. Others were kneeling down and blood was oozing from their noses. There were red and white animals that did not have any legs and seemed to float in the air. And then there were dancers. Many dancers. Some with antelope heads and antelope hoofs. Women were clapping hands and men waving flywhisks. Deeper in the cave there was a group of men dancing around a person lying on the ground, their maleness pointing firmly outwards. A woman was kneeling next to the supine figure, her breasts dangling over it. And of course there was the monster-woman-dancer, who seemed to be the leader of all dancers in the cave; and, as far as Dikosha was concerned, of all dancers in the world. Her painting was the most beautiful of all the cave paintings. It was so harrowing in its beauty that it made Dikosha cry.

She willed it to life, and summoned it to her. At first she was ashamed of herself for being so presumptuous as to summon such an important personage to herself. But as she stood in the middle of the cave, the monster-woman-dancer assured her that there was nothing to be ashamed of. She had long been welcomed as a member of the family, and any member of the family had the right to summon help when the world was becoming too thorny. Then she summoned the hunters, and the dancers, and everyone else from the walls. The activity they were engaged in continued unabated. They spoke and sang in clicks that Dikosha did not understand. However, she could construct images of all the things they were saying in her mind. They could also read her thoughts, which they said were always beautiful.

When darkness fell small fires were lit and the dance continued. Dikosha found herself lying on the ground, and the men were dancing in circles around her, their maleness unflinchingly pointing at her. The song was loud and mixed well with jubilant clicks and laughter. She felt calm, as a woman knelt next to her, her breasts dangling over her, sometimes touching her body.

The dance they were performing was called the Great Dance of the Strong. Its purpose was to heal all the pain that racked her body and her mind, and to banish all her misfortunes. The songs were healing songs, and were variously named buffalo, unclimbable rock, honey, or death. Each one had its own pace, its own rhythm, and its own movement.

The monster-woman-dancer led the women in a frenzied singing that rose in an ear-shattering crescendo. They were sitting in a circle around the fire. Their thighs touched one another, and they clapped hands and breathed very heavily. The men stamped their feet on the ground, dancing around the circle of women. The rattlebones on their legs provided a slow dignified rhythm. They danced on and on for hours without any rest. Soon their buttocks and their bellies began to boil, and some fell on the ground and died. The legs of some of the women trembled. Both men and women staggered and collapsed on the ground.

While they were in a trance they pulled out arrows from Dikosha's belly and thighs with their hands. And her pain went with the arrows. The more arrows they pulled out, the more they seemed to lose consciousness. More men and women fell on the ground and died. Dikosha knew from previous experience that their spirits had left their bodies to make contact with the world of the ancestors. On the way they battled with sickness and death. They would come back in the morning armed with more songs that contained the powers of healing. They would implant those songs in their stomachs and buttocks. Their bellies and buttocks protruded precisely because they were reservoirs of the healing songs.

At sunrise the dance was over. The chief celebrant, the monster-woman-dancer, helped Dikosha to her feet. She sprang up, full of energy. She danced a happy dance. The monster-woman-dancer joined her and they danced around the dead. The dead came back from death and were happy to see Dikosha laughing at last. They all crowded around her and clicked their congratulations, and expressed their hope that she would always be with them as a member of the family, as she had been for the past few years.

Then hunters went out to get food for the people. They did not have to go far, because all was in abundance in the vicinity. A hunter, imbued with medicinal powers, merely needed to point his finger at the rock-rabbits that were prancing about and they froze on the spot. The hunters took only the number they needed for food, and let the others go. Other hunters came back with honey and monokothswai berries. Meat was roasted and a feast was laid out. Dikosha ate so much that she thought her stomach would burst like a balloon.

Dikosha was filled with love for the people of the cave and wished that she could spend all her days with them. She loved the peace that reigned among them. No voice was ever raised in anger, and they did not seem to know any form of violence directed at other human beings. Men did not deem themselves to be more important than women. There seemed to be an equality among them that did not exist in the world of Ha Samane.

As she walked away from the cave she knew that she would come back again. And again. As she had done before. She loving-ly touched the beads made from the shell of an ostrich-egg that they had given her as a gift. She marvelled at the generosity of the people of the cave. She was part of a chain, and so she would bring them gifts that she made with her own hands when she came back for the Great Dance the following week. During the day she would sit with some of the women of the cave and make claypots, while others made beadwork. She gave the claypots to those who had given her gifts before, to show how she valued her relationship with them. They always appreciated her gifts.

How she loved the people of the cave! The most beautiful gift of all was that they had endowed her with the power to see songs.

She caressed the beads, and giggled.

5. The Famo Dance

When Radisene woke up in the morning his whole body was aching and his nostrils were blocked. He hoped he wasn't catching a cold. That would not make his long journey any easier. He went to the bathroom and took a shower. The water was cold. That was always the problem with small-town hotels. But he had no time to complain to the management. He was already late, he would not even have time for breakfast. He quickly dressed in a white shirt, a grey necktie and his trusty grey suit. It showed no signs of age-ing, despite the fact that it was more than seven years old. It was the only thing he had not sold during his horrendous days of unemployment, because he needed it for job interviews. He believed that it brought him luck, so he wore it whenever he was on important assignments.

He paid his bill at the reception desk and ran to the bus-stop, which was only a short distance from the hotel. Fortunately his bus was still there, but it was full and he could not get a seat. He stood in the aisle with the rest of the latecomers who were pressed against one another like sardines in a can. The conductor kept on packing in more and more people. When some women complained that the bus was too full and they could not breathe, the conductor said, 'Should I now leave these people here? Who does not want to get home? You are complaining because you are already in the bus. Move back! Move back!'

The bus was quite rickety and it moved very slowly. In addition to the overload of passengers, the roof-carrier was also overloaded with bags of cabbage, gallons of paraffin, sheets of corrugated iron, live goats, bags of mealie-meal and sundry household goods. At times the driver had to stop because paraffin was spilling, or because a suitcase fell and scattered all its contents on the road. The owners of these things were very angry. They shouted insults at the conductor and blamed him for not tying their property securely. On steep inclines or sloppy roads, the passengers had to get off and walk, until the bus got to the top. Radisene welcomed these moments, for he was able to get some fresh air. It was so hot in the bus that he was sweating and was becoming feverish. His knees were like jelly. Even the songs of the migrant workers and their jokes about the mines whence they came did not relieve his anguish. The fact that some were drinking beer, and the whole bus was filled with its stench, made things no better. From time to time a man would break wind or belch. Or another would shout, 'Tshetshe station!' and everyone knew that he wanted the bus to stop so that he could pee. And with all the beer that was flowing the bladders were loose, and there were many tshetshe stations.

It was evening before the bus arrived at Radisene's destination. The whole journey from Maseru to that distant village had taken him two days. He had had to sleep in a hotel in Quthing, because when he arrived there the last bus to the village had already left. They all left in the morning. If his boss was not so miserly he would have bought a car long ago especially for such missions. Radisene could have completed the whole assignment in a single day if he did not have to depend on the whims of public transport.

In the village he asked the children to direct him to the chief's place. He was led through a maze of narrow paths between home-steads. Here homesteads were built close together, unlike in his home village in the mountains where there were big spaces between homesteads. The arrangement here created a feeling of warmth and cosiness. In every homestead there were many peach trees, and pink blossoms scented the air. The fragrance very much reminded him of Father-of-the-Daughters' orchard at Ha Samane. At that time of the year it also scented the whole village air. Father-of-the-Daughters had many trees of different fruits in his orchard. Everyone in the village had at least one peach-tree, but Father-of-the-Daughters also had apricots, apples and plums.

The thought of all the fruit he used to eat during season made him hungry. He should have eaten before he left the hotel, he thought. But how was he to know that the bus took the whole day on the road. Those who knew had brought with them provisions of chicken and dumpling, and throughout the journey someone would be eating. The smell of the food had tortured him very much and made him feel nauseous.

The blossoms created a longing in him for Ha Samane. He missed his home village. He missed the mountain people. He missed the bucolic life. Most of all he missed Dikosha. He had not seen her for seven or eight years. He wondered what she was doing. Perhaps she was already married. After all, she would be an old woman of twenty-five or so by now. But, no. He certainly would have heard of it from Sorry My Darlie. Sorry My Darlie went home quite often, and never seemed to give up his obsession with Dikosha. He was the main reason Radisene did not go back to Ha Samane. He did not want to go back as a failure and be the laughing stock of everyone there. He had vowed that he would go back home only when he was a success like Sorry My Darlie. The state of emergency had been a setback. He had lost his job and was unemployed for almost two years. He was only just recovering from the depths of destitution, after getting a clerical job with A.C. Malibu, a lawyer in Maseru. Soon he would be able to go home and see his sister.

At the chief's homestead he was welcomed by an old man who introduced himself as the principal councillor, Ramoabi. Radisene introduced himself and asked to be taken to the chief. Old Ramoabi took him to a room where a middle-aged woman was kneading dough. She looked up, and said, 'How can you bring visitors here when I am busy preparing food for my children?'

Ramoabi answered, 'I am sorry, father, but this visitor says he has come from the government about urgent matters.'

Radisene knew at once that the woman was the ruler of the village. He always found it ridiculous that a chieftainess was addressed as 'father' even though she was a woman.

The chieftainess washed her hands and led Radisene to another rondavel. There she served him a dishful of sour porridge and a piece of sorghum bread, which he wolfed down gratefully. Then she asked, 'What does the government want? Surely not more taxes. Our men pay taxes but we do not see any development in this village.'

Radisene answered, 'No mother ... I mean, father. I do not come from a department which deals with those matters. I have brought sad news to one of your subjects, a woman called Matlakala. Her husband has passed away.'

The chieftainess was quite impressed that the government was taking such personal interest in the lives of its citizens that they sent an official – obviously a high-ranking one too, judging by his suit – to inform an ordinary village woman that her husband was dead. She sent Ramoabi to call Matlakala, while Radisene remained giving her details of the death. After a few minutes the old man returned alone. Matlakala had gone to a fuchu party at the other end of the village. The chieftainess ordered that she be fetched from there, but Radisene said he would rather go to find her at the party himself. Old Ramoabi offered to accompany him. 'Go well,' said the chieftainess. 'We are going to prepare a place for you to sleep in this rondavel.'

The fuchu party was held in a four-walled, grass-thatched house. Young men were standing outside in groups, joking among themselves or propositioning young women. Inside the house an organist was playing a very lively tune. He was shirtless and sweat was running in rivers down his back. His drummer was next to him, pounding on a drum made of an old tin container with a rubber inner tube stretched over the top. He also struck with his sticks the bottle-tops that were arranged on a wire tied to the drum. Although the drummer too was sweating like a pig, he was wearing a heavy Qibi blanket. Next to the drummer stood an accordion player talking to a woman and drinking beer from a tin container. He passed the tin on to the woman who swallowed the beer in big gulps. Later Radisene noticed that the accordionist only played when the organist was not playing. They seemed to be competing to see whose music would make more people take the floor and gyrate more vigorously.

As the music hotted up the habitués of the fuchu began to dance the famo dance. A man jumped into the arena singing his praises in the manner of sefela poetry. He was brandishing a stick and had his blanket rolled on one arm. He was geared for a mock fight. To the accompaniment of the organ and the drum, he sang about his origins and his travels throughout the land. He sang about chiefs and the beauty of their villages and the women in those villages. He praised the beauty of his own sister, and boasted that no amount of cattle would be good enough for her bride-price. Sometimes his poetry was a lament about the drought that was savaging the land, leaving it ravaged and naked, and about the blood of men that was being drained by the mines in order to make the white missus look splendid in gold and diamonds.

A woman, also brandishing a stick, jumped into the circle and challenged the man in a mock fight. She too was singing her own praise poetry as she danced aggressively towards the man. Their sticks met in the air and they danced back again, giving each other room to prance around. Her poetry was punctuated by the soulful refrain: 'Sewelelele … ! Awu … welelele!', as she made wild love to the stuffy air. She sang of her exploits when she used to run around with the Russians in Johannesburg. She boasted that she was a whore who had devoured many men, who continued to tell the story of her prowess in their graves. The man responded that he wanted to be taken by her and devoured until he was completely finished and there was not even a trace to show that he once lived in this world of sorrows. The woman would shake her waist, kick her leg up and lift her dress to display her femaleness, around which a white circle called a 'spotlight' had been painted.

'You see that woman who is doing the famo right now?' said Ramoabi to Radisene. 'That's Matlakala, the woman you are looking for.'

'And the man for whom she displays her nakedness, who is he?'

'You know the fighting gangs of Basotho men in Johannesburg who are called Russians?'

'Of course, everyone knows the Russians.'

'He is a very famous Russian. The Russians hire special buses and come to enjoy the famo here during long weekends.'

Radisene pushed his way to the other corner of the room where he would be closer to Matlakala when she finished doing her famo. He wondered how these people could be so happy in such an airless atmosphere. The stench of beer, sweat and tobacco sent his head reeling. He was told that this particular fuchu had been going on for the whole weekend. Obviously some of the habitués did not go home to take a bath. They drank, slept on their chairs, cuddled behind the aloes, ate the papa and tripe that could be purchased from the owner of the fuchu, and danced. The cycle was repeated over and over again for the duration of the long weekend.

At last Matlakala finished dancing. Radisene went over to her side and whispered in her ear, 'Listen, my sister, I have come to see you. I have a very important message for you.'

A group of women nearby giggled naughtily and whispered, 'What a catch! He must have been attracted by her spotlight.'

Matlakala smiled coyly and said, 'We can go outside and talk, my brother.' She led the way to the door. Radisene beckoned Ramoabi to follow. Matlakala was not pleased when the old man joined them. 'You want to talk with me, both of you?' she demanded.

At that moment the Russian came out fuming. He had earmarked the woman for himself, he shouted, and would not allow people who had just arrived and were not part of the fuchu all along to take her away from him.

Old Ramoabi tried to explain, 'This man is from the government. He has a very important message for this woman. We are already from the chief's place.'

At first the Russian did not believe them, and wanted to fight. He thought it was a trick they were using to take the woman from him. But when Radisene said he could come with them to the chief's place and hear for himself the message he had for Matlakala, he decided that she was not really worth the trouble. After all, there were many other women at the fuchu. Matlakala, on the other hand, became impatient and wanted to be told the message immediately. 'What have I done?' she kept on asking. 'What have I done?'

'You have done nothing, my sister. Let's go to your house where we can sit down, and I'll explain everything to you.'

'What is it about? What is it about?'

'It is about your husband.'

Then Mtlakala suggested that they should go to the chief's place instead, where there would be witnesses to anything that Radisene had to say about her husband. On the way she was busy singing about how filthy men could be, for they made promises that they never fulfilled. She staggered along between the two men, as happy and free as the birds of the woods.

When they arrived at the chief's compound they found that she was already in bed. They did not want to wake her up, so they went into the rondavel where bedding had already been prepared on the floor for Radisene.

'Your husband is dead, my sister,' said Radisene. 'He died in a taxi accident yesterday morning.'

Radisene had expected Matlakala to burst out wailing. They always did when he gave them the news. He was used to being the messenger of doom. But she was calm. Maybe it was the beer, he thought. Maybe she was numbed by the fuchu party and its famo dance.

'Did this happen at the mines where he was supposed to be working.'

'Supposed? What do you mean "supposed"?'

'You are surprised that I am not crying? Well, I'll tell you why. I have not seen my husband for many many years. Since he went to the mines he never came back. Sometimes I would hear from people that they saw him in Maseru. When he was on leave he only went as far as Maseru to spend his money with the whores there. He did not send his children a single cent. Now they herd cattle for other people. And you tell me that he is dead. To me, that man died many years ago.'

Radisene told her how much he sympathized with her. He

explained that the main reason he had come was to discuss the matter of compensation with her. Since her husband had died in a car accident she was entitled to get some money which was known as third-party insurance. 'This is the money that passengers who are involved in motor-vehicle accidents get from insurance companies. Every car is insured for that purpose. No car is allowed on the road without third-party insurance. Even though the scoundrel did not take care of you in his lifetime, at least you can get something from his death.'

'What must I do to get that money? And how much is it?'

'All you need to do is to sign the forms that I have here. They entitle me to claim this money for you. We cannot know how much it is. The company assesses and decides how much they will give you. But I can assure you it will be more than one thousand rands.'

Matlakala's eyes popped out at the mention of such a huge amount. She became instantly sober, and demanded that she be given the forms to sign without any waste of time. Radisene took out two forms from his pocket. One was entitled 'Power of Attorney', and he asked Matlakala to sign on the bottom line and Ramoabi to witness. But the old man, having acted as the chief's councillor for many years, was wary of signing things he did not understand. 'What is this "Power of Attorney"? With my little English I know that attorneys are lawyers. What do lawyers have to to do with this?'

'I work for a firm of lawyers. They do the claims for victims of accidents. This document gives them the authority to act for you, my sister.'

'You are a lawyer! I don't have money to pay lawyers.'

'Don't worry, my sister, you don't pay anything. We are paid by insurance companies.'

'I thought you said you were from the government, young man,' said Ramoabi.

'Well, you know that lawyers go to court to appear before the magistrates or the judges. And all that is part of the government, would you not say?'

'Okay, if you put it that way. But we all know that lawyers are liars. How do we know you won't end up charging this poor woman money for doing this work?'

'You are a witness, old man. You heard me say we don't charge a cent for this service. We are a firm of lawyers that is dedicated to working for our nation.'

Matlakala was impatient. She was not interested in a useless debate about lawyers and their crookedness. She wanted to sign the papers and get it over with. She accused Ramoabi of trying to talk the kind lawyer out of helping her to get money from the father of her children who had deserted them all those years ago.

Radisene gave her the Power of Attorney to sign and Ramoabi signed as a witness. Then he gave her the second form, which was headed 'Third Party Insurance Claim'. It had many blank spaces to be completed. Radisene said all she needed to do was to sign. He was going to complete the blank spaces in the office. 'All I want to know now is: how many children do you have?"

'I have two boys,' Matlakala said. 'They are hired out as herd-boys. They live at the cattle-posts in the mountains.'

'Well, my sister, you will hear from us,' said Radisene, noting down these details. 'Here is our office address in Maseru. Don't lose it because you will need to go there after a month to find out about your money.'

Matlakala staggered back to the fuchu, happily singing that she was going to eat the money of the Satan who deserted her. The crickets of the night sang with her.

Old Ramoabi shook his grey head. 'She did not even ask about the body. Women of today are amazing. She did not even pause to think about the funeral arrangements.'

Radisene woke up early the next morning. The chieftainess was already sweeping the clearing in front of her rondavels. He thanked her for her hospitality.

'You cannot go without eating. It is a long road to Quthing, and then to Maseru,' she said.

Indeed, she was right. He remembered the pangs of hunger that had nearly killed him on the long journey the previous day. In one of the rondavels the chieftainess had already prepared bread and tea. As he ate he thought of all the money his boss was going to make just from this single assignment. And he, who had done all the legwork, was going to get nothing, except for the measly thirty rands a month salary. He was not amused.

And he worked hard too. He had to be alert all the time. A.C. Malibu, his boss, had a network of spies throughout the country who informed him of accidents as soon as they happened. Most of these spies were traffic policemen. He paid them a commission for every insurance claim he successfully made as a result of their intelligence. And Radisene had to be ready for the road any time he received information on an accident.

He smiled as he remembered how he had beaten the competition on this assignment. He had been sitting in his office completing claim forms when the phone rang. It was Trooper Motsohi on the line, and he was reporting a new accident on the main road between Maseru and Mafeteng. Radisene still hated him for all the things he had done at the height of the emergency. Moreover, his back still bore the scars of Trooper Motsohi's whip. But ever since his transfer to the Traffic Department, Radisene had been bound to work with him. Indeed, he was one of the most active traffic cops on A.C. Malibu's payroll. Almost every day he transmitted information on a new accident.

Radisene told A.C.'s secretary about the accident and hurriedly left the office. He went to the room he was renting in a big house in Sea Point township and changed into his good-luck suit. Taking only his toilet bag, he rushed to the bus-stop and caught a minibus taxi. They came upon the accident near Morija, a small Evangelical mission town halfway between Maseru and Mafeteng. A minibus taxi had overturned and rolled off the road. Radisene knew immediately that as usual it had been overloaded and speeding. The competition among the different companies was fierce and often led to reckless driving. He asked the driver of his taxi to let him off at the scene of the accident.

Trooper Motsohi was there to meet him, whispering angrily, 'You took your time, eh, Teacher?'

'But I came as soon as I got your message.'

'You bloody well took your time. You need to be here before the ambulance takes the people to the hospital or the mortuary. You know how difficult it is when the victims are already in hospital, when all the ambulance-chasers are flocking around them. I don't want to lose my commission because of your slowness.'

'You know that I depend on public transport, Motsohi.'

'That's not my fault, man. Ask your boss to get you a car. Look, the vultures have descended, and I was having a hard time beating them off.'

Indeed, the vultures were all over the place, waiting to get their share of the spoils of the accident. Some of the vultures were back-yard mechanics who hoped to strip the wreck of all its parts as soon as Trooper Motsohi and two other traffic policemen left. These were competing with the tow-trucks that were already arriving, hoping to profit by towing the wreck away and storing it at their premises. If the owner did not go and pay for towing and storage, then they stripped the vehicle and sold the parts. Then there were the pickpockets and petty thieves who hoped to search the accident victims, especially the corpses, for valuable possessions. And, of course, the ambulance-chasing lawyers and their clerks hoping to get some of the victims to sign Powers of Attorney and claim forms. It was quite essential for the vultures to get to the scene of the accident ahead of the police, or even the ambulance, so as to stake their claim before the law interfered.

Trooper Motsohi led Radisene to the wreck. He told him that the ambulance had already taken the injured to the mission hospital in Morija. 'That's why you don't see the competition here. They all rushed to the hospital to make the victims sign forms. But I got you the biggie. There's only one fatality in this accident, and he's all yours.' The 'said fatality' was lying in a pool of blood next to the wreck. He was covered in a blanket.

Radisene did not want to look at him. 'Why is he still here?' he asked.

'Where do you want him to be, Teacher? He's waiting for you, man. He's all yours.'

'I don't need *him*. I only need information about his next of kin so that I can go there immediately.'

'Come on, Teacher. Where's your sense of humour? He's waiting for the vehicle from the morgue to pick him up. The first thing I did, of course, was to search him. Here, I have all the details about his home village in the Quthing district and his next of kin. I am going to hold on to this information for a while, until I am sure you have reached Quthing. Then I'll release it to the authorities as if I've just found it. That will give you a head start. By the time the competition gets there you'll have made the widow sign.'

Like him or not, thought Radisene, Trooper Motsohi was good. 'How on earth did you get all this information about this man so quickly – even the name of his wife. Surely he wasn't going around with her name in his pocket!'

'I have my ways, Teacher. I am a damn good policeman, after all.'

Radisene had caught the next bus to the southern district of Quthing and arrived around midday. But by then the last bus to the home village of the 'said fatality' had left, and so he had checked into a hotel.

Thinking back on all this, Radisene had to smile at how smoothly the mission had been accomplished. He forced himself to finish the food. Then he thanked the chieftainess once more, and started on the long road home.

He arrived in Maseru at around five in the afternoon. He wished he could go straight to his room in Sea Point and get into bed. His flu was getting worse and he was drenched in sweat. But he knew that A.C. would be waiting for him, and so he made his way to the office in Bonhomme House, the most beautiful building in Maseru. The office was on the topmost floor, which was only four flights up, but he struggled to climb the stairs. It made him feel quite dizzy.

In the doorway he met A.C.'s secretary, who was going home for the day. She told him that a number of clients were waiting for him. He found his office full of widows in black dresses and doeks, and men and women on crutches or with their legs and arms in thick plaster casts. They had all come to find out if their cheques had arrived. Some of them had been waiting since eight in the morning. Radisene was angry that A.C. or even the secretary had not seen fit to assist them. Why did these people have to wait for him?

He went into A.C.'s office and found him dozing at his desk. He was a scrawny old man with a bald head, who wore a white safari suit most of the time. Once in a while he would come in a black suit, and then everyone knew he had a case at the magistrate's court that day. However, he rarely went to court and earned most of his money through insurance claims. People said he had been a great trial lawyer in his day, but he was captured by the bottle and became an alcoholic. He fell on evil days. Then he turned to God, and went on the wagon. He did not recover his once lucrative practice though. His clients had deserted him and his reputation was sullied. He found an easy way out through third-party insurance claims. He had no regrets, for he was making more money than he had ever done as a trial lawyer. He even built himself a mansion, second only to the Prime Minister's, in the posh suburb of Maseru West. His greatest pride was that he was one of Prime Minister Leabua's confidants, and had been involved in the decision to declare the state of emergency when his National Party lost the elections a few years back.

'There you are,' said A.C., waking up with a start. 'See all those people? They are waiting for you.'

'All they want to know is whether their cheques have arrived or not. You mean the secretary couldn't tell them that?'

'Indeed she could. So could I. But only if we knew where you kept the record book and the cheques that arrived in yesterday's mail.'

Radisene remembered that he had left in a hurry and had forgotten to give the record book to the secretary. He had locked it in the drawer of his desk. He apologised profusely to A.C. and fetched the book. Only one client had been paid and her cheque was in the book. Radisene told the widow to wait, and announced to the rest that their cheques had not arrived yet. 'Be patient,' he told them. 'Sometimes the cheques take a whole month, or even two, before they get here. And, of course, if the insurance company disputes the claim it takes longer.'

In fact, there were two cheques in the book, both drawn to A.C. Malibu. One was for five hundred rands, and it was his fee, paid to him directly by the insurance company. The second one was for six thousand rands, and it was compensation to the client for the death of her husband in a motor-vehicle accident. But, as usual, A.C. took half of that amount as well, in addition to his fee. He made out a cheque for three thousand rands and Radisene took it to the widow who was waiting in his office. She was breathless with joy when she saw the large amount she was getting. She would never know that it was in fact only half of what was due to her and that A.C. had stolen the other half. She thanked Radisene over and over again, and asked God to bless him and his good-hearted master, Mr A.C. Malibu.

'There's only one thing, mother,' said Radisene. 'You need to compensate me for my expenses and time when I went to your village to look for you. So you owe me one hundred rands.'

'That is well, my child. But I do not have the money now. I can only change this cheque tomorrow when the banks open. Then I'll bring the hundred rands to you. You know you can trust me. You have been to my house.'

Radisene thought: what if she comes and I am out on an errand? She will give it to the secretary, or even to A.C., and they will know that I have also been milking the clients. He smiled at the widow and whispered. 'I trust you completely, mother. But don't bring the money here. Send it to me by post. Buy a postal order for a hundred rands and mail it to me. Here's my address.'

The widow left with a happy bounce in her feet. No sooner had

she gone than A.C. called Radisene to his office, and told him that
he was doing a very good job. He was seriously considering giving him a raise. He asked, 'This new client from Quthing, how
many children?'

'Two boys.'

'We better say six. He was old enough to have six children,
wasn't he? And they are all under twenty-one, of course, so they
are dependants who must be claimed for.'

Then he asked Radisene to take a packet of candles to the cathe-
dral just across the street to have it blessed by the priest. A.C. was
a devout Christian. Before he went home for the day he lit a con-
secrated candle and left it burning throughout the night in a
candlestick on his big Chubb safe.

The next day Radisene could not wake up. He came down with
a fever and was delirious. Calls of new accidents came to the
office, but no one attended to them. A.C. was furious, for he was
going to lose money to the other vultures. He personally drove to
Sea Point to find out what was happening with Radisene. 'A pretty good time you chose to be ill,' he muttered.

Radisene did not hear him. Instead he was seeing limbs. All
sorts of limbs. Small ones and big ones. The limbs of children.
Mothers. Fathers. Tiny little babies. All piled up together. A mountain of limbs. Thick black blood oozed from the limbs. Yet they
were all laughing at him. The limbs were laughing at him.

When he opened his eyes Misti was sitting next to his bed. At
first he thought he was hallucinating. But she was real enough. She
touched his brow and said, 'At last you are awake, and your tem-
perature is going down. Tampololo heard from her husband that
you were ill, and she told me. I have been coming here for the last
three days and feeding you soup. Last night I came with one of my
doctor friends and he attended to you. There are your medicines. I
am glad you are better now. I must go. There is more soup, and
some scones and fruit on the table.'

'Wait, please don't go.'

'I have been taking time off to look after you. Now that you are better I must go back to work. I'll come and see you again this evening.'

She smiled at him, and walked out of the door. He heard her Volkswagen Golf revving and driving away. He wished he could be sick more often so that his life could be saved by Misti over and over again for ever and ever more, world without end, amen.

6. The Mansion

Snakes no longer cried. They could be seen gambolling and prancing around on the hillsides. In the evenings, when snake families gathered at the fireside, grandmothers told the story of how at one time their life had been a misery. An emaciated girl, who looked very much like them in shape, used to mesmerize them with a dance. Then she would torture and make them do all sorts of humiliating tricks as though they were lap-dogs. To add insult to injury, when she was tired of amusing herself she would skin them alive and roast them. Grandmothers of the snakes, keepers of this sad history, would point at the anthills dotting the hillside and tell the little snakes that they had once been ovens, where many a forebear saw his or her fate. But, as fortune would have it, the emaciated girl found other interests. Anthills began to grow.

Their torturer was not emaciated any more. They would not even have known her if they'd seen her. Perhaps some of them had in fact seen her on her way to the Cave of Barwa – for she continued to go there at least once a week – but did not recognize her. At thirty she had blossomed into a buxom woman, who looked much younger than her years. She still wore her red dress, which did not look a day older than when it left the store many years ago. It was the only dress she was willing to wear. It kept her close to her twin brother, whom she had not seen for more years than she cared to count.

People of the village never stopped wondering about the source of her beauty. No one ever saw her buying any of the creams that young women of the village applied to their faces to make their skin smooth, such as Beauty or Pandora or even Eskamel. Her skin was as smooth as the buttock of a baby, and they said that it was because she was being licked by a water-snake. Why else, they asked, did she go to the Black River so often, sometimes coming back the next day?

At this time Dikosha had begun to speak again. After many

years, and for reasons no one could begin to explain, she had broken her silence. But she spoke only when it was necessary. And she did not consider it necessary to defend herself. So she let the people gossip. She never explained to them that she had another life with the people of the Cave of Barwa. That she ate their honey and their nourishing herbs. That when she was ill she did not need Staff Nurse Mary at the clinic, nor the traditional herbalists and diviners, but was healed by medicine men and women who got their power from the land of the dead and extracted all the sickness from her body in the form of arrows. That she had died many times in the dances of the night, and woken up again in the morning rejuvenated.

People of the village also wondered about the beads that she wore all the time. They were made from the shells of ostrich-eggs. Yet there were no ostriches in that part of the land. Indeed, in the whole country, even in the lowlands, no such birds existed. Those who had travelled in the land of the Boers, working on their farms, said that such birds lived in the Karoo deserts.

Her beauty was a daily topic in the fields where women were hoeing, in the forests where girls gathered wood, in the shebeens where revellers told each other tall stories, and everywhere people of Ha Samane and its neighbouring villages came together for whatever purpose. The general feeling, especially among men, was that her beauty was wasted, since she was not married. Perhaps the ancestors were cursing her with beauty, they said, for she was the child of a night dance.

Indeed, Dikosha was beautiful in the extreme. Hers was an irrational beauty, a crazy beauty. Beauty ran amok on her face, messing it up with ravishing but discomfiting features. It ran loose in the rest of her body, creating curves along its insane path that any red-blooded male would love to rub his body against.

It was this beauty that made Sorry My Darlie mad. His was the madness of unrequited love. He was seen more at the village of Ha Samane than in the lowlands where he was supposed to be playing soccer. Some said he had become useless on the field. But that was not true, because even in his early thirties he was still a force to be reckoned with. When he was on the field he made a difference, as even the deaf could tell from the thunder of the spectators. However, he was seen less often on the playing-fields of the lowlands. He spent most of his time at Ha Samane sitting outside Dikosha's home drooling like a baby, or following her around and begging, 'Please Dikosha, hear me out. I'll do anything you want. I'll be your slave if you want me to.'

She ignored him, and carried on with whatever she was doing as if nothing was happening. People of the village said Sorry My Darlie was Dikosha's tail.

The new tendency in the village was to whisper things about Dikosha, but never to say anything that might hurt her feelings to her face. It all began when Nkgono's skeleton was found in her own rondavel.

No one had seen Nkgono for many years. She had simply disappeared, and people forgot that she had ever existed. Grass and bushes grew in her compound, until it was like a forest. Her rondavels became ruins. People of the village did not bother to ask what had become of her. They thought that she had gone to her own people, as she had always threatened to do when she felt that no one, not even her daughter and grandchildren, cared for her.

Then her skeleton was discovered by some children playing hide-and-seek in the ruins, the bones still dressed in tattered clothing. A neighbour recognized the clothes. That was what Nkgono had been wearing the last time she saw her alive. Then she remembered that Dikosha had been there that day, wailing like a banshee outside her grandmother's house. Other people also remembered how the girl had cried over the ditema patterns. Dikosha's wails must have killed her grandmother, they said. In time people came to believe that if Dikosha wailed, somebody was sure to die. People of the village began to treat her with care and consideration, so that she would not wail at their homesteads.

The elders of the village were disturbed by Nkgono's death. They regretted that no one had bothered to visit her or to socialize with her, merely because of rumours that she had killed her husband with a bedpan and that she was able to manufacture the thokolose hobgoblin from sorghum bread. It was said that she owned the thokolose and sent it to torment her enemies. But many people, some of them members of the Mothers' Union in church, were known to own the thokolose hobgoblin or to fly on a broom at night, and yet no one ostracized them. They lived in communion and good neighbourliness with the rest of the people in the village. It was well known that a man like Hlong, for instance, had the ability to send lightning to destroy his enemies. Yet he remained one of the most popular people in Ha Samane. The elders could not understand why they had singled out Nkgono for the cold-shoulder treatment. 'Are we now like lowland people?' they asked. 'They say in Maseru you can stay in a house for many years without knowing even the name of your next-door neighbour.'

Others justified themselves and said they had taken their cue from Nkgono's own daughter and grandchildren. But one thing they were careful about was that Dikosha should never be given reason to wail like a banshee. They begged her mother, 'Please, Mother-of-Twins, if she wants to paint heathen patterns on your house again, just let her do it without any fuss. We do not want to see people dying lonely deaths like your mother.'

The mind of Mother-of-Twins, however, was occupied with more important things. A few weeks earlier a truck loaded with red bricks had stopped outside her lone rondavel. As usual she was not at home, but off visiting Mother-of-the-Daughters. Children of the neighbourhood ran to call her. When she came and saw the truck she was quite amazed. She thought that the truck-driver and the labourers sitting on the bricks were lost. 'Are you Mother-of-Twins?' asked the driver.

'Yes, I am.'

'These are from your son in Maseru.'

'Bricks? Does he say I eat bricks? He disappears for more than ten years, and then he sends me bricks?'

'They are for your new house. See, here are the plans. More

material is coming. Cement. Roofing tiles. Everything. It is going to be the best house in the village, with many rooms in it. It will even have a bathroom. And he said I must give you this envelope too.'

Her hands shaking, Mother-of-Twins opened the envelope. It was full of banknotes. The truck-driver helped her count them, so that no one should say he had stolen any of them. A thousand rands in all. She was sweating all over and breathing heavily. At first she thought it was a dream. She pinched herself repeatedly, without waking herself up. She asked the truck-driver to pinch her very hard. But he assured her that it was no dream, and that her son was a very rich man in Maseru. She ran to tell Mother-of-the-Daughters, shouting and waving the envelope.

During that week more trucks came with building materials. The builders constructed a shack for themselves with corrugated iron sheets. In the evenings they cooked papa and meat, and played their guitars and accordions, and sang. This created a festive atmosphere around Mother-of-Twins' house, for the young people of the village came and joined in the song. On the days when she did not go to the Cave of Barwa, Dikosha watched these festivities from a distance. Her body moved in a furtive dance. She was sitting as still as a rock, yet inside herself she was dancing a storm.

It was wonderful how the lowland builders never suffered from hangovers, even though they had turned the whole area in front of Mother-of-Twins' rondavel into a nightly fuchu party. They still managed to get up at the crack of dawn and go on with their building. Every day trucks came with more building materials. The house grew at an amazing rate.

Tongues began to wag. What kind of wastefulness was this, people of the village asked. How would Mother-of-Twins and Dikosha occupy all those rooms? People tried to count the rooms, but they always got lost in the process. Until then Staff Nurse Mary's clinic had had the most rooms of all the buildings in the village. The clinic had five rooms in all. Staff Nurse Mary slept in one room, and another one was her kitchen, with a fridge for storing vaccines. The third room was used for storing medicines. In the fourth one patients registered their names and waited to be called into the fifth room, where they were examined either by Staff Nurse Mary herself or, on special days, by the white doctor who flew from Maseru in the Flying Doctor Service aeroplane. So, all the rooms at the clinic had an essential function.

What about the rooms of the new house that was being built for Mother-of-Twins? Surely its rooms were more than ten. What were two people going to do with all those rooms? Even if Radisene planned to come back to the village, the rooms would still be too many for three people. Even if he planned to marry, the rooms would still be a waste. People of the village concluded that it was the same pride they had seen many years ago when he refused to take money from the grandmothers. He was just showing off his wealth. He had the nerve, they observed, to build such a fancy house next to the homestead of Father-of-the-Daughters who had been, until then, the richest man in the village.

'Who says Father-of-the-Daughters is no longer the richest man in the village?' Hlong asked furiously. 'Just because an upstart of a boy builds a fancy lowland house does not mean he is the richest. Do you know how many thousands of cattle Father-of-the-Daughters has? Have you been to the cattle-posts to count his cattle? Anyway, where does this upstart get all this money?'

Indeed, that was the question that was on everyone's lips. People of the village had heard from people who came from the lowlands that Radisene was a lawyer in Maseru. Mother-of-Twins had begun to brag at the feasts she attended that she, a poor village woman, had given birth to a whole lawyer. 'God is big,' she repeatedly told whoever was willing to listen. Behind her back people asked what good was a lawyer if he did not send even a cent to his mother and sister.

Then one day Tampololo came to visit her parents and burst Mother-of-Twins' bubble. 'No,' said Tampololo in her raspy voice, 'Radisene is not a lawyer. To be a lawyer you need to go to the university at Roma for two years, and then to a city called

Edinburgh in a land called Scotland for another two years, and then finally spend yet another year at Roma. Five years in all! Radisene has not gone through all that training. He is not a lawyer. He is a mere servant of a lawyer. He cleans after his master.'

Next time Tampololo visited her parents she gloatingly told the people of the village that Radisene had lost his job. He had been sick with fever and could not do his work. The lawyer lost a lot of money as a result. Her own good husband, who worked very close-ly with the good lawyer since they were both people of the law, also lost a lot of money as a result. Radisene was fired, as he deserved to be, and was once again an unemployed rag. 'You know,' she blustered, 'even this job with the good lawyer … this Radisene got it through my husband. And there he goes and plays with it, when jobs are so scarce in Lesotho.'

People like Misti and Sorry My Darlie always came with posi-tive reports about Radisene's success. Misti said that from time to time she met Radisene and he had established his own company of insurance assessors. People of the village did not understand what that meant. When she told them that he represented people who were involved in car accidents they concluded that no matter what Tampololo said, Radisene was a lawyer after all. Sorry My Darlie, on the other hand, was rather vague about Radisene's work. All he knew was that Radisene drove a Mercedes Benz, which was much more luxurious than his own Valiant. In any case, his Valiant was so old that children sang about its being a sekorokoro whenever it passed. It spent more time parked outside his flat for want of some spare part than it did on the road. Sorry My Darlie really couldn't care less about Radisene's job. All his thoughts were with Dikosha, and the anguish she was causing him.

After ten months the house was completed. At the same time there was a baby boom in the village, a result of the nightly fuchu parties of the lowland builders. The elders laid the blame at the door of Mother-of-Twins. But she was beyond caring. She was liv-ing in the clouds. She had bought herself new seshweshwe dress-es, new Seana-Marena and Victoria blankets, new shoes, and even new pantihose. She had also bought Dikosha two new dresses and a pair of shoes. But Dikosha refused them. She said she was quite satisfied with her red dress. She did not need any of the fashionable blankets either. She was quite happy with an old donkey blanket that she wore in winter.

Mother-of-the-Daughters tried to advise her friend: 'Mother-of-Twins, you are fortunate because you gave birth to a child who cares about his mother. But it is not wise to spend so much money on clothes. You should be keeping some of this money in the post office for a rainy day. That is what we do, you know, in my family. When Father-of-the-Daughters has sold wool or mohair or some old oxen to the butcheries in the lowlands, we do not go crazy with the money and buy all sorts of useless things. We keep it in our post office savings book.'

But Mother-of-Twins was not interested in taking advice from anyone, even from people who were more experienced in the ownership of money, like Mother-of-the-Daughters. She said, 'Mother-of-the-Daughters, I have been poor all my life, I scrounged for food and for clothes. Thank God I had good friends like you, otherwise my children and I would not have survived. Now that God has blessed me with a son who is rich I must enjoy life. I never had these beautiful things before, because I could never afford them. Now that I have the money let me be happy, for life is too short to worry about the morrow.'

The house was by far the most beautiful house that people of the village had seen in their lives. It compared with the very best in the suburbs of Maseru, said those who had been to the capital in the lowlands. Most of the men had been to the mines and had seen buildings just as big or even bigger. But they all vouched that none of those buildings was as beautiful as Mother-of-Twins' mansion. Most of the women and children had never been anywhere outside Ha Samane and the neighbouring villages. To them the house was a wonder of wonders. They imagined that when Jesus said in the Bible, 'In my Father's house are many mansions', he was talking about Mother-of-Twins' house. It was painted white in colour and roofed with red tiles. The best of the houses that people of the village knew were roofed with corrugated-iron sheets, not tiles. It had glass windows, some of which were bigger than the doors. On the floor it had carpets that were as soft as new blankets. More trucks came with furniture: huge beds, tables, sofas and all sorts of strange things. Surely Mother-of-Twins was going to lead a life that was even better than that of Queen 'Mamohato, who was the queen of all the land, and whose husband King Moshoeshoe the Second had palaces in Maseru and in Matsieng in the lowlands.

One of the rooms in the mansion was very special. It was big and had a floor made of very smooth planks. Three of its walls were covered with mirrors. There was no furniture at all in that room. The foreman of the builders explained, 'This is a very special room that Radisene has built for his sister. It is the room where his sister will dance. He has instructed that on the door we must put this plate, on which is printed: DIKOSHA'S DANCE STUDIO.'

Mother-of-Twins thought the whole idea was madness. What would be the point of dancing in the privacy of a room where you would only be seen by mirrors? Dance was meant to be shared and to be enjoyed by everybody. But then Radisene was the owner of the money. If it humoured him to build a dance-room for his sister, there was no harm done.

Dikosha on the other hand was not interested in the dance studio at all. She was not interested in the mansion either. She said she would spend all her life in the rondavel. Mother-of-Twins was angry and accused her daughter of not appreciating all the beautiful things that her brother had done for them. She threatened to destroy the rondavel. But Mother-of-the-Daughters advised her against that. 'Do not provoke Dikosha, Mother-of-Twins. Do you want her to wail like a banshee again? You know what happens when she does that.'

Dikosha never entered the mansion. She lived peacefully in her rondavel, and sometimes in the Cave of Barwa.

7. The Coup – 1986

Radisene was woken in his room at the Victoria Hotel by loud cheers outside. The sound of blaring hooters, happy laughter, songs and ululations drifted into the room. He looked out of his tenth-floor window and down on Kingsway, the main street of Maseru, he saw throngs of people dancing and making whoopee. Many were carrying branches with green leaves. Others were climbing up flag poles and tearing down the national flag. Three armoured vehicles, with armed soldiers sitting on top, were also bedecked with green branches. They were driving slowly down Kingsway and the throngs were singing and dancing around them. Behind the throngs came a cavalcade of cars, deafening the whole of downtown Maseru with their horns. Radisene switched on the radio at the headboard of his queen-size bed. Against the background of martial music, Radio Lesotho blared out the news: there had been a coup.

It had finally happened. The government had fallen. Sixteen years after the National Party had refused to hand over power to the rightful winners of the elections, Leabua's government had been overthrown by his own soldiers. And down on Kingsway people were singing songs in praise of the military. They were marching towards the border post, waving branches of trees and bathing their battered souls in what they thought was a new-found freedom.

Radisene took a quick shower in the adjoining bathroom, and splashed his body with Aramis cologne. He put on his Bang-Bang jeans and his fawn Afro-shirt. The intricate white and pink embroidery on the front and sleeves of the shirt showed the unmistakable hand of Jabbie, who had introduced the West African fashions that had taken Maseru by storm. It was a hot January day, and Radisene felt nice and fresh in his loose attire. A pair of brown Roman sandals, handmade by Rose of Bedco, finished off the outfit perfectly.

Now for his crowning glory. He greased his permed hair and combed it. He took great pride in his perm. It made him look like the rich Johannesburg socialites he had seen in *Pace* and *Drum*. Even grandfathers in Johannesburg permed their hair, unlike the elites of Maseru who frowned upon the practice and regarded it as uncultured and un-African. They often teased him about his hair-style at Lancers Inn, where the top civil servants and businessmen of Maseru assembled for drinks every evening. But he put their derision down to a lack of understanding of the ways of the rich. If Johannesburg tycoons permed their hair, he would perm his as well. After all, he had made it into their class.

He took a lift to the ground floor, smiled at the beautiful receptionists and walked out of the glass doors. The receptionists remained gossiping about his lack of interest in women. 'That money is wasted, my sister,' said one. 'He is so rich and yet you hardly see him with a girl.'

'I thought you could catch any man you want.'

'With this one I have tried, and failed. He treats me like I'm his kid sister.'

'It is because he is gay.'

'Gay?'

'Small feet, my sister.'

Radisene walked across the parking-lot, to a special space that was reserved for his car. He never tired of admiring this awesome machine, a black S-class Mercedes Benz that was nicknamed China-eye by adoring fans because of the shape of its headlights. He drove out of the hotel gate and joined the cars on Kingsway that were hooting their way to the South African border. He was following his curiosity.

On the Lesotho side of the border post the gates were open and the throngs poured through. They crossed the narrow bridge over the Mohokare River, and when they got to the South African side they began to dance and sing in the open parking area. The American ambassador was already there in his cowboy hat and boots, giving interviews to television cameras, telling them that at last the despotic government of Prime Minister Leabua, a government that had caused so much hardship to the citizens, had been toppled.

Radisene wondered what had become of his old enemy, A.C. He had been a close advisor of the government and a confidant of the Prime Minister. Radisene hoped the soldiers were going to lock him up. Not that he was pleased Leabua's government had been overthrown. After all, he did reap some benefits through his wheeling and dealing with government ministers and their permanent secretaries. He just wanted A.C., his main competitor in the insurance claims business, out of the way. Then he would be king of all car accidents from the Tele River in the south to the Mechachane Mountains in the north.

Now the people were singing and dancing around the American ambassador. He was waving and smiling like a benevolent grandfather. The South African soldiers on the verandah of the passport-control building watched the dance with indifference. His excellency made a show of shaking hands with the people and congratulating them, for the benefit of the cameras. He was very excited. It was as if the events of the day touched him personally. It was clear that he had known beforehand that the government was going to be overthrown on that very day.

Although he had never met Prime Minister Leabua, Radisene had grown to like him, mostly because of his comic radio broadcasts. Even his worst enemies used to listen to them religiously solely for their humour. He used to threaten his political enemies that he was going to do a 'fefenene' on them, by which he meant he was going to pounce on them. His words had started fashion trends. The mini-skirt was called a 'fefenene'.

Radisene felt very sorry for Leabua, even though he had never forgotten how his coup messed up his life sixteen years ago. In those days Leabua was still the good boy of the Western world. His problems really started when he decided to play footsie with the bad boys of the East. He established diplomatic relations with Cuba and the Soviet Union. His radio comedy routine became more leftist by the day. The North Koreans built him a stadium and gave military training to the Youth League of his party. Worst of all evils, he was harbouring South African refugees.

South Africa was not amused by all these shenanigans. They ordered him to stop giving succour to the communists who were a danger to South Africa's own security. They reminded him that he had won the very first elections in 1965 with their support. Their Prime Minister, the late lamented Dr Verwoerd, had given him bags of maize which he had rationed out to the starving mountain dwellers, who then voted for him. How could he forget, they asked, that his main rival, Mokhehle, the exiled leader of the Congress Party, had been defeated in those first elections precisely because he was a lackey of Mao Tse-tung of China. How could it slip his memory, they demanded, that it was with their support that he had successfully clung to power in 1970 when the Congress Party had won the elections.

But Leabua was stubborn. He had made up his mind that his future no longer lay with his erstwhile friends. He refused to expel ANC refugees from his country or to break off relations with his Eastern bloc friends. In the meantime the Youth League was becoming arrogant and began to alienate the military by threatening them with harsh discipline if they did not toe the party line.

The South African government grew tired of playing games with Leabua. They sealed the borders and embargoed all goods entering and leaving Lesotho. After a few days there was no petrol in the country, and there was no cabbage.

Somehow the American ambassador knew beforehand that there would be an embargo. Petrol tankers were parked outside his embassy days before the border was closed.

The army generals held meetings with the rulers of South Africa and solemnly undertook to topple the commie who was causing all this trouble. And they did. The people danced, and the borders were opened. Petrol and cabbage began to flow again into the country. The leader of the coup, Major-General Lekhanya, took credit for saving the nation from the throes of starvation and certain death. He became the flavour of the month.

As Radisene drove back to his hotel it made him sad to think that his own people had gone to celebrate the overthrow of their government with the Boers, when he had been taught from the day he was born, like all children of the land, that they were the enemy. Something somewhere had been betrayed.

The car radio was blaring martial music. Radisene was reminded of the first coup, all those years ago, when he had lain on his bed in his small room in Mafeteng, with the radio proclaiming defiantly that whether one liked it or not Leabua was the government. His life now was a far cry from what it was then. He had risen from the ashes of unemployment caused by that first coup to become a very rich man indeed. He was determined to rise further still, and be the richest man in the land. And he had his old enemy, A.C., to thank for it all. If he had not fired him that fateful day, simply because he was ill with fever, he would still be a lowly clerk. He hated A.C. for having been so unjust to him, yet he was grateful that his cruel act had put him on the path to untold riches.

After he was fired, he had established his own insurance claims business and carried on doing for himself exactly what he had been doing for A.C. At first he operated from his small Sea Point room. The insurance companies did not question his credentials. What was important to them was that he knew his job and that his claims made sense. Rarely did they dispute his assessments for compensation. He had learnt all the ropes in A.C.'s office. He resuscitated his church name and Anglicized his real name. His company therefore became known as Joseph Radison, Insurance Claims Consultants. The insurance companies never enquired whether he was a lawyer or not. Perhaps they just took it for granted. In any case, he was not doing anything illegal. There was no legislation that said only lawyers could claim third party insurance on behalf of their clients. However, most lawyers did not like to get involved with third-party insurance claims, because the whole business smacked of ambulance-chasing. They regarded themselves as respectable members of the bar. They had lucrative civil or criminal law practices, even company law practices. Since they did not want to soil their hands with such sordid business they referred all accident victims who came their way to Radisene. And on the very rare occasions when there was a dispute on a particular claim which had to be argued in court, Radisene in turn would brief a real lawyer to appear on behalf of his company.

The only serious competition came from A.C. But Radisene was sure he would win in the end. He was beginning to get more clients than A.C. A lot of the traffic cops who had been on A.C.'s payroll had now defected to his camp, because he was offering them bigger commissions. Even Trooper Motsohi, who had laughed at him at first when he decided to set up his own outfit, was now actively reporting all accidents to him. In addition to the traffic cops, Radisene went a step further than A.C.: he gave kick-backs to tow-truck operators, ambulance-drivers, and various hospital and mortuary workers, for informing him of all the motor-vehicle accidents that came to their attention. And this did not amuse A.C. at all. He sat in his Bonhomme House office weaving plots for the destruction of the upstart.

Now there had been another coup. How would it affect their fortunes, if at all, Radisene wondered, as he turned the car towards the Victoria Hotel, and brunch. He liked the hotel because it was centrally located in the downtown area on the main street. His office was just a few blocks away. Although the Victoria was not the best hotel in town – the best being the Lesotho Sun on the hill above the city, and the Maseru Sun Cabanas – it was quite comfortable. It did not have casinos like the other two, and was less infested with tourists from across the border. It was the headquarters of the ladies of the night, though, and over weekends the walls shook all night long from the music in the basement discothèque.

He tolerated living in the hotel because he was saving all his money to build a mansion in one of the posh suburbs of Maseru. It was going to be greater than A.C.'s mansion. He was determined that everything of his would be greater than A.C.'s. Already his car was a China-eye, whereas A.C. drove an Audi. His office was in the luxurious Lesotho Bank Tower, while A.C. remained in that slummy Bonhomme House. Granted, Bonhomme House had once been the best building in the city. But the architectural face of Maseru had changed over the years. New buildings had sprung up, creating a modern downtown area in the vicinity of the Victoria Hotel. Yes, he was going to build a mansion. It was going to be like the Prime Minister's. Only bigger, with an Olympic-size swimming-pool and a Jacuzzi. It was going to be bigger than the king's palace.

He smiled when he remembered that he already had a mansion in the village – although it was not his really, since he would never live in the mountains again. His life and livelihood were in the city. The village mansion belonged to his mother and his sister. He had received reports that Dikosha had never set foot in the house since it was built five years ago. That hurt him a lot, because he had built it especially for her. He had even built her a dance studio. But then one never knew with Dikosha. She was a woman of her own mind. She was probably angry with him. And who could blame her? It was almost eighteen years since he had left Ha Samane and they had not seen each other in all that time. He had not even seen the mansion he had built for his family.

Sorry My Darlie had been Radisene's only link with his family. The man's burning desire for Dikosha had taken him to Ha Samane quite often. He brought Radisene news of his sister, and so he kept up with her transformations. But even that link had now been broken. Sorry My Darlie's star was no longer shining on the soccer fields of the lowlands. In a particularly dull match, for Sorry My Darlie was ageing, he had received a kick below the belt from an opponent, which landed him in hospital for several weeks. The doctors said that his kidneys or bladder or some such thing had been damaged, and advised him never to play again. He went back to his home village. He had nothing to show for all the years he had spent entertaining the multitudes with his soccer wizardry. Even his valued Valiant had coughed its last and died on the side of the road. It was now used as a fowl-run by people he did not even know.

Radisene thought it might help if he wrote to Dikosha. But he knew that she would not read his letter. He desperately wished he could make her understand that he had not been home in all those years because he had vowed that he would return only as a success, like Sorry My Darlie. But success had eluded him for so long. And when it finally came an important accident would crop up whenever he planned to visit Ha Samane. He had not taken a holiday since starting the business. The roads of the country were killing fields, and there were so many dead bodies, so many riches, to harvest. Taking a holiday would give the upper hand to the likes of A.C., who would enjoy the bountiful crops alone, leaving him to glean the pickings. But he would do it one day. He would go to Ha Samane in a blaze of splendour and glory.

In any case, Dikosha had to bear part of the blame for the long separation. He had tried to get her to visit the lowlands. On two occasions he had sent her air-tickets. But she had turned the offer down.

There was no doubt that he missed her. He could not imagine her now, as a woman of thirty-five. His most vivid memory was of her feet playing in the hearth of the Cave of Barwa. He remembered only the feet, and the red dress rolling in the warm ash.

Thoughts of Dikosha kept running through his mind as he sat behind his desk, staring at a pile of insurance claim forms that he had to complete. He told himself that he needed an assistant. He had reached a point where he could not afford to do both the field-work of running after accidents and the office work of completing forms and attending to correspondence. The fieldwork took most of his time, and he was behind with his paperwork – his chamber work, as he preferred to call it, in keeping with the legal jargon. His reluctance to employ an assistant did not lie in the fact that he would have to share the spoils with him. After all, he was already paying traffic cops so much money that they ran in their own cars. But he was afraid to teach someone the tricks of this lucrative trade, someone who could then establish his own business and compete with him, as he himself had done with A.C.

There was too much excitement in the building. Workers from different offices were standing in the passageways talking about the coup. It was obvious that there would be no work done that day. He told his secretary to lock up and go home. Then he took his bag and went to Lancers Inn, just one block from his office.

There he ordered a beer and joined a group of civil servants who were gossiping about the cabinet ministers of the overthrown government and their whereabouts. Whenever he wanted to hear the latest gossip, especially the inside information from the hallowed ministerial boardrooms and bedrooms, Radisene went to Lancers Inn. Senior civil servants drank there, and their world was so small that they spent their lives gossiping about one another. If one wanted to know who was going to be promoted the following month, or who was going to lose his or her job, one went to Lancers Inn. If one wanted to know which cabinet minister or which principal secretary was sleeping with which head of department's wife, one bought a beer and unobtrusively sat at the counter of the grass-thatched colonial bar.

But deals were also clinched at Lancers Inn. Contractors paid kickbacks to principal secretaries and heads of departments in order to get government contracts. A whole class of new millionaires was created from the ranks of ordinary civil servants at this hotel. Indeed, it had just the right ambience for a man like Radisene.

During the following days and weeks the new military government consolidated itself. Lekhanya became the chairman of the ruling Military Council. King Moshoeshoe the Second, who had been until then a constitutional monarch, was given executive powers. A toothless cabinet was appointed and given ministerial portfolios. But at the head of each ministry was an illiterate soldier of the Military Council.

Highways and airports and other things that bore the name of Leabua were given new names. Even the flag was changed. Those soldiers who were suspected of supporting the overthrown Leabua were locked up, and two of their senior officers were murdered in prison. There was an extensive witch-hunt for all those who were perceived to be a threat to the new government. South African refugees were deported and flown to Zambia. And all was happy and peaceful again with the Boer neighbours.

All these events did not bother Radisene. Governments would rise and fall. New thin leaders would replace old fat leaders. New thin leaders would become old fat leaders. But motor-vehicle accidents would always be there. They were a constant. They were the only reliable things in this unpredictable world. They were for ever.

He was sitting at his desk, which was the size of A.C.'s office, pondering on these developments, when he was rudely woken from his reverie by the sharp ring of the telephone. 'Mr Radison,' said his secretary, 'Trooper Motsohi on the line.' How he detested that Motsohi! His hatred for him would live for as long as the scars were still visible on his back.

'Put him through.'

'Hey, Teacher, you have work to do.'

'Where?'

'On the road to Teyateyaneng. A kombi. But you better hurry. The vultures are descending. I will hold them at bay until you get here.'

He got into China-eye and drove up Kingsway. Just before the main circle, where the highways to the northern and southern districts began, he had to stand on the brakes. There was a big ditch right in the middle of the road. It was so deep that China-eye would have been swallowed by it if he had not managed to stop in time. There was not a single sign to indicate the danger.

It was the same all the time. People in orange overalls were always digging trenches in the roads of Maseru. It remained a mystery what they were looking for. Whatever it was, they never seemed to find it, for the digging went on year after year. Every day they dug in a different part of the city. Sometimes, without warning, they would close the road off with drums. Or they would scatter some small red triangles which would not be visible from a distance. At other times, when they were not in the mood for it, they put up no signs at all.

These mysterious ditches were often left gaping for weeks on end. They should have been a boon to a man of Radisene's profession, for every week they trapped a batch of cars. But he considered them a waste of time since people rarely died in these city-centre accidents. It was the same with the beautiful ladies of Maseru who sleepwalked in the middle of the streets like zombies, especially during the lunch-hour on weekdays. When cars knocked them down they did not die. Radisene was only interested in big claims which involved the deaths of breadwinners with numerous dependants. And, of course, anyone who died in a car accident, as long as he or she was over sixteen years old and as long as Radisene was dealing with the claim, was a breadwinner with many dependants.

Radisene found that he could not reverse because a long line of cars had stopped behind him. They were rudely hooting at him to drive on. He tried to indicate that he could not drive on because of the trench. Those nearest to his car noticed what had happened and tried to indicate to those who were immediately behind them to reverse. It took all of ten minutes to relay the message to the last car in the line, and another twenty minutes before he could extricate himself from the jam and find a different route Teyateyaneng.

He was angry because he had lost a lot of time for no good reason. He knew that Trooper Motsohi would be mad at him. Sometimes Trooper Motsohi seemed to forget who the boss was. It was high time that he was put in his place, Radisene thought. As if his wife was not doing the job properly.

Despite his anger, he had to laugh when he recalled how Trooper Motsohi had come to his hotel room the previous week with a big black eye and a terrible limp. He had been beaten up by Tampololo as usual. 'What did you do this time?' asked Radisene.

'We were eating supper, and she said my chewing was irritating her.'

'Were you chewing with your mouth open?'

'No. I always close my mouth when I chew. But all of a sudden my chewing was irritating her. She said from now on I must eat in a different room. When I tried to reason with her, she jumped at me, grabbed my maleness and twisted it. I screamed in pain, and she rained fists on my face.'

'What do you want me to do? You know that Tampololo never listens to anybody when it comes to beating you up.'

'She is your homegirl, Teacher. Talk with her. But for tonight give me a place to sleep.'

'Only for tonight, Motsohi. I cannot share a room with you.'

The next morning Trooper Motsohi pleaded with Radisene to take him home and explain to his wife where he had spent the night. 'Drive you home, yes, but I'll drop you at the gate. I do not want to be insulted by Tampololo,' said Radisene.

When they approached the front desk on the way out Radisene heard the receptionists giggle. One said to the other, in a whisper that carried to Radisene's ears, 'What did I tell you about him, my sister? He is like that. They spent the night together in his room. And he is so beautiful too, one would mistake him for a girl.'

'Shame, he has a black eye,' said the other. 'It spoils his beauty. A lovers' tiff, I'm sure.'

Radisene did not care what they thought of him. He merely laughed, gave them his key and wished them a good day. Then he drove Trooper Motsohi to his dreaded home and dropped him at the gate. Tampololo would beat him up again, but Radisene did not care, as long as she did not kill him. He needed Motsohi badly on the roads, for he had a nose for a good accident. Who else would have sniffed out this accident on the road to Teyateyangeng?

But when he arrived at the scene the casualties were no longer there. Trooper Motsohi was not there either. The vultures had descended and were fighting over what remained of the spoils. They were stripping the minibus of its parts. One was running away with the battery, and two were struggling over what looked like a water-pump. Another one had a clutch-plate which was still intact. There were pools of blood on the road, and the vultures did not mind rolling in them in their struggle for the spoils.

Radisene found the vultures disgusting. He drove straight to the Teyateyaneng Hospital where he suspected they had taken the accident victims. There he found Trooper Motsohi fuming. 'What happened to you, Teacher?' he demanded. 'I tried to hold everybody at bay. Even when the ambulance came I stopped them from taking the victims away, and pretended that I still had to do measurements of the road and of the skid marks and of whatever else I could invent. But you can't do measurements for ever, Teacher. In the meantime the bastards were dying. I couldn't stop the ambulance guys any longer. You bloody well took your time.'

Radisene tried to explain why he had been delayed, but Trooper Motsohi was in no mood to listen. He was cursing, accusing Radisene of wanting to deprive him of his commission. He had to pay many family debts that had been incurred by Radisene's homegirl, he shouted. Even the bribes that he took from the drivers of overloaded taxis and illegally parked cars were not enough to quench Tampololo's thirst for expensive things. If they failed to get a client from this accident, he added, Radisene would have to pay for it.

Radisene listened patiently to his ranting and raving. When it was finally over, he said coldly. 'You seem to forget that I am the boss here, Motsohi. You can take a hike if you like. I don't need you. I have many other informants, you know that.'

'Of course you are joking, Teacher.'

'I am not laughing. In fact – you're fired! Come to the office and collect your final commission, and never darken my door again.'

'Sorry, Teacher! Sorry! I didn't mean any harm. It's just that Tampololo … Please, Teacher, don't fire me. You know that I left A.C. for you. You can't fire me now.'

At last Radisene had Motsohi where he wanted him: at his mercy.

Turning on his heel, Radisene strode into the casualty ward. Nurses were busy stitching and dressing the wounds of accident

victims, and the only doctor in the ward had his hands full running
from one patient to another. Radisene looked around for the most
promising client. And behind a screen he found him: an old man
whose whole body, including his face, looked like it was made of
caked blood. Two nurses were trying to clean him with swabs of
cotton wool. 'This is the man I am looking for,' said Radisene to
the nurses.

'Oh, are you a relative?'

'Well, not quite. He is my client. I am his lawyer. Can I talk with
him alone just for five minutes?'

'You'll have to wait. The doctor said we must prepare him for
an emergency operation, otherwise he won't make it.'

The caked man opened his eyes slightly and tried to focus on
Radisene. 'What does he want with me?' he mumbled, blood oozing from his mouth.

'Listen, father, I have come to represent you about the third-
party insurance. Since you had this accident you or your dependants are entitled to a lot of money … many thousands of rands.
But you need to sign these papers first so that I can claim it for
you.'

One of the nurses dragged Radisene aside and angrily whispered in his ear, 'Can't you see this man is dying? Have you no
shame? Who gave you permission to come in here anyway?'

'Go and ask the superintendent who gave me permission. And
if this man is dying, that's all the more reason I must talk with him.
You want him to go without getting a cent for his children? And if
he lives, then he'll need the compensation even more. Obviously
he'll be crippled for life. I need him to sign these forms.'

Just then the patient groaned and the nurse hurried back to her
task. Radisene took out his pen and began to ask the caked man for
his name, his address, the name of his chief, the names of his
dependants. The nurses wheeled the man out of the ward and along
a passage that led to the operating theatre. Radisene trotted alongside, scribbling down the information he was struggling to impart
about himself and his family. Radisene pleaded with the nurses to

stop just for a second so that the man could sign the forms. But they ignored him and rushed on. He pressed the pen into the man's bloody hand, but he was in too much pain to grasp it. Then they reached the theatre. As the patient disappeared through the doors, Radisene called after him: 'If any other lawyer comes to you about third-party insurance, tell him that you already have a lawyer!'

As he walked to the China-eye, he decided that he would touch all bases. He would drive to the caked man's village and get his dependants to sign the papers. After all, they were going to be the claimants if he died. Then he would come back to the hospital to check if he had died or not. If he had survived the operation, he would get him to sign as the claimant. He would have to return quickly, in case someone else came and cheated the man into sign-ing. With any luck the fellow would die. But all the same, he could not take things for granted.

The day's assignments having been accomplished, Radisene took an early evening shower, and splashed his body with the usual Aramis. He had two important engagements and had to look his best – especially for the second one. He opened his wardrobe and looked for an appropriate outfit. The rail was full of designer suits, ranging from the funereal to the flamboyant. His grey Sales House suit looked out of place in the midst of all those rich and expensive fabrics. He caressed it. Although he did not wear it any more – his body had grown much too big for it – he still believed that it brought him luck. Before he went on any important assignment he touched it for good fortune.

He selected an off-white suit and a matching wide-brimmed hat. He teamed this with a black shirt, a wide red tie, red socks, and black and white shoes. He thought he looked like a gangster in a Hollywood movie of the fifties, and loved the feeling. The elites of Maseru, who were conservative in their dress, often commented behind his back that he looked like an American pimp when he dressed like this.

First he drove to Lancers Inn and went to the television lounge rather than the thatched bar where top civil servants shared the latest gossip. A few people, mostly women, were relaxing on the sofas with beer or wine, and watching an American situation comedy on the television. He selected a quiet corner and ordered a beer. He looked at the television and wondered what people found so funny in such idiotic programmes, which even instructed you when to laugh.

A few minutes later he was joined by Dr Joe Bale, a burly, bearded man in casual Java prints. Bale was a physician at the government hospital. He took a seat next to Radisene and ordered a beer. Then he took out a sheaf of papers from an envelope and gave them to Radisene, who looked at each one carefully and nodded his satisfaction. 'These are good reports, Joe,' he said.

He was reading a medical report on a woman who had been involved in an accident a week ago. Although the car was badly damaged, both the driver and the woman passenger had received no injuries at all. After the accident they had walked to a nearby hospital, where they were treated for shock and immediately released. There really would have been nothing to claim from the insurance company, and that was not good enough for Radisene. So he'd referred her to the reputable Dr Bale who, on closer examination, found that in fact the poor woman had been paralysed for life. Radisene smiled when he read in the report that she would not be able to walk without assistance and would find it impossible to carry on her trade as a seamstress, since the whole of her right arm had been rendered useless by the accident.

'You have excelled yourself here, Joe,' said Radisene. 'All these reports are quite creative. I have no doubt that you'll get a good commission here.'

'Have you got the cheque for the last reports?'

'Of course I have your cheque. But the death certificates, Joe … please see to it that I get the death certificate for last week's cases promptly.'

'I'll do my best.'

Radisene handed him an envelope, which he put in his shirt pocket without even glancing at the contents.

As he drove to the Maseru Sun Cabanas, Radisene thought that it was really good to have a man of Joe Bale's calibre on his pay-roll. Insurance companies insisted that all claims be accompanied by medical reports or death certificates. It was a great help to know a doctor who could doctor such reports. That was one up on A.C.

As for the police reports which also had to accompany the claims, his traffic cops did all that very diligently. Two up on A.C.

He dropped a couple of coins in the deep pockets of each of the bandits that lined the hotel foyer, pulled each one's arm without success, and walked on towards the bar. Misti was perched on a bar-stool sipping a fruit-juice. What always amazed Radisene was that she dressed quite soberly, and did not straighten her hair by frying it with all sorts of chemicals, as he himself did, yet she always looked exquisite.

'Am I late?' asked Radisene apologetically.

'No, I was early,' she responded with her sunny smile. Radisene thought he was going to melt. He wanted to say something pleasant or smart, but was at a loss for words. Misti had this effect on him. He turned into an utter fool in her presence. But somehow she knew how to make him feel at ease.

'Won't you sit down?' she asked. He pulled another bar-stool closer and sat next to her.

'Are you comfortable here, or would you rather we sit in the lounge?' he asked.

'I'm quite happy here. Anyway, we always sit here. It feels familiar.'

He had been taking her out every two months or so for the past few years, ever since she'd nursed him through his fever. But today was a very special day. 'I thought that perhaps today we should have a meal. They have a good seafood buffet here.' They went through to the dining-room, served themselves, and sat down to eat. Radisene drank a lot of wine, which he hoped would give him pluck. Today it was do or die. If he did not speak his mind today, he would have to for ever hold his peace. That would eat him for all his life, and he would never know happiness.

'Misti,' he began at last, 'we have known each other for many years. I am sorry that I have never told you how I feel about you.'

'I know how you feel, Radisene.'

'You know? How do you know?'

'I am a woman, Radisene. And I have eyes too. I have known it since we were kids back in the village. Then I so much wanted you to come and tell me. I so much wanted you to know that I felt the same about you too. But you know that women were not expected to make the first move.'

'Oh, my God! How could I have been so blind? It is not too late, Misti. We can make up for the time we've lost.'

'I'm afraid it is too late.'

'There is somebody else then?'

'No. There is nobody.'

'Then how can it be too late? I love you. I have loved no one but you all my life. Please marry me, Misti.'

'It cannot be, Radisene. You do not know me. There are things about me that you'll never understand. Some of these things I do not even understand myself. It will never be.'

'I am prepared to accept anything. To take you as you are. Whatever faults you have, to me you are perfect, Misti. I am the one who has a million faults. I am prepared to accept even those things I don't understand. Age is not waiting for us. We are in our mid-thirties. We should not waste this opportunity to spend our lives together.'

But she would not discuss the matter any further. She begged him to understand that she had a very good reason for turning him down, and hoped they would remain friends.

They walked quietly to the parking-lot. Then they shook hands, and she got into her car and drove away. He regretted shaking her hand at once. He should have grabbed her and kissed her very hard. He stood there for a while, feeling lost and numb.

When he got back to the Victoria Hotel he did not go to his room, but went to the bar instead. He was going to drink himself into an absolute stupor. He sat at the bar and ordered one beer after another. He had just lost count when a haggard Trooper Motsohi came in. Motsohi was the last person he felt like seeing.

'Listen, I want to be alone, okay? I have problems that I need to sort out.'

'I have problems too, Teacher. That's why I came here to see you.'

Trooper Motsohi had lost his job as a traffic policeman. Lekhanya's government was rooting out people who were known to be staunch supporters of the overthrown government. Since Motsohi had been closely associated with the Youth League of the National Party he was considered a security risk by the military government.

'You've got to help me, Teacher. When I told Tampololo that I'd lost my job she beat me up.'

'And why should I help you, if I may ask? I lost my job too in your coup sixteen years ago. But did you help me? No! Instead you beat me up. I still have the scars, you know?'

'Awu, Teacher, I thought we had all forgotten about that. We were young and stupid in those days. I am sorry, Teacher, if I hurt you.'

'Go away from me, you little fool! I have been rejected today, and I can't handle rejection. And now you come with your stupid problems.'

Radisene was throwing his fists about, as if he was going to hit his companion. The ladies of the night and the other habitués of the Victoria bar found this spectacle highly entertaining. Especially when Trooper Motsohi went and sat on a stool a little distance away, buried his head in his hands, and began to weep softly.

'What is wrong with him?' asked a lady of the night.

'Don't you know?' said another. 'It is said that they are lovers. They must have quarrelled.'

Yet another one observed, 'Shame, he's so beautiful. He shouldn't make such a beautiful boy cry.'

And the bar burst out laughing.

'You know, Teacher,' sobbed Trooper Motsohi, 'I have made

you rich. I have told you about more accidents than anyone else. I have made you a lot of money, yet you won't help me when I am in trouble.'

'What do you want me to do, man?'

'Give me a job, Teacher. Give me a job so that Tampololo can take me back.'

'You are a masochist, Motsohi. You want to go back to her?'

'I love her, Teacher. I love her with all my heart.'

The sight of Trooper Motsohi in distress, his face smudged with tears and mucus, was not a pretty one. Radisene was moved to pity. He did need an assistant, he recalled, someone to help with the rudiments of fieldwork.

'Okay, man, stop crying. I am going to give you a job. You are going to be my servant. You are going to wash my car. You are going to clean my behind when I come from the toilet.'

Radisene stood up and staggered to the door, but before he reached it he fell on the carpet. Two hotel security guards came and lifted him up. As they helped him to his room tears were streaming down his cheeks.

8. The Musician

Shana just happened. No one knew how. One morning when people of the village woke up, there he was, playing his sekgankula.
He had materialised out of nowhere. Nobody knew where he came
from or whose child he was. He was there. And he was a fact of
life.

Shana was a waif in a tattered grey blanket. His shoeless feet
were as hard as rock with scales of pitch-black dirt. The soles had
cracks that were deep enough to hide a five-cent coin. His little
hands were delicate though, for it was from them that the music
came.

Wherever he was, he played his instrument. The thumb of his
left hand pressed the single string of the sekgankula at different
points to produce different notes. The other hand caressed the
string with a small bow made of hair from a horse's tail. The sound
that resonated from the soundbox made of an old cooking-oil tin
was so beautiful that passers-by always stopped to listen. They
marvelled at how small he was, and yet he carried the wooden
neck of the sekgankula on his tiny shoulders with such ease. The
soundbox dwarfed his head, touching his long tangled hair. The
string shimmered between the soundbox and the neck where the
fingers of his left hand were fervently pressing and stroking.

People of the village said Shana's sekgankula sounded like a
musical instrument of the angels. He sang like an angel too, to the
violin-like music that his fingers produced. All the songs he sang
were of his own composition. Father-of-the-Daughters, who later
took Shana under his wing, and gave him a place to sleep and food
to eat, often told visitors, 'Normally people who compose beautiful songs have atrocious voices and cannot sing their own songs.
But Shana is a wonder among composers. He has the voice of an
angel.'

He looked like an angel too. He couldn't have been more than
ten years old, and he still had the innocent face of all children. Yet

things came from his mouth that were not angelic at all. He sang
about mistresses and the troubles they caused their men, about poisonous women who ran away with other people's husbands, about
modern wives who were too big-headed to obey their husbands,
and about the desires of the body that remained unfulfilled because
modern women had constant headaches.

People were amazed that he knew such songs. 'He composes
them,' Father-of-the-Daughters, who saw himself as an authority
on Shana, told them. 'Yes,' people would insist, 'he composes
them. But how does a child this young know all these things?'
Even Father-of-the-Daughters could not answer that question.
Women wondered how a child so angelic, who had possibly been
brought into this world by a woman, could speak so badly of their
sex. And in such an innocent voice too.

Father-of-the-Daughters had thought that Shana would help to
look after the cattle. But on the occasions when he drove them to
the veld, he sat on an anthill and played his sekgankula. Herdboys
crowded around him to listen. Others joined in on their own sek-
gankulas or their guttural lesibas. Nobody paid attention to the cattle, and they strayed into other people's fields. Their owners had to
pay heavy fines. The herdboys were flogged by their fathers and
their employers. When Father-of-the-Daughters looked into
Shana's angelic eyes he laid aside the leather strap that he had at
the ready and said, 'You will not look after my cattle again, Shana.
Otherwise I'll find myself paying damages to the owners of fields
every day. I don't know what I'll do with you. But you must do
something to earn your keep.'

Sometimes the child stood on the path between the fields and
played a most melancholy song. People of the village said at those
times he was longing for his mother. Others, especially women,
doubted that he had ever had a mother. Trucks loaded with bags
and boxes of supplies for the general dealer's store or for Staff
Nurse Mary's clinic passed and covered him with red dust. Yet he
stood there and played his sekgankula. Some trucks were loaded
with migrant workers going home to visit their families or with

women coming from breaking rocks and building roads in the self-help projects. They waved at him and cheered. More and more red dust piled up on him, until he looked as though he was made of clay. He was inspired to play even more, and to sing of jilted lovers and unfaithful wives.

Dikosha seemed to be captivated by Shana. Whenever she heard the music of the sekgankula she rushed out of her rondavel and sat on the stoep. Shana stood and played for her. He always played for an appreciative audience. And he thought Dikosha was the most appreciative of all the people of the village, for she did not talk. She listened attentively with her mouth open and stared without blinking at the soundbox over his shoulder. He did not mind standing for hours on end playing for her. When he had exhausted his repertoire he moved on to play for the birds of the field, and Dikosha either went back into her hut or to the Cave of Barwa.

She did not go to the Cave of Barwa as often as she used to. The night dances were not as exciting. Fewer and fewer of the men and women with protruding buttocks attended. The names of tourists from the lowlands were encroaching deeper into the cave. Some of these names, with dates next to them so that future generations would know that these important personalities had been to the Cave of Barwa on those particular dates, were written on top of the paintings. They imprisoned them, and Dikosha found it difficult to conjure them for their company. Senseless schoolboys also smeared their own paintings on top of the sacred ones or tried to improve the work of the ancient artists with chalks of different colours.

The monster-woman-dancer told her: 'One day you will not find us here. It is difficult already. The dance is dying.' Every time she went to the cave she thought it might be the last. At first she thought she could save the dance by cleaning the obscene scribblings of the important personalities and the smudges of the misguided schoolboys from the walls. But soon she realized that she could not do that without damaging the sacred paintings, hastening the demise of the dance.

So, when she could not conjure her cave friends, she consoled herself by listening to the music of Shana, and in her mind sang along with him. But she substituted her own words for his, putting the blame for the ills of the world on men.

Sorry My Darlie was jealous that Dikosha was paying so much attention to Shana. He still had not given up hope that one day she would be his. Times were hard on him. He had been unemployed ever since his injury had forced him to stop playing soccer. In those four years he had not set foot in the lowlands. He spent most of his time at Ha Samane, and very little at his home village of Ha Sache. When he was not sitting outside Dikosha's rondavel, with a small safety pin at the ready, he was visiting Grandma 'Maselina.

Grandma 'Maselina was the mother of Father-of-the-Daughters, and her lone rondavel was just behind her son's big compound. She was very old. Those who knew said she was more than a hundred years old. Her face looked like a dried lengangajane peach, and her eyes had the permanent squint of age.

She always welcomed visitors, and liked to tell stories of how she was once a whore in the land of gold, by which she meant Johannesburg and the mining towns of the Free State. 'I used to eat men, my child,' she would proudly announce. She used to run around with the Russians when the land of gold was still young, long before Father-of-the-Daughters was born, and she relished boasting about the Russian wars she had seen with her own eyes.

Grandma 'Maselina had been a singer of the sewelele type of poetry, and it was not unusual for singers of this poetry to make wild claims that they were once whores who devoured men in Johannesburg, only to enhance their image in society. Those who had the real experience would know at once when the claims were exaggerated. They confirmed that 'Maselina's claims were quite true.

Although both Father-of-the-Daughters and Mother-of-the-Daughters pampered her, she always complained that they did not care for her and did not visit her enough. And yet Mother-of-the-Daughters or one of the daughters took her food every day, since she could no longer cook for herself. And from time to time neighbours visited her, for she was the mother of Father-of-the-Daughters. Yet she never stopped complaining that her family had abandoned her. She would die alone in her hut one day, she declared, and they would find her after many years like Nkgono.

Sorry My Darlie spent a few hours of each day sitting with Grandma 'Maselina. When her grandchildren brought her food they knew that he would be there as well, so they came with a little extra. Grandma would eat, and then leave something on the plate for him. That would be his meal for the day. Except when he helped to carry water in big plastic containers on a wheelbarrow for women who brewed beer. Then they would give him some scraps of papa that remained from the previous day or some moroko sorghum chaff that had been sieved from the freshly brewed beer. At least at Grandma 'Maselina's place he ate much better food. There would be fresh papa and milk, and sometimes sour porridge. Once a week there would be papa with gravy and fried intestines from the hens and cocks that the family killed and prepared for the Sunday meal. Every winter Father-of-the-Daughters slaughtered a pig, and Sorry My Darlie got to eat a lot of meat, especially the fat that Grandma 'Maselina left on her plate.

When Grandma 'Maselina bragged about her days as a whore, Sorry My Darlie bragged about his days as a soccer star. His eyes brightened when he remembered those times. 'I used to eat life in Maseru,' he would say, his face reflecting the wondrousness of it all.

People of the village wondered how Grandma 'Maselina could stand the stench of urine that came from Sorry My Darlie. Since the accident on the soccer field he wet himself constantly, and the crotch of his threadbare pants was always soaking. In summer flies buzzed around him everywhere he went. People tended to avoid him – except for Grandma 'Maselina. Her nose was too old to smell anything, people said.

When young children were caught playing house in a manner

the adults did not approve of, Sorry My Darlie was used as an example to scold them. 'If you do naughty things you will pee on yourself and smell like Sorry My Darlie,' a mother would tell her son or daughter. It got to the point that even when children told lies or stole sugar, they were warned by their mothers that their bladders would burst and they would pee on themselves. 'You see how Sorry My Darlie is? It is because he did not listen to his parents when he was your age. He told lies like you.'

When the sun was at its hottest, and Sorry My Darlie sat outside Dikosha's rondavel with the flies buzzing around him and the stench of urine wafting above, Dikosha would peep from the window and shout, 'Get away from here, Sorry My Darlie. You are going to kill me with your flies.' These speaking moments were rare: Dikosha spoke only when she thought it was essential. But Sorry My Darlie would not leave. 'I want to go to my cabbage patch, Sorry My Darlie, but your smell will make me faint,' Dikosha would plead. Still he would not budge. He would look at her with the eyes of a wounded doe.

Dikosha would have to brave the stench to get to her cabbage patch behind the rondavel. She had taken to growing cabbages now that she no longer went to the cave so frequently. No one knew where she had got the seeds or the seedlings. Or even the idea. It was unheard of to plant cabbages in the village – they could only be imported from the Free State. Yet here she was growing them in home soil. Most people laughed at her; she had always been strange, they said. But some, like Hlong of the airfield, said she was an innovator.

Often, when she loosened the soil around the stems of the big-headed cabbages with a stick before watering them, Sorry My Darlie would offer to help, but she would shoo him away. Then Shana would come and play his sekgankula, and the cabbage heads would grown even bigger. Dikosha knew that it was because of Shana's music that she could grow things. Plants used to refuse her before Shana came. She had tried to keep pot plants, but they always died; watering them was enough to make them wilt away.

Although Sorry My Darlie was jealous of the little boy, Dikosha and Shana never exchanged a word between them. Shana came, he ignored Sorry My Darlie, he played his music, Dikosha listened, cabbages grew, he left. Then Dikosha went back into her rondavel and did whatever she did there. Sorry My Darlie would carry on sitting outside. Later he would go off to draw water for the brewers of beer and the owners of feasts, or to sit with Grandma 'Maselina.

One day when Sorry My Darlie was sitting outside Dikosha's rondavel he saw a strange vehicle approaching. It stopped on a strip of land between the rondavel and the big house of Mother-of-Twins. He went closer. Although the vehicle was covered with the red dust of the village, he identified it as a Range Rover. While he was pondering what could have brought it to Ha Samane, two men climbed out. The one was tall and lanky, and dressed in a flowing kente robe and a matching cap. His companion was soft-featured and much smaller. Sorry My Darlie recognized them at once.

'Radison! My old friend, Radison! And Trooper Motsohi!'

'And who are you?' asked Radisene coldly.

'What do you mean, Radison, who am I? You know me, man.'

'This is Sorry My Darlie,' Motsohi said helpfully.

'Who asked you?' Radisene snapped back. Then he turned to Sorry My Darlie and asked him how he was. He was fine, thank you, except for the problems that Dikosha was causing him. Radisene gave him a twenty-rand note. Sorry My Darlie thanked him profusely. Radisene was a real friend, he said, who never forgot his old buddies.

'Where is my mother ... and Dikosha?'

'I don't know, Radison. Neither of them is at home. Please, Radison, talk with Dikosha. She should not treat me like this.'

Radisene ignored his pleas, and walked towards the big house, with Motsohi tagging along behind. Sorry My Darlie followed at a respectful distance.

The mansion was only a shade of its former self. Most of the windows were broken and everything seemed to be falling apart.

Before he went inside Radisene turned and said, 'Motsohi, tell that man not to follow me into the house. I don't want him leaving his aroma here.'

For all these years Radisene had imagined the house as a palace, and he was devastated by what he saw now. In every room spiders had built their webs. Bats hung upside-down from the ceilings. The mirrors of the dance studio were so thick with dust that they no longer reflected any image. The floors were like deserts. Only one room, which had once been the kitchen, was swept clean. It was obvious that this was where Mother-of-Twins lived. She had her bed there, and in one corner stood a big tin trunk that was full of her clothes.

In the beginning, Mother-of-Twins had been very proud of the house. It was the talk of the village, and indeed of the whole district. Tourists who came to see the Cave of Barwa also went to stare at the mansion, and wondered how such an expensive place could have been built in the village. But Mother-of-Twins could not maintain such a big house. It took the whole day to clean the rooms. 'And why should I spend all my life cleaning these rooms?' she asked her friend, Mother-of-the-Daughters. 'No one lives in them except the ghosts that echo even my sneezes.'

People of the village began to laugh at the house. 'What will Mother-of-Twins do with a church like that?' they asked. Their derision was so great that Mother-of-Twins told her friend she wanted to go back to her rondavel. 'The house is too big for one person. I'm afraid of the ghosts. I can't even whisper without them echoing me. I miss my old life. I want to smear cow-dung on the floor, not sweep carpets or scrub tiles.'

But Mother-of-the-Daughters warned her against trying to return to the rondavel. 'Dikosha lives there,' she said, 'and if you try to drive her out or even to move in with her she might start wailing again …'

The house was empty.

Radisene went outside, and asked the children who were begin-ning to crowd around his Range Rover if they knew where Mother-

of-the-Twins was. The children tittered. Then they burst out laughing and ran away shouting that everyone should come and see a
man wearing a dress. Radisene cursed, and muttered, 'They are
barbarians. They have never seen West African costume. I would
have them know that this boubou was designed by none other than
Jabbie himself.' Then he ordered Trooper Motsohi to come with
him to the compound of Father-of-the-Daughters to find out if anyone there knew where Mother-of-Twins was.

'Please, don't go with me there,' pleaded Trooper Motsohi.
'You know that is Tampololo's home.'

'So what? You will come with me, Motsohi. I don't care if it's
the home of God himself.'

They walked to the compound, with Sorry My Darlie slinking
along behind. Radisene was pleased that Tampololo's parents were
going to see how big he was – so big that even their own son-in-
law, who used to be an important policeman in the government,
was now his servant.

Both Father-of-the-Daughters and Mother-of-the-Daughters
were at home, and delighted to see the visitors. They shook
Radisene's hand heartily. Father-of-the-Daughters also shook
Trooper Motsohi's hand and hugged him. Trooper Motsohi, of
course, could not shake his mother-in-law's hand, for according to
custom he was not supposed to touch her.

The old people thought that Trooper Motsohi had come special-
ly to see them, and they peppered him with questions: 'How is
Tampololo? Do you not have any children yet? The two of you
spend a long time without coming to see us. Why didn't
Tampololo come with you?'

'Tampololo is busy teaching,' Trooper Motsohi began.

'That is not the real reason,' Radisene said rudely. 'Why don't
you tell them that she couldn't come with you because you are on
duty now? Get a bucket from the house and fetch water from the
dam over there. It's time for you to wash the car. Make sure you
remove all the dust. I want to see it shine like a mirror.'

Trooper Motsohi crept away without any argument. His in-laws were dumbfounded.

'I am looking for my mother,' Radisene said before they could gather their wits. 'Do you know where she is? Or Dikosha?' Mother-of-Daughters stammered that she did not know where Dikosha was. She might have gone to the Black River or wherever her fancy took her. Mother-of-Twins, however, had gone to work at the self-help project where women were constructing a road.

Radisene had driven past the self-help workers about five miles from the village. They were breaking rocks with huge hammers and building the road one stone at a time. As was always the case in such development projects there were only two men among a whole drove of women. Men generally did not like to work in self-help projects, even at those times when they were not digging the white man's gold. When the farming season was over they preferred to sit under the trees, drinking beer and playing morabaraba.

Most of those who worked at self-help projects were women who held families together and single-handedly brought up children to manhood or womanhood. They were known as the gold-widows, for their husbands spent all their lives working in the mines, coming home for a few days only once or twice a year. Some were real widows whose husbands had died like rats in the deep dark holes of the land of gold. Others were women whose husbands had been conquered by the world, and had established new families in the slums of Johannesburg or even Maseru.

Radisene did not know that Mother-of-Twins was one of those bulldozers-with-breasts, as the road-builders were disparagingly called. He felt angry that his mother, whose son was so rich that schoolchildren sang songs about his fabulous wealth, should end up scraping a living in a self-help project. He did not understand it. What had she done with all the money he had sent her? Had she squandered it with her friends in shebeens?

Radisene thanked Mother-of-the-Daughters for the information about his mother and went to join Trooper Motsohi, who had finished cleaning the vehicle. It was gleaming white and villagers of all ages were standing around it. For many this was the closest thing to a car they would ever see. They had only seen trucks and the ragged Landrovers and Toyota Landcruisers that came to Ha Samane once in a while. When they saw Radisene they giggled. Many of them were young and did not know him. The older ones, who remembered clearly that he was in pants when he left for the lowlands, whispered, 'Has the son of Mother-of-Twins now become a woman?'

Late in the afternoon Radisene and Trooper Motsohi were sitting outside the kitchen door of the big house, passing the time by planning a new business strategy, when they saw an old woman approaching. As she drew closer Radisene saw that it was his mother. She looked worn out and haggard. The hair sticking out from under her doek was completely white. It pained his heart to see his mother like this. He remembered her as a sprightly, slender woman whose only love was to have a good time at the feasts. He had never imagined that his own mother could get so old. Only other people's parents got old. He was even angrier that the years had not touched Mother-of-the-Daughters. What right did she have to look so youthful when his own mother had aged so terribly?

'What happened to all the money that I have been sending you, mother?' asked Radisene, without even waiting for Mother-of-Twins to greet them.

'Is that how you greet your mother, Radisene? You come home after twenty years and you ask me about money?'

'It is because I am shocked, mother. I sent you money so that you would not live a life of poverty. And what do I find? You are working in a self-help project for a tin of cooking oil.'

'I am working in this project not because I am starving, my child, but because I am building something for my community. When we finish the road even buses will be able to come to Ha Samane, and we are going to see more progress in our village.'

Radisene looked at her closely to make sure that it was indeed his mother. No, he did not know this old woman who talked of the 'community' and of 'progress'. Could twenty years change someone so much? Especially someone who had all the means to lead a carefree life?

Mother-of-Twins told him that she had kept all the money he sent her in a post office savings book, following the advice of Mother-of-the-Daughters. She did not need so much money. She generously gave to those who were in need. Even the cooking oil and flour that she received from the self-help project she gave to neighbouring children who lived with their grandmother. They had been orphaned when both their parents died in an accident. A truck had turned over on a mountain road and plunged down a slope.

Radisene's ears twitched like a rabbit's. 'Did you hear that, Motsohi?'

'Yes, Teacher. I'll see this grandmother immediately and make her sign the forms. Poor mountain people. They don't know that they can get a lot of money from this.'

'That's the problem with accidents that happen in the mountains. We never get to hear of them. Anyway, we have our hands full in the lowlands.' And then suddenly remembering where he was, he went on, 'But, mother, where is Dikosha?'

'Well, my child, you know how your sister is.'

'Where is she?'

'I didn't believe her when she said you'd be coming.'

'So she talks now! But I wonder how she knew I would be coming. I didn't know myself until last night, when I decided on the spur of the moment. If I keep on postponing, I said to myself, waiting for a lull in accidents, then I'll never see my dear mother and my dear sister again. Where is she?'

'I don't know,' said Mother-of-Twins. 'But when she woke up this morning she said she was going away because she did not want to meet you. She said she will only come back when you have returned to the lowlands where you belong.'

This hurt Radisene very much.

That night Trooper Motsohi slept in the Range Rover and Radisene slept on his mother's bed in the kitchen of the big house. Mother-of-Twins went to sleep in one of the many rondavels at Mother-of-the-Daughters' compound. Mother-of-the-Daughters laughed, 'You have the biggest house in the village, yet you have nowhere to sleep!'

Early the next morning Radisene sent Trooper Motsohi to a few of the neighbouring homesteads to rent some cattle. He gave him a lot of ten-rand notes.

'My master needs your cattle just for today,' Trooper Motsohi told the neighbours. 'He is willing to pay you good money for them.'

'What does he want to do with cattle for one day? Is he a mad-man? Or some kind of witch? People say they saw him wearing a dress yesterday.'

'When he was young he used to be a herdboy. He loves cattle very much.'

'He should buy his own then. He's rich enough. But of course he won't. We know how mean he is. We remember what he did to those poor grandmothers who tried to give him money. They are all dead now, you know, but even in their graves they don't forget what your master did to them.'

'He is a very busy man, and has no time to own cattle. Perhaps when he is old and retired he might buy a whole cattlepost and herd his own beasts. For now he just wants to rent a few of yours to satisfy his craving.'

In the end some people agreed to rent Radisene a few heads of cattle, because he was paying good money for them. But they instructed their herdboys secretly to watch him, and see to it that he did nothing harmful to their animals. Other people refused. They said they had never heard of anyone renting cattle before. They could not trust him with their prized possessions.

When Radisene played the lesiba and led the cattle out of the village people came out of their houses to stare. A long line of cows, bulls and oxen followed him. He led the cattle to the graz-ing lands above the fields on the banks of the Black River. For that whole day he herded them. In the evening he led them back to their kraals.

The following morning Radisene and Trooper Motsohi got into the Range Rover and began the long drive back to the lowlands. Radisene was happy that he had satisfied his craving for herding cattle. But he was sad that he had not seen his sister. He had had good reason to stay in the lowlands all those years, he reflected. Why had she not given him a chance to explain?

For many hours they were silent, as Trooper Motsohi negotiated the sharp bends in the road. Radisene turned on the radio and listened to the news on Radio Lesotho. As usual it was about the king, the chairman of the military council, some cabinet minister or other. Why was the news always about the rulers? Did nothing else ever happen in the country, or indeed the world? It was like that too in the days of Leabua, he remembered. Ordinary people, who worked hard all their lives, and did both beautiful and ugly things, were not considered newsworthy at all. No event was worth reporting unless it was graced by the presence of some illiterate minister or military councillor.

He switched off the radio and played a cassette of Sankomota. He worshipped the bandleader, Frank Leepa, and believed that his music was the best in the world.

They were always so quiet on these long journeys, Radisene observed to himself. Perhaps they had nothing in common except road deaths. He stole a glance at Trooper Motsohi. What was in his mind? He was a pitiful sight. Suddenly Radisene felt sorry for having treated him so shabbily in front of his in-laws. He would not tell Motsohi that, for it would spoil him, but he vowed not to treat him like that again. Poor beautiful face! It was marred by Tampololo's fists.

Why did Tampololo beat this man so much? Radisene had bumped into her earlier that week, and she really did not strike him as such a bad person. He had gone to the CNA to buy some stationery, and there was Tampololo admiring the cuddly toys. A saleslady was demonstrating a new type of teddy bear to a group of children. It was big and fuzzy and snow-white. It had a red heart on each paw. When the saleslady pressed one of these hearts with her finger the teddy bear played Christmas carols. Tampololo laughed. She was as excited as the children. She took the teddy bear and pressed it herself. When the music started she laughed again.

Radisene joined her. She seemed genuinely happy to see him. She smiled, and talked very close to his face, her body almost touching his. Her perfume was intoxicating. She constantly touched his hand as she explained how much she loved cuddly teddy bears and stuffed animals of all kinds. She had a collection of them. And of dolls too. She had given them all cute names. Radisene concluded that a woman who loved dolls and stuffed animals could not be so bad.

She pressed the heart again and the teddy bear began to play 'O come all ye faithful'. She hummed along for a few bars, then burst out laughing. It was a throaty, full-bodied laugh, and Radisene fell in love with it.

He stole another glance at Trooper Motsohi.

9. **The Great Drought**

The land had not seen rain for more than two years. In the height of summer only small matted grass remained on what had once been lush grasslands. Cattle found no joy in it, for it was dry and devoid of the sweet juices. They ate because they had to eat. Still, it did not satisfy their needs. The bones of the cattle stuck out at every conceivable corner and one could count their ribs. Those were the lucky ones. Their relatives were dead. More of them died every day, and the people were tired of eating stringy meat.

The sun stubbornly stood above the heads of the farmers as they tried to scrape the land with their ploughs. But they could only tickle the surface. The hard ground mockingly laughed at their feeble efforts. They lifted their eyes to the heavens, to the very God they did not care about when all was well, and prayed for rain. But rain refused to come. Even when the ministers of the Evangelicals called for a Sunday of prayer, and the Good Fathers of the Catholics held mass after mass, the rain simply refused to come. It was a drought of the world.

King Moshoeshoe the Second, who had been so good at calling for prayers for rain, was no longer in the country. He was languishing in England, where Lekhanya had banished him in one of the countless power struggles that had continued to rage ever since the very first coup led by Leabua twenty years before. Moshoeshoe's supporters said that was why the rain would not come, because their king had been cast into foreign lands, leaving his poor people like orphans. Those who did not give a hoot for the monarchy said it served him right: he should not have involved himself in politics in the first place. In any case, they added, he was a freeloader who was supported by their hard-earned taxes and did nothing in return.

The usual queues of donkeys laden with bags of maize were no longer seen at the mills. People had run out of maize to grind. Their grass-woven silos were empty, and so they were forced to buy maize-meal from the general dealers. The dealers had run out of white maize-meal long ago and only yellow meal was available. This was imported from South Africa, which is turn imported it from overseas countries. Normally yellow maize was considered fit only for feeding animals. But at times like these people resorted to eating it, cooking what they called red papa. At first it tasted terrible. But as the drought continued unabated their palates got used to it, and it ended up tasting even better than what they remembered of white papa.

At Ha Samane too, as in every village in the country, the sun stood still. But the fields of Ha Samane were green. It was the same every time there was a drought. The village was not affected. The extension workers from the government said that it was because the soil was moist deep down. The people of the village said the soil was fertile because it had been drenched by the tears of the goldwidows – those whose husbands had died in the mine shafts in the bowels of the earth or been swallowed by the city of gold. Of course, there were goldwidows in every village in the land, and in every town. Why the tears of the women of Ha Samane should be different, no one could say.

Rain was the main topic when visitors came. 'We do not see any rain,' complained Father-of-the-Daughters to Radisene, who was visiting Ha Samane again. 'We do not know how we'll plough the land.' Although he complained like this his silos were overflowing. Drought or no drought, he always had a bumper harvest, for he used a lot of manure from his kraals and different types of fertilizer that the extension workers advised him to buy from the farmers' cooperative. The tears of the goldwidows merely supplemented his own efforts. 'Is it refusing to rain even in other parts of the country, or is God only angry with us here in this valley?'

Radisene assured him that there was drought all over the country. 'Even in the Free State the Boers are crying because of this drought,' he said. 'You are still lucky in this valley for your fields have some greenness in them, even though it is not as luxuriant as it would be if the rains were merciful. All along the road, as I was driving from the lowlands, I saw things that would make a grown man cry. I saw crops that merely peeped from the ground, only to be scorched and shrivelled by this sun of hell.'

Radisene had started coming to the village regularly. Three things had drawn him back to Ha Samane. The first was that he had again tasted the joys of leading cattle to the grazing lands, and no longer wished to be without them. He came back every other weekend to do some herding. It must be said that weekends were the best time for accidents in the lowlands. Overloaded taxis were always racing to get more passengers. Drunken drivers were the kings and queens of the roads. No one obeyed the traffic rules. The roads became racetracks where the youths displayed their reckless skills. And orphans were created in the course of all this merriment.   But Radisene left Trooper Motsohi to attend to all these accidents. For him the craving for cattle was too strong.

The second reason Radisene came back to the village was that he hoped Dikosha would finally agree to talk with him. But she was adamant: she wanted nothing to do with him. She did not disappear entirely when he was around, as she had done during his first visit. She decided that she belonged to the village, and especially to her rondavel, and she was not going to run away again on account of a stranger who belonged to the lowlands. But when Radisene came to the village she locked herself in her house; and she remained there until he left. He knocked until his knuckles hurt.

Radisene appealed to Mother-of-Twins to talk with his sister, but she said she had no time to waste on spoilt children. She was too busy with her community affairs and her development projects. In addition to road construction, these included dam building and communal gardens. Women of the village had taken their cue from Dikosha's cabbage patch, and were cultivating cabbages, carrots and spinach in a communal garden. And they were doing this on their own, without anyone's assistance, unlike the lowland communal gardens which were supported by the Germans and the Americans and all sorts of white people who came from across the seas.

Mother-of-Twins did not have time to waste sorting out Radisene's problems with his sister. She spent most of her day at the dam, which she and some other women of the village were digging. The soil was as hard as rock. Yet the women persisted. One day, they knew, they would wake up to find the dam full of the tears of the goldwidows.

When he saw he would get no help from his mother, Radisene thought about breaking down the door and forcing his way into Dikosha's rondavel. But he was strongly warned by the people of the village, especially by Mother-of-the-Daughters, not to do anything that would make Dikosha wail like a banshee. 'Do not force her to see you,' Mother-of-the-Daughters advised him. 'We never force Dikosha to do anything she does not want to do, for we know the dangers of that. Sooner or later she will change her mind, and agree to see you. Her moods change from time to time. It is because she was conceived at a night dance.'

Although he could not make sense of what Mother-of-the-Daughters was saying, he took her advice and stopped bothering his sister. He desperately wanted to be in the good books of Mother-of-the-Daughters and Father-of-the-Daughters. That was the third reason he came to Ha Samane so regularly. He wanted to cultivate the old people, so that they would accept him as their new son-in-law, the husband of their daughter. The daughter in question was not one of those who had never received any higher education – they were all married to mountain men who looked after cattle or worked in the mines; it was their only educated daughter, Tampololo. Yes, Tampololo had left Trooper Motsohi and was living with Radisene in his room at the Victoria Hotel.

The old people did not know about this yet. Radisene believed that no one in the village knew. But they would know soon enough. It was already the scandal of the day in Maseru. Mountain people who frequented the lowlands would surely bring the gossip to Ha Samane. By then he hoped to have made such a good impression on Tampololo's parents that instead of being angry, they would be happy that they had gained a son-in-law who was much worthier than a snivelling ex-policeman.

Radisene's affair with Tampololo had happened quite unexpect-edly. Early one morning the reception desk called to say he had a visitor. He went down, and found Misti waiting for him.

Although Misti had rejected his proposal, hope burned eternal in him that one day she would relent and be his wife. They often met by chance at the Maseru Café, where they had both gone to buy the Sunday newspapers. When the papers were late, which was often, he would sit in her car to wait and they would talk about the weather. He did not mention his love for her again, but just once he vowed that he would wait for her until she changed her mind. And when she did, he said, she would know where to find him.

And now here she was, coming towards him across the lobby. His heart skipped a beat when he saw her smiling face. Surely there could only be one reason for such an early morning visit ...

They took a lift to the penthouse lounge. The bar would only open at ten, but the staff fell over themselves to be of service. Misti said she would have a cup of coffee, and he ordered a fruit-juice for himself. They engaged in some small talk, while she seemed to be mustering courage to tell him whatever it was she had come for. Radisene was dying with curiosity, but he kept it in check.

'You know, Radisene,' Misti finally said, 'I have always thought of you as somebody very special.'

'You are special too, Misti. That is why I love you so much.'

'I love you too, Radisene.'

'You do? I told you once that I was going to wait for you. I told you that one day you would realize that we were meant for each other. I knew this day would come.'

He leaned over to her side of the coffee-table, and took her hand, but she pulled it away.

'I have loved you since we were kids, Radisene, but things will never work between us. I am leaving town for some time. When I come back I'll be different.'

'What do you mean, Misti? You can't lead me on, and then dash my hopes like this.'

'I'm sorry if I led you on. I didn't mean to. I just wanted you to know that I care for you, that I turned you down because I had no choice in the matter. My life is not my own. I have been called by the ancestors. I am going to be a lethuela diviner.'

Radisene laughed, but the laughter died on his lips when he saw the look of distress that crossed her face. 'I am not joking,' she said.

'But you are an educated woman, Misti. You can't be a lethuela.'

'When the ancestors call you, they don't ask whether you are educated or not.'

Then she told him the whole story.

She was in her thwasa period now, possessed by the spirits that were forcing her to go for training as a lethuela diviner. The spirits often seized her and shook her violently, making her grunt like a pig and gasp for breath. This thwasa had started many years ago. At first she resisted it. Sometimes it subsided and she thought it was over for ever. But it would come back again. When the spirits seized her, she sometimes got sick with strange ailments which could not be cured by Western doctors. Those who knew about these things told her that she was being called by the ancestors to be a traditional doctor. She laughed in their faces. A traditional doctor? She was an educated woman with a B.Sc. degree. The whole notion was ridiculous.

Then she began to have visions. She saw strange figures that other people could not see. She heard voices that other people could not hear. She saw an old woman in the regalia of a traditional doctor. She was a vague image, and Misti could not distinguish her features. The old woman just appeared in front of her, and then disappeared without saying a word. She told her parents at Ha Sache about these strange happenings.

Her mother cried and said, 'Why don't they spare my child after we have sacrificed so much to send her to school?'

Misti's father tried to comfort her: 'There is really nothing we can do about it, Mother of Misti. When the ancestors call, they call. You know that her grandmother, who died long before she was born, was a diviner too. She must be the one who is calling her to follow in her footsteps. We must be proud that she has chosen our child among all her numerous grandchildren.'

Mitsi's mother could not be comforted though. She blamed her husband's side of the family for causing all this trouble. On her side of the family they were God-fearing Christians, and there were no diviners among them. 'If her grandmother wants a lethuela, why doesn't she choose one of her many good-for-nothing grandchildren who have refused to go to school? Why does she choose my child who has a whole B.Sc.?'

Finally Misti made up her mind that she would go for training and become a diviner. That night she was shown in a dream a woman who was mixing herbs and throwing bones of divination on an ashy floor. This woman was in a cave, and she was wearing the diviner's regalia of animal skins and beads. When Misti was able to see her face, she knew her at once. She didn't remember her name, but she was sure it was the girl who used to sit at the desk in front of hers at primary school, thirty or so years ago. She had grown much older, of course, but it was definitely her.

Now Misti had not seen this girl since their primary school days and did not know where she lived. But she had the urge to wake up and go to her, wherever she was. So she rose in the darkness, put on an old dress and sweater, and walked out of her apartment.

She walked on the road for many hours. She did not know where she was going. She just walked and walked and walked. Although her feet were bare, the gravel roads did not hurt her. When the sun rose she had gone past Teyateyaneng, forty kilometres from her home. She walked all day on the Main North Highway, with the tar burning her feet, but causing her no pain. There was no hunger or thirst in her. Only the hunger for the road.

Buses and taxis passed her, but she did not stop them. The spirits that possessed her demanded that she walk that road. Once the driver of a passing car recognized her and stopped. She walked on. He hooted and called her name, but she kept on walking. It is not her after all, he decided, it is just someone who looks like her.

When night fell she had passed through the district of Leribe and was in Butha Buthe. She had covered more than a hundred kilometres on her bare feet. She arrived at the village of Qalo and went straight to an old homestead fenced with reeds. She had never been in Qalo before, but she knew exactly where to go. At the door of one of the rondavels she hesitated. A voice invited her in.

'She knew that I would be coming.'

'How did she know?' Radisene asked. He had been listening attentively, slowly sipping his fruit-juice.

'I don't know. She knew my name too. She told me that she had been chosen to be my mentor. I have taken leave from my work at the hospital and will be joining her for a month. I must wear the white single-stringed beads of the acolyte and begin my training immediately. That's why I came to see you … to say goodbye.'

'Goodbye? You are not leaving for ever, Misti. You are not going to your death. You'll come back, and we'll be friends again.'

'I am glad to hear you say that. You make it easier for me. I know that at least as a diviner I'll have peace of mind.'

After Misti had driven away, Radisene remained standing in the hotel parking-lot. He did not know what to do next or where to go. He knew that things would never be the same again between him and Misti. He had lost her for ever. All of a sudden his wealth seemed meaningless. What was the use of his expensive toys – the Range Rover, the brand-new Mercedes S500 – if he could not share them with Misti? And the house that he was ready to build, the house that was going to cost millions, what would be the use of its sumptuous chambers if they were not to be graced by her elegant presence?

He walked slowly back to the hotel and lingered in the reception area, gazing at the window displays of the boutiques. He was debating whether he should go up to his room and go back to sleep, or go to the dining-room for the same old boring breakfast, when he heard Tampololo's throaty laughter. He spotted her in a video rental shop. She was talking with the young woman behind the counter, as loud as ever, gesticulating sweepingly with her arms.

She was very excited to see him. 'You can help me to choose,' she said, laying a hand on his arm. She thought the movie he selected was 'very naughty', and she could not wait to see it. 'Do you have a VCR in your room?' she asked. 'Well, let's go and watch it there.' And that was that.

They spent that whole day in Radisene's room, her soft body cemented to his. They ordered mixed grills from room service and ate them in bed. She laughed a lot. She was such a free spirit that he could not help wondering why he had wasted all his life without her. Her voice was the most captivating part of her. No, it was not raspy, he decided. It was husky. Husky was sexier.

They watched the movie, and added their own groans and moans to the soundtrack. Then they talked about the problems of the world. The war in Angola. The negotiations for the democratization of South Africa. The problems with the monarchy and the soldiers in Lesotho. He was surprised how much they had in common. In the conflicts of the world they supported the same sides. They discovered that they loved reading the same novels. They both enjoyed the stories of Mbulelo Mzamane, Njabulo Ndebele and Sipho Sepamla. 'Are we being sexist in our tastes?' asked Radisene.

'Not me. I love Miriam Tlali too. And Alice Walker. Her poetry! "Horses make a landscape look more beautiful".'

'Walker is my favourite. You see what I mean when I say our union was made in heaven? Do you know about her campaigns against female circumcision in Africa?'

They talked about female circumcision. They both agreed it was horrendous that women should be mutilated like that just to please men. 'We are fortunate that we don't have that kind of thing here in Lesotho,' said Radisene.

'How do you know? You haven't been to a female initiation school, have you?'

'Surely we would have heard of it by now if it was practised here. Don't you think so?'

'Well, I haven't been to an initiation school either, so I don't know. But I can tell you of the mutilation that does happen ... something we all did when we were little girls.'

She told him that young girls were encouraged by older girls and young women to pull the pages of the book that contained the mysteries of life, until they were long. As the girls played their games, out of sight of everyone else, they pulled each other like that, every day, until the pages were stretched and hanging out. The longer they were, the happier the future of the girls would be, for girls were taught that when they got married these long pages would please their husbands, and their marriages would last for ever.

'Which is a myth,' said Radisene.

'Even so, many little girls deform their Lesothos for the imagined benefit of men.'

'Their Lesothos?'

Tampololo laughed. She told him that the femaleness of little girls was named after the country because that was where people came from. Hers, of course, could not be called a Lesotho. It had seen many things.

They laughed, but both agreed that it was really a serious matter. It was important to educate the people against such practices. If Tampololo was willing to establish a group that would engage in educational campaigns, Radisene said, he would be willing to use some of his vast fortune to fund it. Tampololo was impressed. She had never met a Mosotho man who held such progressive ideas on the relations between men and women. She wondered where a village boy from Ha Samane had learnt all these things which had created an anti-sexist attitude in him. Perhaps it was from the works of authors like Alice Walker?

In the evening Radisene drove Tampololo to her house. He knew that Trooper Motsohi was away in the district of Qacha's Nek tracking down the victims of a bus accident that had happened the previous day. Tampololo packed all her clothes in suitcases and Radisene helped her to carry them to the car. They drove back to the hotel, and did not leave the room for the next three days.

When Trooper Motsohi came home two days later, he was devastated to discover that Tampololo had left him. The neighbours were quick to inform him that his boss had helped her to move out. He went straight to the Victoria Hotel, and knew at once from the giggles of the receptionists that something was wrong. He took a lift to the tenth floor and knocked at Radisene's door. 'Go away, Motsohi,' shouted Radisene. 'I'll talk with you tomorrow at the office.'

Trooper Motsohi knew then that his wife was in the room. He hammered on the door and kicked it with both his feet. 'I know Tampololo is in there, Teacher! Open up, you wife-stealing bastard!'

'Motsohi!' Tampololo finally shouted. 'You will stop that nonsense if you know what's good for you. Do you want me to come out there right now and deal with you?'

Trooper Motsohi fell silent. After a while he began to plead softly, 'How can you do this to me, Teacher? When I've worked for you so faithfully for all these years? Tampololo, please come back home! I love you, Tampololo, please come home!'

But Tampololo did not go home. She stayed with Radisene permanently. And that gave Radisene a third reason for visiting Ha Samane: to curry favour with Father-of-the-Daughters.

On this particular weekend, however, he had a fourth reason too. He had brought a cheque of the grandmother who lived next door to Mother-of-Twins. This was the old woman who had to take care of two grandchildren, after their parents had been killed in a truck accident.

Radisene made an occasion of the cheque presentation. He slaughtered three oxen and invited all the people of Ha Samane and the neighbouring villages to a feast, which he said he was making for the orphans. All the important people of the village were there: Hlong, the postmaster, Staff Nurse Mary, some teachers from the primary school, and of course Father-of-the-

Daughters, who was the master of ceremonies.

The church choir sang a new song composed by the conductor, a young teacher who had recently joined the primary school, and who fancied himself as a composer in the league of the classical masters such as J.P. Mohapeloa and M.M. Moerane. The song was about Radisene. It said that he was the pride of Ha Samane and that nations of the world envied his fabulous wealth. It went further to compare his wisdom with that of King Solomon of the Bible.

It was not a bad song really, although people of the village were quick to notice that it sounded very much like the song the children used to sing about Sorry My Darlie at the height of his fame. They agreed, however, that there was nothing wrong when a composer as good as the young teacher stole a little bit from a song with proven popularity. It was a sign of his giftedness.

After the song Father-of-the-Daughters called upon Radisene to make the presentation to the grandmother. Radisene made a brief speech, explaining to the people the nature of his work. He said he was a lawyer who represented poor people who were involved in accidents. He sacrificed all his time to work for the nation. That was why he did not charge his clients any money. And a lot of his clients, he added, were people who did not even know that there was any money due to them. Without people like himself the insurance companies would have been quite happy to shut their mouths and bank more profits for themselves.

Then he presented the old woman with a cheque. 'This piece of paper, grandmother, is not just paper. It is money. Ask the postmaster to read for us how much it is. He will also advise you how to put it in his post office bank where you can withdraw only the amount you need for your grandchildren from time to time.'

The postmaster came forward and read aloud, 'Ten thousand rands.'

People thundered their amazement at such a huge amount. Women ululated and men did the tlala dance. The choir burst out into its song in praise of Radisene, son of Mother-of-Twins, brother of the beautiful Dikosha, pride of Ha Samane.

Normally Radisene would have kept half of the amount paid by the insurance company for himself and given the client only five thousand rands. But this time he had decided to give the old lady the full amount in order to make a great impression on the people of the village, but more especially on Father-of-the-Daughters. He was not losing anything, because as usual the insurance company had paid him an eight-hundred rands fee for lodging the claim.

During the feast, when people were eating meat and drinking beer brewed by the team of Mother-of-Twins and Mother-of-the-Daughters, men of Ha Samane approached Radisene and offered to rent him their cattle for the next day. 'We know that before you leave for the lowlands you'll want to herd cattle,' they said. Radisene said he would only rent from those men who had let him use their cattle that very first time he had sent Trooper Motsohi to ask them. He would never rent cattle from those who had first refused. They begged him and said they were sorry. 'We need the money because of this terrible drought,' they pleaded. But Radisene would have nothing to do with them.

Before the people left in the evening Radisene announced that he had been very much impressed with the church choir. He gave them the job of singing for him whenever he visited the village. The young teacher was assigned the task of composing more songs about him. And, of course, he was going to pay them well for their services. They were his personal sycophants. The choir members shouted with joy. They were even more excited when he promised that he would also pay their way to the lowlands one day, to sing for him there and to have their beautiful music recorded by Matsepe Massa of Radio Lesotho.

Unfortunately, there were some who were not impressed with all the events of the day. They said that Radisene was merely trying to absolve himself for what he had done to the grandmothers all those years ago.

Radisene, on the other hand, was pleased with himself. His only regret was that Dikosha was not there to see him at the height of his greatness. He walked to her rondavel, hoping to catch a glimpse of her, and found Sorry My Darlie drooling on her stoep. As soon as he'd finished eating the meat at the feast he had come to sit in his usual spot.

'Have you seen Dikosha today?' Radisene asked.

'Yes, she's in there. When I came her whole head was visible at the window because the little boy, Shana, was serenading her with his sekgankula.'

Some young women who were passing by laughed to hear this. It was obvious that Dikosha was smitten with Shana, they said. When she disappeared, he disappeared. When she reappeared, he reappeared as well. One said, 'What does Dikosha do with a child like that?' Another said, 'What does she *see* in a little child like that?' The third one laughed and said, 'And the scales of dirt on his feet! They have become part of his skin. If they were to be removed, he would bleed.'

Radisene turned his back on their idle gossip and went to his mother's dilapidated mansion.

10. The Great Snow

It finally happened. The people of the cave were totally imprisoned by the scribblings and graffiti on the sacred walls. Dikosha was powerless against the most powerful people in the land, and against the tourists from across the seas, who took their cue from the high and mighty and desecrated the cave with their vain names.

On the day she learnt of the final imprisonment Dikosha sat on the warm ashes on the floor and summoned her friends with all her might. But they could not come. She tried again and again, but the monster-woman-dancer and her people stayed behind the scrawls. Dikosha knew that this was the end of her healing dances of the night with the people of the cave. It was not only the death of the dance, but the death of a lifestyle as well. Her world and her life with the people of the cave had been destroyed for ever. She would have to find a new way of expressing herself and a new life in the world that was far away from this place. She would not come here again. It would be too painful to reawaken all the memories of a beautiful and peaceful life that had been rudely dashed by vandals.

She walked out of the cave, daintily touching her ostrich eggshell beads. They would be the only reminder of the idyllic life she had led. The beads ... and the gift to see songs with which she had been endowed by the monster-woman-dancer.

She walked on the frozen water of the Black River like a puny, red-dressed Jesus, and crossed to the other side. Her bare feet ploughed into the snow, which swallowed her legs almost up to the knees.

It had snowed almost every day for two weeks and mountains of snow had piled up. Everything was at a standstill. The trucks that delivered food to the general dealer's store could not move an inch, and the store had long since run out of groceries. The main problem was paraffin, which was absolutely essential for cooking at this time since women could not go and gather wood on the snow-covered hillsides. Many families did have Primus stoves which had been brought back by returning migrants, but they were stored and forgotten somewhere since all the cooking was done in three-legged pots outside or on the hearth in the kitchen rondavels. Now people remembered their Primus stoves and dug them out. But without paraffin they were useless, and the paraffin ran out at the general dealers during the very first week of the snow.

Ha Samane and the neighbouring villages were cut off from the rest of the world. Even the planes could not land at the airfield. The only people who had any contact with the outside world were Hlong and Staff Nurse Mary, who spent the whole day sitting at their CB radios, appealing to the government in the lowlands to send relief supplies to the mountain people, otherwise they would die of starvation.

Food had never been a problem for Dikosha when the people of the cave were still there. She had all her meals with them. Even when a number of days passed without her going to the Cave of Barwa, the honey and the herbs she had eaten on her last visit would sustain her. But now that that lifestyle was dead, she would soon be required to think seriously about such mundane things as eating.

Her cabbage patch was still there with its big-headed cabbages. Even in the middle of such a vicious winter they flourished. Shana continued to play his sekgankula for them, and they defied the cold and the snow. When she still had the comfort of the cave she used to give some of the cabbages to Shana and he would take them to his guardians to cook for the family. Some of them were used by Mother-of-Twins, who was free to cut off a head or two for herself from time to time. When the communal garden to which the old woman belonged had enough vegetables she did not need Dikosha's cabbages, although she always said that she preferred them because they had the most savoury taste. Sorry My Darlie was also given an occasional cabbage, until Dikosha got to know that he often exchanged them for beer at one of the shebeens. Now that the lifestyle of the cave was dead, she would have to eat some of the cabbages herself.

After struggling up the hill over what would normally be the grazing lands, and through the paths of the lower part of the village where the snow covered the murals of the houses and made the rondavels look like igloos, Dikosha arrived at her home. As usual Sorry My Darlie was sitting outside, his teeth gnashing noisily, and his eyes bulging with cold. Dikosha shook her head and said, 'You know, Sorry My Darlie, one day you are going to catch your death in this cold.' And she walked into the rondavel and locked the door.

She had to lock her door because Radisene was in the village, and he hadn't given up hope that one day she would want to see him. From time to time he came to knock and to plead with her to open up. Once or twice he had tried to force the door open, but then he remembered Mother-of-the-Daughters' advice.

In fact, Radisene had been marooned in the village. He had come two weeks ago on one of his regular visits. Then it had suddenly snowed, and he could not drive back to the lowlands. His supplies of the delicacies that he always brought with him to the mountains had run out, and he had been reduced to eating papa and cabbage like everyone else.

His main problem was that he was bored. He could not herd cattle because of the snow. Herding cattle involved too much work in weather like this. The herdboys had to shovel the snow from the grazing lands so that the cattle could scrape at the matted icy grass. Those farmers who had stored the stalks after harvesting the maize rationed them to the milk cows and supplemented their diet with a lot of salt. The cattle suffered, and the bones stuck out all over their bodies. What made things worse was that this snow of the world had followed the drought of the world.

Radisene was lonely and fed up with the snow. He had no one to talk with except Mother-of-Twins. She, however, was busy with her community work. She visited the sick and the destitute, and shared with them the little food she had. She did not bother to go to the communal garden because the snow had killed all the vegetables. Unlike Dikosha's cabbage patch, the communal garden could not survive the weather.

Once or twice the sycophantic church choir came to sing Radisene's praises composed by the enthusiastic schoolteacher. But the enthusiasm waned as the snow piled up.

One person who could have kept Radisene company was Father-of-the-Daughters. The two men had become close lately. When the old man first heard that Tampololo had left her husband for Radisene he had been very angry – not because he particularly liked Trooper Motsohi, but because he believed in the good old-fashioned family values. He considered it a sin that the two children were living together, and yet they were not married. It was shameful that his daughter, who had been brought up so well, had run away from her husband to live with another man, whoever that man was. The ever-present fear of what the neighbours would say about this scandal gnawed at the family, especially at Mother-of-the-Daughters. And Radisene was not the most popular person in the village to have as some kind of a son-in-law. Even though he was rich and had tried to do good things for the people of the village, they had never forgiven him for what he had done to the grandmothers twenty-one years ago.

But in the course of that year, as the children continued to live together and insisted that they were deeply in love, both Father-of-the-Daughters and Mother-of-the-Daughters accepted what they could not change. Radisene also had a way of ingratiating himself with them by bringing them nice presents. He spent a lot of time sitting with Father-of-the-Daughters under the big gum-tree in the yard, talking about the affairs of the land, and especially about how Lekhanya's fellow soldiers had removed him from power at gun-point and replaced him with Major-General Ramaema, who had promised to call a free and fair election in the next two years. Most of the exiled Congress Party members were back, and soon there would be constituency demarcation and voter registration in the whole country.

The two men would sample the European beer that Radisene always brought with him from the lowlands. Then Father-of-the-Daughters would express his fears that now that politics was coming back again in the country, people would kill one another as they did in 1970. Radisene would remember 1970, and Trooper Motsohi, and Potiane, and Roll-Away. He would smile and say, 'Perhaps we are now mature enough not to repeat 1970. In any case we need democracy in this country. The bloody soldiers are so corrupt they have looted the national coffers empty and covered themselves with layers and layers of the fat of the land.'

Sometimes, out of the blue, Father-of-the-Daughters would ask, 'Hey, son, how do you see this Mandela thing in the Republic? Do you think the Boers will just give him power without fighting?'

Radisene would respond sagely, 'They have no choice, father. Why do you think they released him after twenty-seven years in jail? It is because they can't contain the situation any more. The people are tired, father. They want to be free. The Boers cannot rule any more now; their government is in a mess. And the countries of the world are pushing them to talk with the blacks.'

'Maybe we too need our own Mandela. Don't you think so, son?'

'Well, at least the elections are coming, father. Perhaps a new leader will win. Perhaps we will get a government that serves the interests of the people and not of its pocket, like the previous governments we have had in this country.'

Father-of-the-Daughters would nod in agreement.

But when the snow came Father-of-the-Daughters could not keep Radisene company any longer. He left for the cattle-posts on the second day of the snow. He was worried about his herds and wanted to make sure that the herdboys who lived permanently on those distant mountains were taking care of his wealth properly.

For most of the day snow imprisoned Radisene in his mother's tumbledown mansion. He sat in the kitchen alone, listening to Radio Lesotho on his portable radio. He had a searing pain in his heart when he remembered that only a few blocks away from the studios, from which the programmes he was listening to were broadcast, was the Victoria Hotel. On the tenth floor of that hotel was his room. And in that room was Tampololo, waiting eagerly for his return. He could imagine the room full of all sorts of stuffed animals and cuddly bears of different sizes. Oh, how he missed his Tampololo!

And, of course, he missed her body. He had never in his wildest dreams imagined the joys of a woman's body against his own. His deep, dark secret was that until Tampololo, he had never known a woman before … in the biblical sense, that is. He could not tell his friends that he had kept himself for Misti, only to be deflowered by Tampololo. He did not want to be the laughing stock of all Maseru. He was in his forties, and deemed to be a man of the world, with enough money to sow wild oats everywhere he went. How could he explain his unsullied state to the world without appearing ridiculous? He could not even explain it to himself. He put it down to the teachings of the Good Fathers when he was a young altar boy.

Now he regretted the wasted years. If he had only known what untold ecstacies he was missing! He remembered that first morning when they watched the video, and how he had hollered for his mother and promised to buy Tampololo the whole world, including her personal train with its own railway line. He missed Tampololo. He missed walking hand-in-hand with her at the LNDC Shopping Mall, with the nosy people of Maseru gawking and sniggering and pointing fingers.

Shame, the people of Maseru. They had a village mentality. They made everyone else's business their own. That was their greatest pastime … to stick their noses into other people's business. They knew everything about everyone, and especially what went on in their bedrooms. If there were no romances like Tampololo's and Radisene's what would they talk about? Their lives would be excruciatingly boring.

Radisene listened to the seven o'clock news. He heard that the government was going to send its two army helicopters to drop food supplies in the mountain regions. Through the Red Cross friendly nations of the world had donated grain and powdered milk which would be dropped at various villages. However, the two helicopters were not enough to serve the whole country, and so the government had asked the South African government to help. Fortunately there were already South African helicopters flying over the mountains of Lesotho without anyone's permission, scouting the area for cattle rustlers. These would help to drop food supplies as well.

At last! They should have thought of this a week ago, thought Radisene. Many families had run out of food, the poorest people of the village had resorted to eating snow.

He walked to the window and looked across the white strip of land between the mansion and Dikosha's rondavel. The moonlight reflected on the snow and filled the whole area with a dreamlike lustre. Dikosha's house was a silhouette against shimmering flakes. Radisene could see the yellow light of a paraffin lamp at her window, and knew that even in this icy weather the window was open.

She loved the untainted air of the night. Nights were peaceful and full of beautiful dreams. Hers were very lucid dreams, in which she invoked the imprisoned people of the cave to play with her again. Often she made Shana feature in those dreams, and he played music for them. And indeed, as Shana snored in the herd-boys' rondavel at Father-of-the-Daughters' homestead, Dikosha featured in his dreams too. He played music for her, and for some strange men and women who had protruding buttocks. For most of the night Dikosha's house was filled with the music of her dreams.

Shana's songs became more and more beautiful. Dikosha willed him to stop singing about the infidelities of women and to sing instead about the beauty of sadness. When she summoned him in her dreams she taught him songs she had composed, and he sang her words to the music of the sekgankula in his waking hours. People of the village and Shana himself thought these new songs were his own compositions.

People staggering home from shebeens in the small hours, or answering the call of nature behind the aloes, heard strains of a sekgankula from Dikosha's place. They wondered what Shana was

doing in there at that time of the night, and what kind of an irre-
sponsible guardian Father-of-the-Daughters was to let a little boy
like that spend his winter nights in a woman's chamber ...
although in reality they never really thought of her as a woman.
Those who could count remembered that she was in her forties,
and could have been a grandmother if she had done what all
women were created for: to marry and settle down and look after
her husband and children. Yet she did not look like a woman. She
looked like a girl who had just reached her twenties, a hauntingly
beautiful girl in an unfading red dress.

Mother-of-the-Daughters was surprised when she heard
rumours that Shana was spending his nights in Dikosha's house.
She was certain that Shana spent the evenings with the family and
slept at night in the hut reserved for the herdboys. And all the boys
vouched that Shana was there every night. Mother-of-the-
Daughters knew that they would not lie to protect him. They did
not like him, because he did not work and received special treatment. He spent the whole day playing his sekgankula, and herded
cattle only when he felt like it. They would have been happier, in
fact, if the rumours were true, and Shana was in trouble for a
change.

Mother-of-the-Daughters wondered why people of the village
would want to tell such lies and accuse her family of irresponsi-
bility. She vowed that when Father-of-the-Daughters returned
from the cattle-posts he would sue the rumourmongers for damaging the name of his family.

The snow continued to fall.

The helicopters promised by the radio arrived in due course and
dropped bags and boxes of food in the vicinity of Staff Nurse
Mary's clinic. The chief of the village, Chief Samane, helped by
ministers of the two main denominations in the village, rationed
the food to the hungry families. The mothers and grandmothers
came with empty sisal bags, hoping that they would be filled with
maize-meal. But to their disappointment each family could only
get a dishful of yellow maize-meal and a small bowlful of pow-

dered milk.

That afternoon Father-of-the-Daughters returned from the cattle-posts. His face was haggard, and his thick Qibi blanket was full of mud. He was wearing a gumboot on one foot, but the other foot was bare and lacerated. His horse walked very slowly. It was obviously tired and hungry. Men who saw him shouted their greetings and asked him what had happened to his other boot. He snapped at them, 'You people of Ha Samane, don't you ever get tired of asking stupid questions?'

In the evening strange men in grey donkey blankets passed through the village. They were cattle rustlers driving a big herd of Friesland cows whose udders hung almost to the ground. In their attempt to dodge the helicopters that were looking for them, the rustlers had lost their way in the mountains and found themselves at Ha Samane.

The men were hungry and asked for food from some homesteads. Throughout their journey they had lived only on milk from the cows and on meat from those that could not survive the long road, leaving a trail of feasts in their wake. And many of the animals had died along the way, since they were not strong enough to traverse snow-covered mountains and cross icy rivers.

The men of Ha Samane quickly called an emergency meeting at the chief's place to discuss the rustlers. A hot debate ensued as to whether or not the rustlers should be given refuge in the village. A man who argued in favour of helping them said, 'After all, they are running away from the Boers. The Boers stole our land. If you see that whole Orange Free State, then you know that in the days of Moshoeshoe it used to belong to Lesotho. And the Boers stole it from us. It is only right that we should steal their cattle.'

'Those are politics of the Congress Party', shouted one man.

The chief said he was governed by the law, and was a servant not only of the people but of the law. 'What will the mounted police say when they hear that I, Chief Samane, a gazetted chief of a Christian village, gave refuge to cattle thieves? And they are sure to hear of it because many of you here have wagging tongues.'

Father-of-the-Daughters, who had changed into clean clothes and a Lefitori blanket, agreed with the chief. 'I am an owner of animals,' he said. 'I therefore have no time for rustlers. Their theft has no mercy. They do not only steal from the Boers.'

'That is so,' agreed Radisene, who was quite pleased to play a role in the affairs of the village. 'Even now as we are speaking here, I am sure they are spying on your kraals to see what cattle to steal next time.'

The meeting decided that the men should be told to leave forthwith. Hlong was asked to use his radio in the morning to inform the mounted police that the rustlers had passed through Ha Samane.

Before the men of the village could leave, Father-of-the-Daughters stood up and said he wanted to speak. 'I have an urgent case against Hlong. I want the chief to call the kgotla tomorrow to hear my case.'

'But tomorrow is Sunday,' protested the chief.

'Yes,' agreed another man, 'some of us are Christians. We go to church on Sundays.'

'We have heard cases on Sundays before when the matter was urgent and was likely to spoil the peace of the village. My case against Hlong is urgent. It can be heard after church.'

Hlong was open-mouthed with surprise. He did not know anything about this case. He could not remember doing anything wrong to his friend, Father-of-the-Daughters. 'What case is this against me that cannot wait until Monday?' he asked.

'You will know soon enough. I am suing you in your capacity as the father of two herdboys in one cattle-post.'

The chief said the kgotla would meet the next day after church.

Normally the kgotla met on the rocks under the tree which was next to the kraal of the chief's homestead. That was also where the men who considered themselves the chief's councillors sat and played morabaraba all day when there were no disputes to settle. But this Sunday afternoon they could not sit there because of the snow. Somebody suggested that the case should be held in one of the big rooms at Staff Nurse Mary's clinic. The men, led by the chief, proceeded to the clinic, but Staff Nurse Mary drove them away. 'You can't turn the clinic into a kgotla,' she said. 'This is a place for nursing the sick, not for settling village arguments.'

The men left, mumbling something about women who were too educated for their own good. Then someone suggested that since Radisene had a big house, surely the kgotla could meet in one of the rooms. Indeed, Radisene thought, the kgotla could meet in Dikosha's dance studio. That would enhance his standing in the village too. It would take a bit of time to clean the place up ...

But before he could respond Hlong objected, 'No, we can't meet there. That is not a neutral place. We know that Radisene is Father-of-the-Daughters' lawyer. We also know that the same Radisene does dirty things with this man's daughter. So you see, dear friends, if Father-of-the-Daughters says he is suing me for whatever he says I have done, then we need a neutral venue. How do we know what medicines they have put in that house, so that I will lose the case?'

'You would know about medicines, wouldn't you ... since it is well known that you are a wizard who sends lightning. And who told you that Radisene is my lawyer? Where was he when your children did terrible things to me? And if you talk about my daughter again I will sue you until you remain only with the clothes you are wearing.'

'Hey you, Father-of-the-Daughters,' shouted Hlong, 'why do you want to spoil my name like this? I will sue your pants off too. Ha! Medicines! Don't you know that I am a Christian? I am a man of the church, Father-of-the-Daughters. A man of the living God. I do not touch medicines with my hands.'

The men of the village laughed, for everyone knew that, Christian or no Christian, Hlong was an expert at sending lightning to destroy enemies. Some had privately voiced their doubts at Father-of-the-Daughters' wisdom in suing such a man. But they concluded that perhaps Father-of-the-Daughters had stronger medicines. That was why he was so wealthy and Hlong was not.

'Whoever heard of a lawyer in a chief's court?' asked the chief. 'I think Radisene must go. We don't need lawyers here.'

'You are right, morena,' Radisene replied. 'The law does not allow lawyers to appear before a chief's court. Lawyers like us appear only in front of the big judges at the high court in Maseru. I am not here as a lawyer, father. I am here as a man of the village. All men of the village are expected to participate in the affairs of the village, especially in the kgotla, whether they are lawyers or not.'

Everyone agreed that Radisene should stay, for it was his right as a man of the village to participate in the kgotla. His cleverness as a lawyer would not distract the men from digging out the truth of the matter and reaching a judgement that was fair to all.

The kgotla finally met in the Evangelical Church, after the Mothers' Union had concluded their deliberations on a tea party they were organizing for a visiting minister.

'Fathers of the village,' said Father-of-the-Daughters, addressing the kgotla, 'my complaint is against Hlong. I am suing him for damages that this court will decide upon. His two sons destroyed my property, namely one of my precious gumboots.'

Chief Samane turned to Hlong. 'Hlong, do you know anything about this case?' he asked.

But Hlong did not respond. He merely looked at the chief. The chief called his name again, but still there was no response. Then Radisene suddenly remembered it was Sunday. On Sundays Hlong only answered to his church name. This fact had obviously slipped the chief's mind.

'Perhaps he will respond if you call him Petrose,' suggested Radisene.

'Petrose, do you know anything about this case?' the chief said with a sigh.

'Morena, I know nothing about it. He didn't say I destroyed his gumboots, did he? He said my sons did.'

'Well, you know that in our custom as long as the sons are not married they are the father's responsibility. They can be a hundred years old, but if they are not married they cannot answer any case on their own. Even if they impregnate a woman, they can only appear as witnesses. You are the one who is accused and who must pay damages. But let Father-of-the-Daughters explain to us what happened.'

'I was caught in a snowstorm at the cattle-posts. Hlong's, ah, Petrose's boys came and tore one of my gumboots with a knife.'

'Where is this gumboot now?' asked one man.

'They threw it away. I only have this one that remained as evidence.' He brandished the gumboot that was not torn.

'They just came and tore your gumboot without provocation?'

'When you look at me, at my age, do I look like a man who can provoke children?'

The men were all shocked at the rude behaviour of today's children. Various men made speeches, asking the same old question. 'What is the world coming to, when children of today cannot respect their elders?' Hlong apologized profusely for what his sons were alleged to have done. But he insisted that the court could not find against him because he had not been given the opportunity to call his witnesses. It was only fair that the two boys should come from the cattle-posts and give evidence on their behalf.

'Not on their behalf,' said the chief. 'On *your* behalf. You are the accused, not them.'

But Father-of-the-Daughters was adamant: the case was straightforward. The court should find against Hlong, without any waste of time, and award him damages.

'That would not be fair, morena'; Radisene suggested. 'We need to hear all the evidence before we can award damages. It is important that Ntate Hlong, I mean Petrose, should come with his witnesses.'

All the men of the kgotla agreed with him. And one angry man demanded. 'What was urgent about this case that we had to listen to it on Sunday?'

Father-of-the-Daughters responded, 'Things must be discussed while they are still hot. Would you have preferred that I took my stick, and went to the airfield and settled this matter with blood?'

On their way home Father-of-the-Daughters was grumbling. 'How can you, of all people, child of Mother-of-Twins, turn against me in the presence of my enemies?' he kept on asking.

Radisene tried to explain that the law was the law. It tolerated no favouritism. 'All sides must be heard before any judgement can be passed,' he added.

'And yet you say you want to marry my daughter? How can you betray me like that, child of Mother-of-Twins? Don't you know that winning is everything in a court case? Where does fairness come into it? Do you think I spend my life attending court cases in order to lose? And you call yourself a lawyer!'

Radisene thought of Tampololo, and blamed himself for the indiscretion of giving a legal opinion at the kgotla. He apologized to Father-of-the-Daughters and promised that when the case continued he would not interfere again.

That evening those people of Ha Samane who loved social occasions, and were undaunted by mountains of snow, rode their horses to Ha Sache. Others went on foot. It was the night of the tlhophe, when diviners from all over the region gathered to dance through the night and drive out evil spirits from those who were possessed. They would also make predictions of the future and cure sicknesses.

Radisene rented a horse and picked his way over to Ha Sache. Misti would be one of the graduands tonight, and he was looking forward to seeing her. Maybe he would even get a chance to talk with her.

The tlhophe was held in a big four-walled house at Misti's home. It was jam-packed with people. Others crowded around the door outside and in the clearing in front of the house. The rumble of cowhide drums and the rattle of gourds filled the air.

Radisene squeezed himself into the house and watched the diviners dance. Misti was dancing between two fat women. She was wearing a red skirt made of some rough calico, with white beads sewn in intricate patterns onto the hem. Above the waist she wore only a bra, and there were many strings of white beads around her neck and at her wrists and ankles. She also wore what looked like a tiara of white beads on her head. She danced in her bare feet, stamping the ground like a woman possessed. Radisene wondered if she felt any pain hitting the floor like that with her toes and heels. Sweat ran in rivers down her face.

An older diviner used a broom to sprinkle some medicinal liquid on the audience. The air was filled with the smell of strange herbs. One of the fat women began to divine. She spoke about people who had evil intentions for the family, and about witches running loose outside and ready to pounce on the innocent at any moment. From time to time she challenged the audience by shouting, 'Vumani!' The audience shouted back their agreement: 'Siyavuma!' Then she went into a frenzy, bellowing like a hurt bull. Misti and the other diviner began to bellow too. The sound that came from Misti was deep and hollow. It was as though all her insides had been wrenched out. Radisene felt humiliated on her behalf. He wanted to leave. He didn't want to see her like this.

All around him people seemed to be in different states of trance. He thought he saw Dikosha's face across the room. But when he tried to push his way in her direction, she was no longer there. He looked hard at every face in the room, but couldn't see her any more.

He forced his way out, and went to fetch his horse which he had tethered on a stump. Past the aloes that partly fenced the homestead he saw a woman standing alone, weeping. 'What is the matter, mother?' he asked. But she did not respond. Going closer, he saw that it was Misti's mother. Her whole body was shaking with sobs. He held her hand and said, 'Don't cry, mother. Misti will be fine. This is what she wanted to do.'

After almost a month the snow was beginning to melt. People had survived all this time on relief supplies from the Red Cross dropped by army helicopters, mostly from South Africa. The government had declared a state of emergency in the mountain areas and many nations had donated food. The mountain people knew that some of the food did not reach the poor and destitute, but ended up in the warehouses of important people in the government. The people of the mountains were not stupid. They knew these things, but they did not have the power to change them.

Radisene was a very worried man. He had never before been away from his business for such a long time. He was sure that accidents had happened and no one had attended to them. He couldn't trust Trooper Motsohi to act without supervision. On top of that the man was still sulking over the little matter between Tampololo and his boss. But Radisene had no doubt that when he returned to the lowlands Trooper Motsohi would still be around. He had nowhere else to go. And working for Radisene was a way of staying close to Tampololo. Motsohi had not given up the idea of winning her back.

The first truck that got through to the general dealer's was a joy to everyone, and especially to Radisene. It showed that the roads were at last passable. Radisene asked the truck-driver to help him jump-start the Range Rover, and then he kept the engine running to charge up the battery. He wanted to be ready to leave the next day.

That afternoon Chief Samane summoned the men of the village to the kgotla to finish Father-of-the-Daughters' case, as the witnesses from the cattle-posts had arrived. Father-of-the-Daughters had lost interest in the case in the meantime: he was now involved in another case at the local court, which he found more exciting because it was about fields and cattle. However, he had to complete what he had begun, and so he duly arrived at the kgotla.

To start with Father-of-the-Daughters repeated his accusations, and the men of the village repeated their angry words against the children of today who had no respect for their elders. Then the two witnesses, a boy of about sixteen and his brother of about fourteen, were asked what they had to say for themselves. Did they not know that Father-of-the-Daughters was one of the most respected fathers of the village?

The elder boy spoke timidly, 'We are sorry for what we did.'

'You are sorry!' bellowed the chief. 'Is that all you can say?'

'Why don't you ask them first why they did it, before you

pounce on them like this?' demanded Hlong.

'That's exactly what we want to know, Petrose – or whoever you are today.'

'You can call me Hlong. It's not a Sunday today, is it?'

'So,' said the chief, turning to the boys. 'Why did you do it?'

'It was the only thing we could do, fathers,' pleaded the younger boy.

The boys told their story. They had been looking for some calves which had strayed during a snowstorm when they saw a horse which looked very familiar. It was neighing and raising its front legs as if it wanted to call their attention. They tried to think hard whose horse it could be, but couldn't place it. As they approached the animal they saw that it was standing on the edge of a crevice. Looking down between the rocks they saw a man with snow piling up on him. He must have fallen from his horse in the blizzard and passed out. They climbed down and removed the snow from him. To their surprise they found that it was Father-of-the-Daughters, the very friend of their father's. They tried to pull him out, but one of his legs was caught between two rocks. The rocks held tight and refused to yield. The only way they could free him was to cut the gumboot he was wearing with a penknife. Only then were they able to pull him out of the crevice.

They took Father-of-the-Daughters to their hut at the cattle-post and gave him hot gravy. After a while he came to his senses. The first thing he wanted to know was what had happened to his gum-boot. 'He was very angry when we told him,' said the younger brother.

'From what I hear, Father-of-the-Daughters, these children saved your life,' said Chief Samane. 'And yet you have the gall to sue them?'

'What kind of procedure is this?' Father-of-the-Daughters burst out. 'How can you make a decision that these children are innocent even before the men of the kgotla have deliberated on the matter?'

'Do you agree that things happened the way the children claim they did?' asked one man.

'Of course they happened that way. I was caught in a snowstorm as I said, and Hlong's children tore my gumboot.'

'But they saved your life.'

'Where is it written that when people save your life they must destroy your property? Which law is that? Is that in the Laws of Lerotholi? Do I need to remind you that our courts here are based on the Laws of Lerotholi, which in turn are based on our customary law? Do the Laws of Lerotholi say that people must just destroy your property when they are saving your life?'

The men of the kgotla did not feel like wrangling with Father-of-the-Daughters any more. The case was dismissed.

Father-of-the-Daughters was not happy with the decision. He announced that he was going to appeal to the local court which, he assured the men of the village, was manned by people who knew the law … unlike the chief's kgotla which was full of ignorant people who were easily swayed by their fear of Hlong's medicines. If he lost the case at the local court, because sometimes the court presidents were easily bribed by the likes of Hlong, he was going to appeal until he reached the judicial commissioner's court and then the high court in Maseru.

Hlong, on the other hand, was very angry that his time had been wasted. 'I know that litigation has become a sport among us,' he fumed. 'But this man has wasted my time and my money. I am a servant of the government. I have no time to play with. I had to spend time and money fetching these boys from the cattle-posts. Who is looking after my cattle in the meantime? And you have heard this man. He says he is appealing against your decision. This means that I will spend all my life running around the court rooms of this country. Who will control the airfield during all that time?'

Hlong stormed away. Father-of-the-Daughters also mounted his horse and rode away. The men of the kgotla remained behind mumbling that it was not wise to make a man like Hlong angry.

As he rode home Father-of-the-Daughters could smell the rain in the air. Dark clouds had gathered above him. He was glad that at last the remaining snow was going to melt away. But in an instant these comforting thoughts vanished from his mind as a tremendous flash of lightning shattered the still mountain air and thunder engulfed him. The horse reared and for the second time in a matter of days Father-of-the-Daughters found himself flung to the ground. The horse bolted. He picked himself up and stumbled after it, but another bolt of lightning struck the earth in front of him and hurled him flat again. He got to his feet groggily and reeled about in a frenzied sort of dance, while the earth shook and lightning crashed all around. Then all of a sudden it was quiet. He ran home like a scared rabbit.

As soon as he got home he called one of the herdboys and gave him instructions. 'Run to Hlong's house and tell him that I am no longer going to appeal against the decision of the kgotla. I am withdrawing my case against him.'

The next day he went to see Radisene off. 'Go well, son of Mother-of-Twins,' he said. 'I hope you will always remember that you made me lose a case.'

Radisene hated to be called son of Mother-of-Twins. Other men were called after the father of the house, and he had to be called after his mother. He knew that when Father-of-the-Daughters addressed him that way he was not happy with him at all. He would have to make amends somehow. He could not afford to have the father of his beloved Tampololo mad at him.

11. The Great Rains

The rains finally came, breaking the drought of many years. Those who believed in King Moshoshoe the Second said it was because he had returned from his enforced sabbatical. They were now lobbying for him to be reinstated in his rightful position as monarch of all the land. Moshoeshoe's son, Mohato, who was now called King Letsie the Third, had been sworn in as king in his father's absence. But his throne was full of political thorns and he wanted his father to take it back. The government was adamant that Letsie was the permanent king, and Moshoeshoe was reduced to a mere chief. Those who did not believe in the institution of kingship felt that this dispute was a waste of time and money. The whole institution should have been done away with long ago, they said. A poor country could not afford to maintain an institution that did not benefit the people but only ate into their pockets. They saw a republic as the only answer, where leadership would be bestowed on people on merit, and not because they were born of certain individuals.

Nevertheless, everyone welcomed the rains. During the drought water had been rationed in Maseru. People could not fill their swimming-pools or wash their cars. Water was available only in the early morning and in the evening, for one hour at a time. In towns like Mafeteng people walked for miles in search of water. Yet those in power boasted all the time of the white gold with which the country was endowed, which they even sold to South Africa. But people did not see any of this white gold inside the country, and they were dying of thirst. Now the rains were back, and people got relief. It rained so much that the Mohokare River which separated Maseru from the Orange Free State overflowed. The snow that was melting in the mountains added more water to the rivers throughout the land.

From the windows of his house in the Maseru suburb of Florida Radisene could see the muddy waters of the Mohokare, almost covering the poplar and willow trees that grew on its banks. He could also see bodies floating in the water, carried along by the strong currents. These were people who had been swept away by flood-waters while trying to cross the river high up in the mountains or were gathering wood along its banks. The river carried these bodies for miles, sometimes dashing them against rocks and stripping them naked, swirling them along with stumps of wood and uprooted trees. After a long journey through many districts the Mohokare would vomit its unwilling passengers into the Senqu River, which in turn would vomit them into the sea. But people said the sea never accepted corpses. It took pride in its cleanliness. It therefore spewed them onto the shores to be cleared away by birds of prey.

Radisene thought that if the rains continued for another few days the water would certainly reach the house. He would love that. He would be happy if the floods covered the whole house and destroyed it. He did not really like the place. It was not a bad house in itself, with three bedrooms, a study, a bathroom and toilet, a second toilet, a big living-room, and a kitchen with a dining area. But he had come to live in it against his will.

More than a year had passed since Radisene had been marooned in the mountains because of the snow. He had returned home after a month to find that Tampololo had checked out of the Victoria Hotel. She had taken everything with her, including his own clothes. There was a note at the reception desk giving an address in Florida, where she could be found.

Radisene had driven to Florida, to a red-brick house that stood in its own yard a few hundred metres from the Mohokare River. It was an old house of the type that used to house white civil servants in the colonial days. It had a beautiful view of the river and of the evergreen Free State farms on the other side. He knocked and Tampololo opened the door. She was very happy to see him back, and kissed him over and over again. She told him excitedly that she had decided to rent them a house because a hotel room was too small for them.

'You are renting this house?' asked Radisene, not quite believing his ears.

'Yes! Isn't it wonderful?'

'Don't you think you should have waited for me before you took a decision like that?'

'Oh, come on, Radisene! I knew you wouldn't mind. You wouldn't want our son to grow up in a hotel room, would you?'

'Our son?'

'Of course. I am pregnant, silly!'

Radisene did not know whether to laugh or cry. It had never occurred to him that he was capable of putting a whole woman in the family way. He was dazed. Tampololo had been married to Trooper Motsohi for many years, but they could not have children. And here he was going to be the father of Tampololo's child. He hugged and kissed her. A child was good news indeed. There was no way that Father-of-the-Daughters and Mother-of-the-Daughters could fail to bless their union now that there would be a child. They had always complained that Tampololo was not giving them any grandchildren, whereas even the youngest of their daughters already had children of their own.

Radisene was not happy about the house though. It had always been his plan that when he moved from the Victoria Hotel he would go straight to his mansion. And he was almost ready to build it. His site had already been surveyed, and he was waiting for the lease documents from the Department of Lands and Surveys. He also felt that Tampololo should have discussed the move with him first. Instead she had acted on her own in a matter which affected his life as well. But he decided to keep his unhappiness to himself. He did not want to pour cold water on her good intentions.

During the period when she was pregnant life with Tampololo was absolute bliss. They fussed over each other, and were together most of the time. She was always so understanding, so considerate and generous. Radisene never forgot how fortunate he was to be loved so intensely and selflessly by a woman like Tampololo.

The baby was born at a private clinic in Bloemfontein. It was a girl. As soon as the nurse called with the news, Radisene drove to Bloemfontein. He arrived at the clinic with a bouquet of flowers and went straight to Tampololo's ward. She was not excited to see him. He had expected the usual hugs and kisses, but she was distant and cold. He put it down to the ordeal of bringing a human being into the world.

As they drove home Radisene babbled about how beautiful the baby was, how she had taken after her mother who was the sweetest woman he had ever known, how the baby would have a great future limited only by the sky itself, how she was going to be the prime minister of Lesotho, and how when Mandela had finished negotiations with the Boers and South Africa was free and Lesotho was one of its provinces she was going to be the president of South Africa. Through all this prattle Tampololo sat quietly in the back seat, breast-feeding the baby. Finally Radisene asked, 'Awu, Tampololo, what is the matter? You are unusually quiet.'

She snapped at him, 'What is there to talk about?'

'Ourselves. The baby.'

'The baby, eh? The bloody baby! Do you know the agony I have gone through while you were sitting in Maseru having a good time? Have you ever tried giving birth? And don't you see that this is a girl?'

'Of course it's a girl, Tampi. A beautiful girl too. Like you.'

Tampololo began to shout at him. And her voice was no longer husky – it was raspy. What was she going to do with a girl, she demanded. She had wanted a baby boy. Her family needed a boy. All her siblings were girls, and their children were girls too. It was left to her to provide her family with a boy, and she had let them down. Or rather, Radisene had let *her* down. 'You are useless, Radisene!' she croaked. 'Useless! Useless! Useless! You can't even make a boy!'

That was their first big argument. But it was not the last. Since then they had argued almost every day about things that Radisene felt were petty. It was a rude awakening: he discovered that his goddess had human flaws.

Some of their biggest fights were on Sunday evenings after the soccer matches that were played at the Setsoto Stadium or the Pitso Ground. She was crazy about soccer, especially when her team, Bantu FC, was playing. She would leave the baby with the nanny and go with her friends to the stadium. She came back from these outings staggering from too much wine and singing, 'Bantu, Bantu, bamnyama, a matsho Matebele', a song in praise of the Mafeteng team, where the citizens nicknamed themselves the black Ndebeles. Then she would snatch the baby from the nanny and dance around with her – if Bantu had won, that is.

Radisene tried appealing to her maternal instincts: 'Tampololo, please, you are going to injure the child.'

'You shut up,' she would yell at him. 'You are jealous because you support Matlama.'

'Of course I support Matlama. Bantu is useless.'

'You are the one who is useless. Take it from me – I have to share a bed with you. You can't even make a boy!'

Gibes like this hurt Radisene. He would try to take the baby from her. There would be a tug of water, until the nanny stepped in and rescued the child. Tampololo would slap Radisene. Radisene would hit Tampololo with his fist. Then a full-scale battle would ensue, with the baby screaming and the nanny imploring them to stop behaving like spoilt children. She was no match for him, but in the end he often retired to his study to nurse a bruised ego or a bleeding nose.

When Bantu lost, Tampololo would not speak with anyone. She would not even cook the evening meal. If Bantu lost to Matlama it was worse. She would throw plates and pots around, and bellow at Radisene, calling him useless, and saying that he had merely scored a lucky goal like the useless Matlama which he supported.

The rain had subsided, and on the Free State farms Radisene could see a faint rainbow over the yellow sunflowers. Even in his study, with the windows closed, he could hear the deep rumbling of the overflowing Mohokare. He prayed for the kind of floods that he had seen on television ravaging whole cities along the

Mississippi River. Heavy rains were always good for car accidents, especially with the wild drivers and potholed roads the country could boast of. Thinking about accidents made him restless and he decided to go to the office.

Tampololo had left the baby on the sink unattended, while she was cooking something on the stove.

'You should not leave the child like this,' he said. 'she might fall.'

'This baby is not stupid like you, Radisene,' said Tampololo.

'I'm going to the office,' he said, ignoring the taunt and walking out of the door.

Behind him Tampololo shouted, 'Hey, you, don't close that door as if you are closing your mother!'

He had no intention of banging the door. But in response to her admonition he banged it so hard that the baby screamed and a cup on the sink crashed to the floor.

Outside it was drizzling in drops so tiny they would not get one wet. It was the kind of drizzle that the people called the spittle of a fly. He got into the Range Rover and drove to his office in the Lesotho Bank Tower.

There were no new claim forms to complete. Business was in a slump. It had all begun when he was marooned in the mountains. Accidents happened while he was away, and as usual traffic cops and ambulance-drivers phoned his office to report them, but there was no one there to attend to them. The secretary would look high and low for Trooper Motsohi, but he was busy drowning his troubles in some dark shebeen in Thibella. He only came to work when he felt like it. 'What's the use of coming to work when Teacher is not here?' he said when the secretary complained to him. 'I come with details of accidents and signed claim forms and powers of attorney. But they just sit there. He is the only one who knows how to complete and send them to the insurance companies. Plus I don't have money to go to the villages to hunt for widows.'

Indeed, Radisene had not left any money for that. He had planned to spend a weekend at Ha Samane, not a month. He had sent messages to the police in Maseru on Hlong's radio, asking them to inform his employees that they would have to do the best they could in his absence. But most of the work would simply have to wait for his return.

Unfortunately his traffic cops and ambulance-drivers could not wait. They needed their commission too badly, and so they transferred their allegiances to other ambulance-chasers. A.C. Malibu got most of them. Even Trooper Motsohi tried to join A.C. again, but he would have nothing to do with him. 'You betrayed me when you defected to Radisene,' A.C. said. 'Now that things are bad you want to come back to me. No ways!'

Since then Radisene had slowly tried to rebuild his business. But competition was tough. In addition to A.C. there were a few other upstarts, ranging from qualified lawyers with weak practices to charlatans like himself who had gained their experience as legal clerks. They all wanted a piece of the cake, with the result that he found nothing but crumbs in his in-tray.

It was time for a hospital visit. Perhaps he would be lucky enough to find one or two clients there. He preferred the smaller hospitals in the districts, where it was sometimes possible to find an accident victim who had been overlooked by the competitors. He told his secretary that he was going to Mafeteng. But first he changed into the black suit that he kept in a cupboard and put on his dog-collar. Today he would be a priest who had come to pray for the patients. The hospital authorities had got wise to the ambulance-chasers, whom they referred to as scavengers, and they did not allow them into the wards. But ever since adopting his clerical disguise, Radisene had been able to come and go in the wards as he pleased.

The Mafeteng Hospital was reassuringly busy. He walked through the casualty section, talking briefly with each patient and muttering a brief prayer before proceeding to the next one. First he went through the male ward, asking each man what was ailing him. Some had stab wounds received in fights over women, while others had been hurt in robberies and car-jackings. At last he came to the victim of a car accident and asked, 'And did anyone approach you about your rights . . . insurance rights I mean?'

'Yes,' was the reply. 'A lawyer came at the scene of the accident and said that since I was the driver I could not claim compensation.'

'Oh, you were the driver, were you? He was right. You were not a third party in this accident. Only third parties can claim. God bless you, my child.' And he moved on to the next patient.

He did come across a few accident victims who were genuine third parties. But they had already been signed on at the scene of the accident by one of A.C.'s scavengers.

He moved to the female ward and repeated the process. Here there were women who had been scalded with boiling water in fights over men, wives and girlfriends who had been battered by their partners, and young girls who had been raped and stabbed with knives. There were a few accident victims too, but unfortunately none of them were eligible for third-party claims.

The scene of the accident really was the best place to get clients, Radisene reflected. But how were you supposed to know about them if you did not have traffic policemen or ambulance-drivers on your payroll?

It was becoming too putrid in the wards. Why were government hospitals always so filthy? He went out for a breath of fresh air. With his good humour somewhat restored, he decided that he should try the mortuary. He went to the man in charge and told him that he wanted to bless the corpses.

'I have seen priests come to pray for the patients here,' said the man, 'but I have never heard of one blessing dead bodies.'

'Well, priests work in different ways. I prefer to pray for the dead, so that their souls may be forgiven, and may at last know peace.'

The man was impressed with this priest's dedication. He unlocked the door.

'I wonder if you could show me around?' said Radisene. I always like to give individual attention to each one, and also to find out if possible how they met their death.'

'Well. I don't really know about most of them,' said the man. 'I only work here. But I'll come along with you and do my best to help.'

The corpses lay on concrete slabs. They were wrapped in off-white linen or some canvas-like material. Radisene had to unwrap each one in order to see whether it had injuries that were consistent with a motor-vehicle accident or not. After unwrapping the corpse he uttered a few words of prayer, asking the Good Lord to forgive its sins, and to make the poor soul choose the narrow road even though it was full of thorns.

Much as he admired the priest's dedication the mortuary attendant did not relish this ritual. He asked to be excused. 'Okay, you can stand outside if you're so squeamish,' said Radisene, 'I'll call you when I need you.'

Radisene carried on unwrapping corpses, mumbling meaningless prayers over them, wrapping them up again. At last he came across a mangled corpse with its body parts in pieces. The man had clearly been an accident victim. There was a band on one wrist where his name, village and chief were written. Radisene noted the information down.

There were still more corpses to unwrap, but he could not take it any more. The putrid atmosphere was beginning to overwhelm him. He shot out of the door and promptly vomited. The mortuary man ran for a waste-paper basket, but he was too late. Somehow it tasted like 1970, Radisene thought as his stomach heaved. The taste brought back the memory of the night he was dead drunk at Mr Qobokwane's, and Trooper Motsohi and his friends escorted him home.

When he left the hospital he drove to Ha Ramokhele. The houses were still standing, as dilapidated as ever. The whores stood outside, as their mothers had done before them, and like sirens lured unwary travellers with songs of the beautiful things they would do to their bodies if they were to stray into their chambers. Mr Qobokwane's red house was still there. It looked much smaller than he remembered it. But then twenty-three years later everything would look smaller, wouldn't it? Even Mr Qobokwane had shrunk into a shrivelled old man with bloodshot eyes and fluffy grey hair that grew only in patches on his small head.

He was happy to see Radisene. 'It's nice to see you, man,' he enthused. 'We haven't seen you since you became a millionaire. You didn't think you should share your fortune with your old friends?' He laughed, and asked Radisene to buy him a nip. Radisene offered to buy a half instead, and to sit with him and share a drink for old times' sake. He didn't feel like driving to Maseru just yet, and being harassed by Tampololo for one thing or another.

Mr Qobokwane took out a half-jack of brandy and two glasses from the cupboard. Radisene asked for ice or water. Mr Qobokwane laughed and said he had turned into a weakling since he became a millionaire. Real men drank brandy without mixing it with anything. But he got him a jar of water. While they drank Mr Qobokwane teased him about Tampololo. 'We hear that you now share blankets with Motsohi's wife. You are a brave man indeed. Even Roll-Away, a whole district commander of the police force, was afraid of her.'

'Talking of Roll-Away,' said Radisene, trying to steer Mr Qobokwane away from the topic of Tampololo, 'what happened to him?'

'Don't you know? He died only six months ago. Poor Roll-Away. He died a poor and broken man. Not that we are better-off ourselves. We are all poor and broken. What with all the changes of government, he lost his job in the police. Then he worked as a messenger at the Catholic mission, where he died a lonely man. Yes, we are all poor and broken. You know that Mrs Qobokwane left me too . . . for a younger man? They go for younger men these days, and they call them teaspoons.'

Radisene had a warm feeling inside him as he drove back to Maseru in the evening. He had not wasted his day. He had at least met an old friend and reminisced about old times. There were also prospects of a client, if A.C.'s scavengers had not already approached his relatives; and, of course, if his death really was due to a motor-vehicle accident in which he was a third party. He would have to drive to his village early the next day. He could no longer leave such sensitive jobs to Motsohi. He was a man on a mission ... a mission to resuscitate Joseph Radison, Insurance Claims Consultants, and restore it to its former glory. And he was determined to succeed.

If he failed though, it would not be the end of the world. If the insurance business didn't pick up, why, he would just build himself a smaller mansion, and use some of the money that was left over to start a new business. Perhaps he would buy or build a hotel. Liquor was a sure-fire profit-maker.

'Who is she, Radisene?' Tampololo greeted him with the question at the door.

'Who is who?' asked Radisene.

'The slut you have been seeing in Mafeteng? You lied and said you were going to the office. I went there, you know, and your secretary told me that you'd gone to Mafeteng.'

'I went to Mafeteng to look for clients, Tampololo.'

'Since when do you look for clients? You do absolutely nothing in that office. It is the people you employ who do all the work. What is Motsohi's work if you are the one who looks for clients?'

He wondered why she had gone to the office. If she'd wanted anything she could just have phoned. He had observed that whenever he was away she got edgy if he didn't phone. She wanted to get in touch with him all the time, even if there was nothing important to talk about. For the first time he thought he'd put his finger on the problem. She was consumed by jealousy.

He remembered one day when she had burst into the office unannounced and found him interviewing a client. She stared at the client, a sixteen-year-old girl who looked as though she had dropped out of the pages of a teen fashion magazine, and shouted, 'So this is what has been happening behind my back? You claim that you have come to work, whereas you lock yourself in your office with sluts.'

'This is just a child, Tampololo,' pleaded Radisene. 'She is a dependant of an accident victim.'

She realized that she had made a mistake. But she was too proud to apologize. Instead she stood there with her arms akimbo, and said, 'Well, maybe not this time. But I'm watching you, Radisene. I know what you men are capable of.'

Yes. That was the problem. She loved passionately and was consumed by jealousy. But Radisene could not understand why she seemed to derive so much pleasure from hurting those she loved … why she belittled all his efforts to do things for the improvement of the family. Yet when he was not there she ran absolutely crazy with longing for him … tormented by loneliness … Perhaps one day she would gain some measure of security. She would learn to accept that for him there could be no one else.

The next morning Radisene told Tampololo that he was going to Qalabane in the Mafeteng district to see a prospective client. 'Mafeteng again!' screeched Tampololo. 'Does the Mafeteng slut know how much you hate her home-team, Bantu FC, the black Matebeles?'

'There is no Mafeteng slut, Tampololo. I am going to work there. I am not even going to town, I am going to the village of Qalabane.'

'When are you going to spend time with your child. You don't even buy her toys. When I take her to the park she cries for the toys of other children.'

That was a new one. He did not know what Tampololo was talking about. The child had so many toys she could have opened her own toy shop!

When Radisene got to Qalabane he learnt that the man had indeed died in a car accident. Just before dawn he had been staggering from the Las Vegas Disco at the Hotel Mafeteng when he was knocked down by a car driven by some drunken teenagers who were also from the disco. Radisene wondered what the heck a man that age had been doing in a discothèque with children.

Within an hour of the accident A.C.'s scavengers were there and got all the details about the dead man's next of kin. They went to Qalabane, and there they discovered that the situation with his dependants was a complicated one. The man had a wife with whom he lived. He had four children by her. But on other days he went to live with his mistress. There was a dispute over the corpse, each woman claiming she had the right to bury it. This dragged on while the body, in its many pieces, remained on the concrete slab in the Mafeteng Hospital mortuary, where Radisene had discovered it almost three weeks after the accident.

Finally the relatives of the deceased and the elders of the village decided that the funeral would be held at the first wife's place. She and her children were declared the rightful heirs of all he owned. The mistress was adamant that she was going to attend that funeral because she had a child with the man. As far as she was concerned, she was as good as any widow.

A.C. had taken his cue from the decision of the elders and recognized the first wife as the rightful claimant in the third-party insurance. He personally came and made her sign all the necessary forms.

Radisene arrived at Qalabane on the day of the wake. The man was going to be buried the next day. When Radisene was told about the dispute he decided to stay for the wake, and talk with the mistress.

In the evening people assembled under a big tent and sang hymns. Those who were moved by the spirit stood up and preached about the glory of the Lord and the good deeds of the deceased. Others reminisced about him, and told jokes meant to show that he was a good man who was loved by everyone.

The coffin was put on a table and people queued to see the deceased for the last time. Normally this ritual was done on the very morning of the funeral. But because there were fears that by the next day the corpse would have decomposed beyond recognition, those who wanted to see it were asked to do so at the wake.

The mistress also queued to take a last look at her lover. When her turn came, the corpse smiled. Those who saw it screamed and ran away. There was a great commotion at the wake, as everyone began to talk about the corpse that had smiled at the mistress. Some even swore that it had not only smiled – it had also winked. The wife and her supporters were angry that the dead husband had not smiled at the person who really deserved it – the mother of his four children. But they consoled themselves and said, 'He can smile at his mistress as much as he wants, but she is not getting a cent of the insurance money. The lawyers have signed with us, and not with her.'

Radisene introduced himself to the mistress. At first she was reluctant to talk with him because she said lawyers were liars. 'Right now they want to give all the money to her. Yet this man loved me more than that old hag. Why do you think he smiled at me, and not at her?'

'That's why I want to talk with you, my sister,' said Radisene. 'I come from a different firm of lawyers, and I think we can fight this.'

'I don't have money to pay lawyers.'

'I won't charge you a cent. If we succeed I will be paid by the insurance company.'

The woman began to tell Radisene about her late lover. He had made his living repairing radios in the camp – by which she meant the town of Mafeteng – and supported both families. She felt that she was entitled to the insurance money because he had often told her that he loved her, and was only staying with the old witch because of the children.

'Well,' said Radisene, 'just give me the facts and not your opinion of her. Does your child attend school?'

'She passed Standard Seven with first class. But we didn't have money to send her to secondary school. Some people wanted to give her a bursary, but they first wanted to see our certificate of marriage.'

'So she couldn't get the bursary because you were not married?'

'Only a week before he died we went to the Zionist Church

where the bishop is his friend. They had worked together in the mines. We signed a piece of paper, and he was ready to take it to the bursary people. But he died before he could do that, and now my little girl will not go to school.'

'Do you have the piece of paper you signed? I want to see it.'

They drove to her house on the other side of the village. Radisene stayed in the car while she went to fetch the paper.

It was indeed a marriage certificate. Radisene could not hide his excitement. He knew that he had already won his case against A.C. Even with his meagre knowledge of the law, he knew that a marriage solemnized in church or by civil authorities was recognized by the law above a customary marriage. He had ascertained that the first wife was a customary-law wife. All the insurance money would go to the mistress, who was in fact the legal spouse. He was surprised that A.C., with all his legal knowledge, could be so careless as to overlook such facts. Perhaps he had been too lazy to investigate the matter and had taken it for granted that the senior wife was the lawful heir. Radisene was going to disgrace him. He was going to destroy him once and for all. Joseph Radison's prestige would rise again. All the traffic cops and ambulance-drivers would come back to him. Once more he was going to be the king of the roads.

The mistress, who was no longer a mistress, did not understand what Radisene's excitement was all about. She did not place any importance on the piece of paper from the Zionist Church. She was not even a Zionist for that matter. Nor was her dead lover. They had merely gone to the bishop to ask for a favour as old friends, and they had paid him a little something for his trouble.

Radisene assured her that the Zionist paper was the most important paper in her life. 'I am one hundred per cent sure, my sister, that all the money will come to you. That other woman will not get a cent,' said Radisene, giving her the power of attorney and the claim forms to sign.

On the way to Maseru he was happily singing along with Frank Leepa and Sankomota.

'Hello, Mr Mafeteng,' Tampololo greeted him at the door. 'Father is waiting for you in the living-room.'

And there was Father-of-the-Daughters watching the marvel that was television, and playing with the baby. He had taken a break from his recreational litigation and come to the dreaded lowlands to see his grandchild: 'Because if I wait for you to bring her to Ha Samane I'll wait for the rest of my life.'

'We are certainly going to bring her one of these days, father.'

'You have not been there for more than a year now … since that big snow. Is it because of that case that you spoilt for me?'

'No, it is not because of that case. It is because when I got home I found that my business had been destroyed by my absence. I am trying to rebuild it now. That's why you see me coming home so late at night. Things are shaping up well, and when it picks up I'll be able to go back to Ha Samane.'

'You know that Tampololo is complaining about you?'

'Tampololo is a very jealous woman, father. Now that you are here I hope you'll talk with her. She does not respect me at all. She treats me like a piece of rag.'

'You are a man, Radisene. You are the one who wears the pants. You ought to know how to control women.'

'This is a modern world, father. We don't control women, and in the same way we don't want them to control us.'

'Well, if that's what you think … then don't come crying to me.'

12. The Great Mist

Spring was the time when birds drank nectar from aloe flowers and got drunk silly. Their chirping went out of tune and they flew in erratic twirls. Those who had taken more than their little bodies could carry flew into trees or the walls of houses. They were easy victims for the boys, who had their fires ready for a roast.

The boys also drank the juice of the aloe flowers, and immediately ascended into a state of euphoria. They saw things that no one else could see. Some even claimed that when they were euphoric they played games with the thokolose hobgoblins that escaped from the bedrooms of their owners to steal a few thrills with the herdboys. The hobgoblins did naughty things, like milking cows into their mouths, and riding on the calves.

Generally these were happy times in the village of Ha Samane. Like yawning, laughter is infectious. The euphoria of the boys diffused itself into the air that people breathed and everyone was filled with good feelings. Even Dikosha, who was determined never to be happy, was seen on one or two occasions giving what looked like a smile to Sorry My Darlie.

Sorry My Darlie too was filled with cheerfulness. Dikosha's vague smile gave him more hope that she was finally coming around to accepting him as a worthy suitor. The flies that hovered in the vicinity of his loins sensed the high spirits and buzzed even louder. And the stench that was unleashed from his body by the warmth of the sun ran wild and attacked innocent passers-by. They merely laughed and did not take offence. The days were too beautiful to spoil with finicky attitudes.

Shana's music created further elation. To Sorry My Darlie's chagrin he continued to play outside Dikosha's window. His music annoyed Sorry My Darlie, who would go off to draw water for the brewers of beer or to sit with Grandma 'Maselina. But he would go back to drool outside Dikosha's house when he thought the upstart had left to play for the birds in the fields and on the hillside.

Of late Shana had taken to singing about the mist. People were beginning to forget about the mist until Shana's songs reminded them of its dangers. He sang about a menacing mist that killed without mercy. In his songs people ran away from it and fell down precipices, or were suffocated by it.

Shana was genuinely afraid of the mist. Even when he saw it far away, surrounding distant hills, he ran away with all his strength and hid himself under the bed in Father-of-the-Daughters' bed-room. People thought he was being unreasonable. When asked to take cattle far from the village, he would plead, 'Please … not that far … what if the mist comes?'

Father-of-the-Daughters would respond, 'For generations we have feared the mist. Up to now it has not done anything. You are just lazy, that's all. You just want to eat, and not do any work but play your sekgankula.'

The goodwill that permeated the air of Ha Samane extended to erstwhile friends and erstwhile enemies, Hlong and Father-of-the-Daughters. They exchanged visits and chit-chatted about every-thing under the sun.

One Sunday afternoon, when Petrose returned from church and from his meetings of the elders of the church, they sat under the bluegum tree in Father-of-the-Daughters' yard. They drank the foaming beer brewed by the expert hand of Mother-of-the-Daughters. As women passed on a footpath that led to the lower part of the village, then to the Black River, and finally to Ha Sache, the two friends gossiped about their looks.

'She is so ugly she looks like something that has come to fetch us,' said Father-of-the-Daughters of a woman with whom they had just exchanged greetings in a most friendly manner.

Petrose laughed, and responded, 'Her husband too is just like that. They are the ugliest couple at Ha Sache.'

'Well, you know that Ha Sache is full of ugly people. But as for her husband … he is a man … he has the right to be ugly.'

'Indeed a man is never ugly, as long as he has cattle. The beau-ty of a man is in his cattle.'

Father-of-the-Daughters told Petrose about his visit to the lowlands for the umpteenth time. It was a long time since he had returned from visiting his daughter, but he still had not stopped talking about it. He said he did not wish his worst enemy a life in the lowlands. 'They have all these wonderful things, including something called television which is a bioscope in your own house. Yet their lives are miserable. They lack the joy and the freedom that we have here in the mountains.'

'And the cattle and the fields,' said Petrose. 'That is what I hate about life in Maseru. You have to eat from your pocket all the time.'

'Yes. It is a dog-eat-dog life in Maseru, Hlong … I mean, Petrose. Their lives are so sad that laughter has to be induced, and there are people who are paid a lot of money to make people laugh.'

'Now you tell me, Father-of-the-Daughters, what kind of life is that where people have to buy laughter? Is it not supposed to be a free gift of God, that we all have and we all must share? I have always said so too when I am in the lowlands – when I see the pedlars of laughter called comedians and actors – that it is no life for a human being.'

'I think Tampololo must come back here. After all, we have a secondary school now and they need teachers.'

'What about her husband?'

'Which one?'

'Is it not that child of Mother-of-Twins who is a lawyer in Maseru?'

'Petrose, I do not know. If somebody told me that they are no longer together and Tampololo has gone back to her policeman I would believe him. When I was there they fought all the time. That child of Mother-of-Twins is not a man. I tried to advise him. The problem with my age, Petrose, is that I have accumulated so much experience about life, yet no one wants to learn from it for they think I am an old damn fool.'

'That is the problem with the children of today. We are there for them, but they refuse to use us as a stick to feel how deep the water is, so that they may cross the river safely.'

Although it was still early in the evening the two friends decided to part and go and take a rest. They had had their share of happiness for the day. In the old days they would have sat for the greater part of the night, until they got drunk, and then they would have gone to hunt for feasts, night dances and shebeens, not only at Ha Samane, but also in the neighbouring villages such as Ha Sache. But now, in the days of their maturity, they liked their happiness in small doses – in fleeting moments that made the experience more enjoyable – like stolen moments of illicit lovemaking.

At dawn the following day Father-of-the-Daughters woke Shana up. They were going to drive some cattle to a distant cattle-post. It was necessary from time to time to decrease the number of cattle in the village by taking some of them to the cattle-posts. The grazing lands of the village could only accommodate a small number, so each family kept only those oxen that were used for ploughing, cows for milking, and a few bulls for servicing the cows. Father-of-the-Daughters' cattle had increased so much that they were becoming unmanageable. It was absolutely essential that he drive almost half of them to join his herd of more than a thousand at his cattle-post.

Since he had materialized in the village, Shana had never ventured further than the fields and the hillside. He protested that he was afraid to go to the distant mountains. But Father-of-the-Daughters barked at him, 'Don't be a weakling, Shana! Be a man! You have no reason to be afraid because I'll be there with you.'

While Father-of-the-Daughters was busy with his ablutions, Shana ran to Dikosha's rondavel and played his sekgankula outside her window. At first Dikosha thought he was playing in her dreams. But when she realized that she was awake she knew that the Shana of flesh and blood was outside her window. She opened the window, and he stopped playing. And for the very first time since they had known each other he spoke to her, 'Please keep my sekgankula for me … until I return. I am going to the far away mountains. I will see you when I come back.'

They set off before sunrise. Father-of-the-Daughters rode on his horse while Shana walked beside him. They drove the cattle towards the horizon where mountain peaks kissed the pink and purple sky. They travelled for many hours, climbing one mountain after another, and crossing steams and rivers. Sometimes they stopped for a while so that the cattle and the horse could graze and drink. Father-of-the-Daughters gave Shana a piece of steamed bread and some sour porridge from a billycan.

Late in the afternoon they descended into a gorge, and all of a sudden everything looked white. It was the mist. Shana shivered, but Father-of-the-Daughters urged him on. The boy resisted. He wanted to turn back. Father-of-the-Daughters would not relent. 'Come on, stupid boy! We still have a long way to go!'

The mist was rising, and Father-of-the-Daughters also began to be fearful. Shana held tightly to the hind leg of the horse. It kicked him away. He stood up with the mist swirling around him and plucking at his clothes. Then he turned and ran as fast as he could. But the mist was at his heels. It caught up with him and threw him to the ground. The mist began to suffocate him. He let out a muffled scream, and kicked his legs, fighting against the mist, as it wrestled him over and over. Then suddenly he was still. His body lay sprawling on the ground, his face contorted by a frozen scream.

People were surprised to see an exhausted Father-of-the-Daughters returning with his cattle early the next morning. He was leading his horse by the reins, and the limp body of Shana lay across the saddle. He had to stop all the time and explain to inquisitive people who were going to the fields that Shana had been killed by the mist. Then he consoled himself, and those who said they were crying with him, with these words, 'It is sad. He was such a beautiful boy. He had such beautiful music in him. But what can we do? What can we say? We begin to die the moment we are conceived. And we have no say in the matter.'

Even before Father-of-the-Daughters entered the village with

the sad news, Dikosha knew that something terrible had happened
to Shana. She had felt pain in her whole body the very moment
Shana was killed. At the time she did not know what the pain was
all about. That night she had tried to evoke Shana in her dreams,
but he would not come.

When she heard what had happened she blamed Father of the
Daughters for letting the mist kill Shana. She bitterly told Sorry
My Darlie, who was drooling in his usual spot, that taking the cattle to the cattle-post had just been a ploy to kill the boy far away
from the eyes of people. Sorry My Darlie spread that story in the
shebeens, and soon people of the village were talking of how
Father-of-the-Daughters had used a poor motherless child as medicine in order to gain more wealth.

Dikosha was very much affected by Shana's death. She remembered his beautiful songs. Dikosha could see music. It was a gift
that she had, that people envied. Ordinary people, who had not
been conceived at a night dance, could only hear music, but she
could see it. The people of the cave had enhanced her gift even
more. All songs looked different, she said. Even the same song
when sung by different people could look different, depending on
how good or bad the singers were. She said that Shana's sekgankula had produced such beautiful images for her.

Now Shana was gone.

The funeral was a big one. Many people brought their curiosity.
They wanted to hear the speeches that would be made. Father-of-
the-Daughters spoke both as the father and as the nurse. A 'nurse'
at a funeral was not necessarily a person who had looked after the
deceased when he or she was ill. Any person who was the last to
see the deceased alive, and who had inside information on what
caused the death, was the nurse. Since Father-of-the-Daughters
had actually seen Shana die he became the nurse, and was required
to tell the people attending the funeral what had happened.

Men of the village made speeches in praise of Father-of-the-
Daughters. They said his heart was made of gold, and he was a
shining example to other wealthy people, for he had taken a poor

motherless child and made him his own.

After Shana's coffin had been lowered into the deep hole and the hole had been filled with soil, the priest said a short prayer for the soul of the little boy. It had not been easy to get the priest to administer the funeral rites, for he said Shana was not a member of his congregation. In fact, he was not a churchgoer at all. Father-of-the-Daughters, himself not a churchgoer, had to contribute some money for the repair of the leaking church roof before the priest would agree.

Throughout the funeral Dikosha stood alone a little distance from the rest of the people and listened to the speeches, the hymns and the prayers. She was beginning to feel restless. She had not danced for years, except in the Cave of Barwa when the cave-dwellers were still there and in her dreams – worlds which were far removed from the world of the funeral. New dance steps had come and gone while she stood on the sidelines. Her bones were aching for a dance. Just a few steps might quench the thirst.

Suddenly she jumped up and danced. The proceedings of the funeral stopped, as everyone watched her. She danced like a woman possessed ... like the whirlwind of August. She raised helical dust to the skies, which could be seen for miles around. It was visible even in distant villages.

She danced her last tribute to Shana. Then she walked away to her rondavel. People of the village applauded in spite of themselves.

Later they observed that she did not go to wash her hands in the aloetic water at the boy's home, as was the custom. Neither did she partake of the beef and samp that was part of the funeral meal. For everyone else it would have been considered rude not to eat the funeral meal. But for her, the people of the village said, 'Well, Dikosha is Dikosha. She does what she likes, even if it is against custom. It is because she was conceived at a night dance.'

Throughout that spring and summer she played with the darkness. She, the keeper of memories, sat in her hut, with all the windows closed and played with the absolute darkness that she created. She devised a number of games with which to amuse herself. She tickled herself with a feather. Shivery currents danced up and down her spine, and her whole body tingled with untold pleasure. She closed her eyelids tightly, so that darkness created stars and rings of different colours and made them float before her eyes. She laughed – it was the first time she had ever laughed – and tried to catch these spangles. But darkness snatched them away before her hands could touch them.

When she was not in her room playing with the darkness, she went to wherever dancing could be found. She was seen at the tlhophe dances, where the drums of the mathuela diviners throbbed. She danced alongside the Zionists as they drummed themselves into a frenzy, possessed by Holy Spirits. She joined the mokgibo dancers as they responded to the rhythm of a lone drum interwoven with singing, whistling and handclapping. She danced with the little girls, who could easily have been her grandchildren although she didn't look much older than them, in the songs of the pumpkin and the monyanyako dance. She danced the dances of the men: the fast-paced ndlamu of the Matebele, and the graceful mohobelo with both its SeMolapo and SeMatsieng variations. She even danced the famo dance of the fuchu parties of the night, to the rhythm of the organ or accordion and drums.

She danced until the following autumn, when she suddenly confined herself to her house, and played and danced only with the darkness. She had felt in her bones that Radisene would be coming, and she did not want him to lay his eyes on her. She did not want to lay her eyes on him either. She was going to sit in her room until he went back to his lowlands. She would quench her thirst for dance by dancing only with the darkness. She would return to the village dances when he was gone again.

Radisene, Tampololo and the baby arrived at Ha Samane early in March. The schools were closed for a week because of the elections. The lowlands were a hive of activity, with more than fourteen parties canvassing for votes. In the mountain areas things were less hectic since only the two main parties, the Congress

Party and the National Party, had the resources and the following to canvass there.

It was rumoured that there was going to be violence in Maseru. People said that sections of the army were not pleased with the new democratic order. They complained that the government was being returned to the civilians even before some of them had had the opportunity 'to eat', by which they meant 'to accumulate wealth by looting the coffers of the state'. They felt that the Western governments were being unfair when they threatened to withhold further aid if the soldiers did not hand over power to an elected civilian government. The hotheads among the soldiers were threatening to disrupt the elections, or even to make a coup.

Radisene did not want to be anywhere near Maseru during the elections, and so he convinced Tampololo that they should spend the election week in the mountains. She agreed because she had not been to Ha Samane for quite some time. She had gone back to teaching at the Catholic high school in Maseru after a maternity break of a year. But now, thanks to the elections, she had a week's holiday, and she was happy to spend it with her parents.

Not only was Radisene running away from potential violence during the election, but he wanted to take a well-deserved break from the war with A.C. Radisene had won the case of the corpse that smiled. There was a settlement of fourteen thousand rands for the mistress – of which only half went to her, of course. A.C. felt very humiliated. He, a qualified lawyer with a B.A. and an LL.B., had been outsmarted by a numskull who had never even seen the doors of a law school. He vowed that he was going to destroy Radisene once and for all.

Radisene took this to mean that A.C. was going to have him killed. He had reason to take the threat seriously: A.C. had connections with military men in high places, which he had cultivated during his days as an adviser to the now dead prime minister Leabua. Radisene hoped that by the time he returned to the lowlands A.C.'s anger would have subsided, and he would be big enough to take everything in a sportsmanlike spirit of good competition.

Tampololo insisted that she was going to stay with her parents and Radisene should stay with his mother in what she laughingly called 'the home of the bats'. Radisene was glad of the breathing-space. He needed some respite from her shrill jealousy.

Only a day before they left for the mountains they had gone to the OK Bazaars at the LNDC Shopping Mall to buy supplies for their holiday, when Radisene saw Misti between the shelves of groceries. She was very excited to see both him and Tampololo. She was on a lunch-break from her job at the government hospital and was wearing a white laboratory coat. There was no sign of the paraphernalia of the mathuela diviners, except for a string of white beads at each ankle. She joked that she was enjoying her dual practice both as a traditional doctor in the African mode and as a medical laboratory technologist in the Western mode.

Radisene was surprised to notice that Tampololo was cold towards Misti. The two women had once been friends.

After Misti left, Tampololo snapped at Radisene, 'Sies, you had to laugh with her until she saw your wisdom teeth.' Radisene did not respond, but continued to take items from the shelves and put them in the trolley. Tampololo became livid. She burst out, 'I am talking to you Radisene! Don't you dare ignore me. You think I don't see what is happening between you and that witch-doctor? You think I don't know that Misti was your girlfriend?' People stopped and looked and listened and giggled. 'You know what your biggest problem is, Radisene? Your biggest problem is women!'

A combination of anger and hatred swelled in Radisene's chest. He felt like jumping on her and throttling her until he squeezed the last drops of life out of her body. But he just carried on pushing the trolley up and down the aisles.

Father-of-the-Daughters slaughtered the pig that had been ear-marked for winter to welcome his daughter and grandchild home.

And girls sang songs of the mist.

13. The Coup – 1994

Trooper Motsohi fancied himself as some kind of politician. His drinking comrades in the dingy shebeens of Thibella held him in high esteem. He had once been a policeman, and had worked for lawyers. He was therefore their political sage.

The main topic of conversation in the shebeens of Thibella, and in the whole country, was the announcement by King Letsie the Third that he was suspending both the constitution and the one-year-old Congress Party government of prime minister Ntsu Mokhehle. He had chosen a new ruling council composed of politicians who had lost to the Congress Party in the elections the previous year. The chairman of the council, and therefore the de facto prime minister, was a young ex-convict who referred to himself as a human rights lawyer.

'This is a coup, gents,' said Trooper Motsohi to his drinking comrades. 'This guy has made a coup against a government that was elected by the overwhelming majority of the people.'

'His coup will fail,' said the shebeen queen. 'We want Mokhehle back. The Congress Party swept all sixty-five constituencies in the elections last year. Now this young king wants to put the National Party, which lost every single constituency, back in power through the back door.'

'What are his reasons for removing the government of the people?'

'He says he is dissolving this government because from his observation it has lost popular support.'

Everyone found the notion hilarious. How could the Congress Party have lost popular support within only a year of a landslide victory? They wanted to know how the young king measured this loss of support. 'Is support not measured at the ballot-box?' asked one man.

'I think the young king just wants to bring his discredited friends back into the government and his father back to the throne.

He knows that he has the support of the soldiers.'

Indeed, from the very day the Congress Party had taken over the government they had had problems with the military establishment. The soldier simply did not want to recognize the new government or cooperate with it. The army split into cliques and they fought among themselves. Many of their members died, including a prominent politician of the Congress Party. Then they sent some of the members of the cabinet into temporary exile in South Africa. The police also went on strike. Supporters of the Congress Party believed that all this was a concerted effort to overthrow their government. In spite of all these problems they had held tenaciously to power, until the king took the drastic step of dissolving the government.

Trooper Motsohi was one of the people who vowed that they would not take the king's action lying down. He was now an ardent supporter of the Congress Party, and hoped that they would one day reinstate him in his rightful position as a traffic policeman of his majesty's government. He felt that the National Party, for which he had worked during the first coup of 1970, had let him down. He had first become vocal in his support of the Congress Party when the election results were announced and he heard that they had swept to power. Since then he had not looked back.

When he heard that a national stayaway from work and a demonstration were being organized for the next day, he had no trouble convincing his drinking comrades that it was in the interests of the nation that they participate. He himself was going to be there in the black, green and red colours of the Congress Party.

The next day thousands of people marched down Kingsway, waving green branches and singing protest songs. Some were wielding posters and placards denouncing the action of the king, and demanding a return to constitutionality.

Trooper Motsohi was at the very head of the demonstration, wearing his Congress Party colours and holding a placard with the declaration: 'Today is the end of monarchy. Lesotho is now a Republic.' He was doing the toyi-toyi dance that he often saw South African protesters do on television. He danced even more vigorously when he thought the television cameras were on him.

The demonstrators had left Kingsway and were on a strip of road that led to the gates of the king's palace when they were confronted by soldiers. Without any warning the valiant soldiers opened fire. People ran helter-skelter. Others fell to the ground bleeding. Trooper Motsohi was shot in the leg. He limped back to Kingsway, leaving a trail of blood. A television crew from South Africa was interviewing people in the street. The interviewer approached Trooper Motsohi with a microphone. 'I see you are bleeding. What happened?'

'They shot me. Those bastards shot me.'

'Did you see the person who actually fired the shot?'

'Oh, yes, it's a soldier I have seen before in one of the shebeens. He also shot the woman who was marching next to me. He shot her dead. They've killed a number of people. Even the Boers no longer use live ammunition on protesters. But these ... our own people ... shot us dead!'

That evening Radisene arrived home to find Tampololo in a jovial mood. She was like that, Tampololo. Sometimes she would be full of joy and laughter. She would tease him, and joke with him and the baby. Everyone would be happy at home, and wish that it could last forever. But it would not. All of a sudden her face would harden, and she would not even respond when Radisene or the nanny greeted her. As soon as visitors came she would laugh and be happy for their benefit, and they would never forget how sweet she was and how lucky Radisene was to have such a wonderful wife who loved people. When the visitors left she would revert to her sour and sullen self. Perhaps something has made her angry ... something one of us said, Radisene would think. But he never knew, for she kept whatever was eating her to herself.

On this day Tampololo welcomed him with a cup of tea. She had not done that in ages and he was delighted. The tea would certainly refresh him. He was exhausted, having spent most of the day at the building site inspecting the foundations of his mansion. He had employed an excellent construction company, but he liked to be there too, to see to it that they were following his plans to the letter. He had decided to build the original mansion of his imaginings, rather than the scaled down version he was contemplating when his business was down. Not that business had picked up. It was still in a slump. But he was convinced that things would improve with the new reputation he had gained after trouncing A.C.

Tampololo and Radisene sat in the livingroom and watched the news on South African television. They were keen to hear the latest developments in the saga of the young king who thought he owned the country and its people and could do anything he liked, even if it flew in the face of democracy. Everyone knew that if you wanted to hear what was happening in Lesotho, you did not tune in to the local radio or television stations. The Lesotho media reported on events in the country two weeks after they happened, and with a twist that had received the blessing of the political authorities. People were forced to depend on the South African media and the BBC for Lesotho news. Things were worse now that the king's people had taken over the radio station and were broadcasting news from the point of view of the new ruling council.

South African television reported that all Western governments had suspended aid to Lesotho until the restoration of the legitimate government. The trade union movement in South Africa was also threatening to close the borders between Lesotho and South Africa if the Congress Party was not restored to power, and to prohibit their members from handling goods moving into or out of Lesotho. The king and the overthrown prime minister had been summoned to Pretoria for a meeting with Presidents Mandela of South Africa, Masire of Botswana, and Mugabe of Zimbabwe. The young king's actions had destabilized the whole subcontinent.

Then the focus shifted to the events in the city. There had been a general strike and a demonstration. Bishop Tutu of Cape Town had flown in to try and mediate, and had made Congress Party members angry when they thought he was biased in favour of the king. 'Hey, Tampololo,' shouted Radisene, 'is that not Motsohi among the demonstrators?' Indeed, it was Trooper Motsohi toyi-toying his heart out. Then all of a sudden there was shooting. And then there was an angry Motsohi being interviewed and giving his opinion about the callousness of the law enforcement authorities. 'The blood of all these people who are dead,' he was saying, 'will be on the king's conscience for ever! It is as good as if he pulled the trigger himself.'

Tampololo laughed. 'I didn't know that he was now a political activist. Isn't he still working for you?'

'I'm not sure. He comes to the office sometimes … when he is broke and needs a few rands for beer. I use him as a messenger now and then, for local errands. Sometimes he washes my cars. But I no longer send him to look for clients. He's always drunk.'

Late that night, when Tampololo was marking her students' exercise books and Radisene was preparing to go to bed, there was an urgent knock at the door. Radisene opened, and a sweat-drenched Trooper Motsohi stormed in. 'You've got to help me, Teacher,' he panted. 'They're after me.'

'Who's after you?' Asked Tampololo.

'The army boys. They invaded the shebeen where I drink, but I escaped.'

'What would the soldiers want with you?' asked Radisene.

'They saw me on television. It's bad outside, Teacher. There is a six-to-six curfew, you know? They're chasing curfew-breakers with whips, and shooting at some of them. They heard me say that I saw the soldier who killed one of the women. Now they want to kill me. You've got to hide me, Teacher!'

'Oh, no, you can't hide here. They know you work for me. They'll come and look for you here.'

'But you've got to help him, Radisene,' pleaded Tampololo.

'You can't let them just kill him like a dog.'

It was so unusual for Tampololo to plead for anything.

'But what can we do?' asked Radisene.

'Maybe you should drive him to Ha Samane. He can hide in your mother's mansion until things cool down in Maseru.'

'At this hour of the night? No ways! You heard that there is a curfew out there. I'll give him money tomorrow, then he can go seek his own refuge wherever!'

'Please, Radisene … please. Most of the soldiers know and respect you. They won't even search your car if you happen to come across a roadblock. Please, Radisene …'

She was so beautiful when she begged. And so lovable.

Radisene drove the Range Rover through the streets of Maseru, with Trooper Motsohi covered by sisal sacks at the back. Fortunately the few soldiers he passed on Kingsway did not stop him. When he was out of the city he gave the wheel to Motsohi who drove for the whole night. They reached Ha Samane the next day, just before midday.

Mother-of-Twins, assisted by Trooper Motsohi and Sorry My Darlie, shoveled out the dirt in one of the bedrooms of the mansion and cleaned it. That was to be Motsohi's bedroom. Radisene decided to take a nap on his mother's bed and catch up on the previous night's sleep. But before that he asked about Dikosha.

'Oh, Dikosha is Dikosha as you know,' said Mother-of-Twins in a tired voice. 'She is well. But she has taken to a new habit now. They say she listens to the confessions of men.'

Indeed, between the dances and the playing with the darkness Dikosha had added a new activity. It began when men were inexplicably drawn to her rondavel. 'I was just passing and saw your door open,' they would lamely say. She invited them in and closed the door. In the darkness of her room they began to speak about their beautiful and ugly deeds, and to confess their dark secrets. She merely listened and said nothing. But when the men left they felt relieved.

Strangers gravitated towards her house.

When a migrant came to the village from the mines, he first went to Dikosha's house for confession. She listened to confessions from men for hours on end. When these men finally walked out they had relieved themselves of all the burdens of conscience. But sometimes they were drained and exhausted. Some walked slowly and somberly, while others walked with a spring in their step that spoke of fulfillment.

When there were no men to confess she went back to catching the stars that floated in front of her eyes in the pitch-darkness of her room. Then she danced with the darkness. She held tightly tightly to the darkness, until her nipples became all firm with pleasure and she was breathless with exhaustion.

Late that afternoon Radisene was woken by his mother's voice, 'Wake up, Radisene! You have visitors.'

They were two huge dark men in flowing West African robes. Their boubous were made of a cloth so rich that even Jabbie could only have dreamt about it. They introduced themselves, and said that they were from Nigeria. They had paid Radisene a visit at his office in Maseru that morning, but they were told that he had gone to the mountains. Their business was very urgent, and so they had chartered a special plane to fly them to the village. They suggested that he fly back to Maseru with them. They would not reveal the nature of their business, but they assured him that it was a profitable one. Judging by the boubous Radisene was inclined to believe them, and so he left his Range Rover parked in Father-of-the-Daughters' yard and flew back to Maseru with his mysterious visitors.

They decided to hold their discussions in the cosy surroundings of the Lesotho Sun, where the Nigerians had a suite in the most expensive wing of the hotel, the one normally reserved for visiting heads of state and other dignitaries.

'Well, we'll be on the level with you,' said the bearded, fat-faced Nigerian.

'We don't believe in beating about the bush,' added the clean-shaven, high-cheekboned one.

'We are involved in a scam and we need your assistance. There is a big share for you,' said the bearded one.

They said they were from Toronto, but had recently opened an office in Johannesburg. In Canada they had insured the clean-shaven one for five million dollars. They had paid the premiums for four months. Now the time had come for the clean-shaven one to die, in order that the bearded one, the sole beneficiary of the policy, should get his five million dollars.

Radisene was taken aback. He asked, 'You mean your friend is willing to die so that you can get all that money?'

The Nigerians laughed in their booming voices. 'Of course I won't die,' said the clean-shaven one. 'That's where you came in. We need a death certificate to the effect that I am dead. I was a tourist in Lesotho, you see, and then I fell ill and died … or perhaps I died in a car accident. Your country, like our Nigeria, is famous for its glorious car accidents.'

'All we need from you is to use your connections to get a death certificate. If it's a car accident we'll also need a police report. A car accident sounds more convincing, and you deal with those a lot.'

Radisene was fascinated by the suaveness of the Nigerians. And their ingenuity. 'They make our own little crooks look like Sunday-school teachers,' he muttered under his breath.

'What did you say?' asked the bearded one.

'It sounds like a great idea. But it's very risky for me and my career. What's in it for me?'

'How's half a million dollars? Remember, we incurred a lot of expenses on this. We paid high premiums for four months. And our air-fares to South Africa. And I have to fly back to Canada as a grieving relative to claim the insurance money.'

Five hundred thousand dollars! For one small job. That was almost one and a half million rands. Radisene excused himself: he had to make a telephone call. He went to the public phones near the reception desk and called his old friend, Dr Bale. 'I need a death certificate urgently. The man died in a car accident. Please organize it at once, man … and a police report of the accident.'

'You have the police connections,' said Bale.

'Not any more. Not at such short notice. Surely you can organize a police report? Just take one of the reports lying around there and make one of the victims my man here.' He gave him the name of the clean-shaven Nigerian.

'What's all the urgency? You are on to something big, eh? Listen, I want five thousands rands for this … up front. Not commission, but up front.'

'Okay. As long as I get the death certificate first thing in the morning.'

Radisene went back to his friends and told them that they would get the documents in the morning. They ordered whisky and toasted their success.

'You've done this kind of thing before? asked Radisene.

'We do it all the time,' said the bearded one. 'Our insured people used to die in some remote Nigerian village or other. But now the Canadian insurance companies have gotten wise to the game. They scrutinize the claims of people who die in Nigeria with great suspicion. That's why we have decided to let a few die in this part of the world for a change.'

And his partner added: 'We'll be doing more business with you … as our special insurance consultant. We're going to have people dying in South Africa, Swaziland, and Botswana in future. We won't need to come here every time – we'll just mail you the particulars and you can send us the death certificates.'

When he left the Nigerians Radisene went straight to Lancers Inn to celebrate. He was in a very generous mood, so he bought everyone drinks. He sat with the civil servants, sharing jokes with them and listening to their gossip. They treated the whole controversy with the king and the prime minister as a joke. Some said the three presidents of the neighbouring countries needed to discipline the young king and his soldiers. Others said that the Congress Party government was weak and had distinguished itself by its indecision. The years of exile had taken their toll on Mokhehle, they said, and he was too old and ailing to have a firm grip on the government. His party also was riddled with cliques and rivalries. The pessimists among them said there was no hope for the country whether the Congress Party was restored to power or not.

At eleven the bar closed, and an extremely intoxicated Radisene was dropped home by one of his drinking companions of the evening. Tampololo greeted him with a sarcastic laugh, 'Ha, Mr Mafeteng … or is it Mr Misti … Some people were looking for you. Nigerians.'

'Hello, my Tampi … my beautiful Tampi … We are going to be multimillionaires …' He danced into the house. He tried to embrace Tampololo but she stepped aside, and he fell on the floor. He did not get up again. Tampololo put off the lights and went to bed.

He was woken by the ringing of the telephone. For a moment he was utterly bewildered to find himself lying fully clothed on the floor of his lounge, but a pounding headache gave him a sharp reminder of how he had got there. He looked at his watch. It was ten o'clock. There was no one else in the house. Obviously Tampololo had already left for school, and the nanny had taken the baby to nursery school. The dear heart would have tried to wake him up, but he imagined Tampololo snapping at her, 'Leave him there. You have no business to disturb his beauty sleep.'

The phone kept on ringing in a most irritating manner. He lifted the receiver. It was as heavy as a rock. 'Hello,' he whispered in a hoarse voice.

'Mr Radison,' said his secretary, 'there is a white man here who has been waiting for you since eight. His name is Hindson. He says he needs to see you urgently. He is from the insurance company.'

Radisene washed his face with cold water and drove to the office.

Hindson said he was from the insurance company's head office. 'I have come in response to a complaint by a lawyer, a Mr A.C. Malibu.'

'O yeah?' said Radisene gearing up for a fight. 'What does he want?'

'A short while ago Mr Malibu came to see the directors of our company in Johannesburg,' said Hindson. 'He told us that we had been dealing for years with someone in Maseru who was not qualified to handle insurance claims and was robbing clients of their money. I'm sorry to say that this someone was you. As you know, dealing with someone who is not a qualified lawyer has serious implications for our clients: a client with a complaint will not be able to approach the Law Society, for one thing.

'I must say that we have never had any complaint about you or your dealings with clients. We were very surprised indeed to hear that you had no qualifications. But our investigations showed that you have not been admitted to the high court as a legal practitioner and are not a member of the Law Society. We therefore give you one month to wind up the business you are doing with us. So as not to prejudice our clients we'll honour the claims that are already in the pipeline within this period.'

And Hindson departed.

'Well, girlie,' said Radisene to his secretary, 'it seems we'll have to shut up shop.'

'You don't seem too bothered, sir,' whimpered the secretary, who saw her cushy job flying out of the window.

'Bothered? I'm a winner girl. A.C. can never destroy me. I'll be earning millions in other ways. Don't worry your pretty little head about your job. You'll stay on as my personal secretary.'

The phone rang. It was A.C. 'How was your meeting with the man from head office, Mr Joseph Radison, Insurance Claims Consultant?' he gloated.

Radisene was at a loss for words.

'You know,' A.C. continued, 'I could kick myself that I didn't think of destroying you this way years ago. I knew all along that you were an upstart with no qualifications, yet it never occurred to me to report you. Ah well, you know what they say: better late than never.'

Radisene hung up on him.

The next day Radisene flew back to Ha Samane to fetch his Range
Rover. As he got off the plane Hlong came limping towards him.
'Hey, Radisene,' he said, 'did you hear what happened to Father-
of-the-Daughters?'

'No. What happened?'

'It is terrible! It is terrible!'

'What happened, Ntate Hlong? Is he alright? Is he dead?'

'I advise you to go to his house and find out yourself.'

Radisene feared the worst. He ran as fast as he could to Father-
of-the-Daughters' compound. Several other people were walking
sadly into the compound when he got there, and he joined them.
They passed Mother-of-the-Daughters, who was sitting on the
stoep with her head bent down in sadness. They greeted her
casually and walked into the house. Father-of-the-Daughters was
sitting on a stool. He was relating the story for the umpteenth time,
bound to repeat it every time new people came to console him.

'Mother-of-the-Daughters was attending a meeting of the burial
society at Mother-of-Twins' house. You know that they are organizing a stokvel to raise more funds. So the meeting went on until
it was late.'

'So? What happened?' the people egged him on.

'So, it was late when Mother-of-the-Daughters left the meeting.
She could have asked the boy who now lives at Mother-of-Twins'
house … the boy who used to be our son-in-law … to accompany
her. But he had arrived earlier quite drunk, and said he was going
to sleep. Children of today drink too much. You know this young
man is here … our former son-in-law, I mean … they say he is here
running away from soldiers in the lowlands. I do not know why.
After all, he was a policeman himself …'

'We don't care about your son-in-law, Father-of-the-
Daughters,' people said impatiently. 'We want to know what happened to Mother-of-the-Daughters.'

'Everything was calm when she left Mother-of-Twins' house', said Father-of-the-Daughters tiredly. 'And the stars twinkled brightly, believing that it was a peaceful night.'

'And then what happened, Father-of-the-Daughters?'

'They raped her,' shouted Father-of-the-Daughters. 'The mother of my children was raped!'

Radisene's blood began to boil with anger. Who would do such a dastardly thing to such a kindly old lady? He remembered her sitting on the stoep outside, shoulders stooped in shame, and both men and women passing her as if she did not exist, on their way to sympathize with her husband.

The anguished voice of Father-of-the-Daughters interrupted his thoughts. 'Who could have thought such a thing was possible in this village? We live in a world that has no mercy for a man …'

People went away angry. 'Who could do this to Father-of-the-Daughters?' one man demanded. 'To such an important personality in these parts? A man known far and wide for his generosity and his modesty, even though he's the wealthiest man in the village?'

'Ha Samane is becoming like a lowlands town where people are afraid to walk after sunset,' a woman said bitterly.

Some people suspected Sorry My Darlie. But others said it could not be. His stench, and the flies that did not seem to sleep even at night, would have given him away.

In spite of the urge to herd cattle, or to go and plead at Dikosha's door, Radisene took his Range Rover and drove back to the lowlands.

14. The Trials

Father-of-the-Daughters sat in the gallery and listened attentively to the proceedings of the case. Next to him sat Tampololo. He had tried to dissuade her from coming. 'You may hear things that the ears of a child should not hear,' he said.

'I am not a child, father,' she replied. 'I am a woman.'

Radisene was there too. And Hlong. And Mother-of-Twins. And a few other people from Ha Samane who wanted to hear for themselves how the magistrate would decide the fate of the man who violated Mother-of-the-Daughters. They had ridden their horses to the magistrate court at the district headquarters, which the villagers referred to as 'the camp'. Some got lifts on trucks or in Radisene's Range Rover.

Mother-of-the-Daughters was in the witness box. Her evidence was brief. The prosecutor asked her a few questions about the night of the rape and she answered quietly. But she could not understand why the magistrate, in his own questions to her, seemed to emphasize the fact that when the rape happened she was drunk. She was not drunk, she said. They had had a few drinks, as they usually did at their burial society meetings. But she was not drunk. In any case, she didn't think it mattered whether she was drunk or not. What mattered had been that she was violated.

The magistrate turned to the accused. 'Motsohi,' he said, 'do you wish to cross-examine the witness?'

Trooper Motsohi – for it was none other than that former traffic policeman and son-in-law – declined. 'The old woman has not pointed a finger at me. She said clearly that she could not identify the rapist because his face was hidden under a balaclava.'

The next witness was a young migrant worker. 'I was carousing with Trooper Motsohi on the evening of the rape,' he said. 'We went from shebeen to shebeen drinking beer and looking for good-time women. Motsohi kept telling me that he was physically attracted to Mother-of-the-Daughters. "If I were to get inside her I would never come out again. I would stay in there for ever," he said. I thought he was joking, of course. I didn't imagine that a handsome young man like that could be obsessed with a woman old enough to be his mother.

'The next day when I heard that Mother-of-the-Daughters had been raped I asked Motsohi to his face if he was responsible. At first he said he knew nothing about it. But after a few drinks he boasted about it, and said, "Yes, I did it. If Tampololo won't have me, then I am going to help myself to her mother." '

The migrant had reported the matter to Chief Samane, and Trooper Motsohi was arrested by the men of the village. They drove him in front of the horses to the police post like an animal. He was screaming for his mother and for forgiveness as their whips ate into his flesh.

Trooper Motsohi took the stand in his own defense. He denied everything. 'When Mother-of-the-Daughters was raped I was fast asleep,' he said. But under the heavy cross-examination of the prosecutor he broke down and confessed that indeed he was the culprit. He blamed drunkenness for his behaviour, and asked for the court's forgiveness.

The magistrate, a weasel-faced old man, gave his verdict. 'The accused has committed a rape, which is a hideous crime,' he said. Then he looked benevolently at the gallery, where Mother-of-the-Daughters was sitting. 'But the victim must be flattered that at her advanced age she should be the subject of desire of a handsome young man.'

Mother-of-the-Daughters was outraged. 'I have been violated,' she called out, 'and the court is making light of the matter!'

The magistrate scowled: 'The witness is being contemptuous of this court by addressing it like that from the gallery. However, I will let that pass. The court was only trying to be complimentary. It is obvious to this court that the witness has no sense of humour. `

'As I have already mentioned, rape is a serious crime. But there are mitigating factors that have to be taken into consideration in this case. The victim is an experienced woman who was not a virgin at the time of the crime, and she therefore suffered no serious injury. She was also drunk when the crime was committed. It is well known that drunken women sometimes invite such actions. I therefore sentence the accused to three months' imprisonment suspended for two years.'

The people of Ha Samane gathered outside the court to discuss the sentence. 'You tell me, my child,' lamented Mother-of-the-Daughters to Radisene, 'you are a lawyer … tell me, don't I have the right to drink? Has my own husband, Father-of-the-Daughters, ever complained about my drinking? Is it the law of the land that I must not drink?'

'The magistrate does not know what he is talking about,' Radisene consoled her.

The general feeling was that Motsohi deserved the death sentence, especially because he had raped his own mother-in-law. According to custom it was taboo to touch your mother-in-law. You were not even supposed to shake hands with her. What Motsohi had done was unheard of. But at least he was going to stay in jail for two years. Two years was better than nothing.

'What two years?' asked Radisene.

'We all heard the magistrate sentencing him to two years,' said Father-of-the-Daughters authoritatively.

'You did not hear well, father. Motsohi is a free man. What the sentence means is that he can go free, but for the next two years he must not be found guilty of a similar crime. Otherwise he'll have to serve a three-month sentence.'

The people laughed sarcastically at Radisene's interpretation of the sentence. He might be a lawyer, they said, but this time he did not know what he was talking about. No man who rapes another man's wife like that can go free.

But their derisive laughter died on their lips when they saw Motsohi sauntering past them, and out of the gate. He was as free as the waters of the Black River.

The people of Ha Samane walked quietly away.

Father-of-the-Daughters was dazed. 'It is your fault, child of

Mother-of-Twins. You brought this devil in our midst.'

Radisene did not reply. It was an unfair comment, he thought, for the devil had once been Father-of-the-Daughter's own son-in-law. But he could understand the old man's anguish.

Hlong muttered, 'Perhaps your son-in-law has a much stronger medicine, Father-of-the-Daughters.'

Radisene was glad that the court had adjourned quite early as he planned to visit the site to see how his mansion was coming along. But first he went to the bank to transfer some money to the building contractor's account. The foundations were almost finished and the contractor would need some money to start work on the walls.

An unpleasant surprise awaited him at the bank. 'I'm very sorry, sir,' said the girl behind the counter, 'there is no money in this account.'

He laughed and said, 'You must be making a mistake. Maybe you punched a wrong number on your computer.' He gave her the numbers for his current and his savings accounts.

The girl punched the numbers into the computer again. 'Both these accounts are empty.'

'I want to see the manager,' barked Radisene. 'Now!'

The manager consulted his records. 'These funds have been transferred to Switzerland according to your instructions,' he said.

'What instructions? I never gave such instructions!'

The manager showed Radisene the file. There was a letter authorizing the transfer. It was on Radisene's letterhead and the signature was undoubtedly his. It requested the manager to transfer all the funds in his accounts to Switzerland for the purchase of irrigation equipment for a farm that he intended to start at Ha Samane. It further requested the manager to obtain approval for the transfer urgently from the Central Bank of Lesotho. The letter was accompanied by invoices for the irrigation equipment. 'As you can see,' said the manager, 'I did as I was told.'

Radisene's heart sank. 'My Nigerian friends ...' He remembered that they had asked for his account numbers so that when they had cashed in on the insurance scam they would transfer the money directly into his accounts. They had also asked for one of his letterheads and a specimen signature. They said it was essential for them to have these as they were going to do big business together. He had signed on the letterhead and given it to them.

Radisene was shattered. How could they be so heartless, he asked himself. They had robbed him of his share from the insurance scam. To add insult to injury they had stolen all his money. There was nearly a million rands in those accounts, and they had taken the lot.

That evening Tampololo was on the warpath. She was kicking everything in front of her and blaming Radisene for what had happened to her mother. 'You took that man to Ha Samane to rape my mother,' she screeched.

'You said I should take him there, Tampololo,' said Radisene.

He was worn out. His head was buzzing with his problems. How was he going to pay the builders for the work they had already done? Perhaps he would have to sell his Range Rover. No, he needed that to earn his living. Perhaps he would have to sell the Mercedes Benz. And what was he going to do with the foundations for such a big house. Should he go to the police? How could they help? How would he explain his involvement in a scam to defraud insurance companies in Canada? Perhaps he could alert the insurance company and at least get even with the Nigerians. But how would he know which insurance company it was among the thousands of companies in Canada?

'You are lying, Radisene! You are lying! I didn't ask you to send that man to rape my mother!' Tampololo was shouting in his ear. Her raspy voice grated on his eardrums. But strangely it sounded very distant, as though it was in a dream. It echoed over and over, until it faded away. Yet Tampololo was standing right there next to him, shouting and foaming at the mouth. He could not hear a word. He just saw her lips moving, and her eyes bulging.

Finally his voice came back. He pleaded, 'Please, Tampololo, don't shout at me.I have lost all my money. The Nigerians have stolen it all.'

He told her what had happened.

'How could you get involved with Nigerians?' she asked. 'You know very well that they are all crooks!'

He felt bitter towards the two Nigerian crooks who had robbed him dry, but he was not going to let Tampololo paint the whole nation with the same brush. In their happier moments they had often discussed prejudice and the dangers of generalizing about a people. He told her so.

She sneered, 'Isn't it generous of you to defend them when they have stolen every cent you own? Stupidly generous! You know very well that they are drug peddlers.'

'Indeed!' said Radisene. 'Wole Soyinka and Chinua Achebe are traffickers. Beautiful people like Buchi Emecheta and Tess Onwueme are drug queens!'

'You can be as facetious as you like, Radisene, but you know that every day in airports around the world Nigerians are arrested for smuggling drugs. How many South African beauty queens and models are in jail in Thailand for smuggling drugs on behalf of their Nigerian boyfriends? Only last night when we were watching the news the Gauteng premier, Tokyo Sexwale, was complaining about the problems that the Nigerian drug barons are causing his province ...'

'And that makes every Nigerian a drug trafficker?'

'Obviously not every Nigerian is a crook. But those who do take up crime as a career become the best criminals in the world. They are ingenious. Just last week on *60 Minutes* there was a story about a Nigerian who operated in his basement in New York ... or was it Connecticut? ... and traded in stocks and shares worth billions of dollars, with nothing to his name but a telephone and a computer.'

She had turned from a tormentor into a civilized debater. That was Tampololo. Shouting one moment and discussing issues reasonably the next. Screeching like a bird of prey ready for the kill, then purring like a pussy-cat. The problem was that one never knew when she was going to be in what mood.

'What are you going to do?' she asked.

'I don't know. But I'm a fighter. I wont' give up.'

He was surprised at his own coolness. He should have been a burbling lunatic by now. Losing a million like that would make any man mad. He hoped it was not the calm before the storm.

The following day he stayed at home. He was in bed most of the time, contemplating what to do next. It was December and soon he would be required to pay his secretary's salary. And the office rent. But the salary was the most important thing. How would he manage to pay?

In the evening he sat in the kitchen as Tampololo cooked the evening meal. Between checking the pots she was feeding the baby, who was playing on the floor, and they were both laughing and chasing each other around the chairs. Radisene was lost in his thoughts about money.

Suddenly the room was full of smoke. She rushed to the stove and pulled the pot from the plate, but it was too late. The food was charred. She kicked the baby, 'It's your fault that the food is burnt! No one else around here is willing to feed you when I'm busy!'

That was another problem with Tampololo. She burnt everything she cooked, and when that happened she became angry with everyone. Most times Radisene preferred to cook his own food.

Radisene picked up the screaming baby from the floor. 'You are going to kill this child, Tampololo!'

'Bring back my baby, you useless thing!'

They struggled over the child, until Tampololo sank her teeth into Radisene's cheek, to make him let go. She locked herself and the baby in the bedroom. That night Radisene slept in the guest-room.

The next morning Tampololo packed her suitcase and left. 'I'm going home to Ha Samane to spend Christmas with my raped parents and my fatherless baby. I'll see you when I come back in the new year. Have a merry Christmas.'

He offered to take her to the airport. She thanked him for the offer, and said she had already called a taxi. Then she was gone.

He was alone. He was free at last – at least until the new year.

He went into the bedroom. Tampololo's stuffed animals were all over the place as usual. How he hated those fluffy teddy bears. He found them embarrassing, especially when Tampololo wanted to be driven around in town hugging a big teddy bear in the back seat of his car. She liked to take her dolls everywhere she went. He remembered that it was the teddy bears that had first attracted him to her, that day in the CNA. How strange that those were the very things he had ended up hating about her.

Like her laughter, which he found so irritating. At first he thought her husky voice was very sexy, but now he found it annoying. She sounded like a man who was trying to talk like a woman. In the CNA that day her smile had been so sensual and her demeanor so regal, that he had instantly fallen in love with her. Now that smile amounted to a sneer, and her demeanor was downright rude.

Radisene opened the wardrobe to look for his Sales House suit, which he had for more than twenty years now. He had not seen it for quite some time. Maybe that was why he was having a run of bad luck. He needed to touch it to change his fortunes.

That suit was not in the wardrobe. He looked everywhere for it, but couldn't find it. He was becoming frantic. He went to the servants' quarters behind the house to look for nanny. Maybe she would know where his suit was. 'Oh, that old suit,' she said, 'Tampololo said it was of no use any more because it was old-fashioned. She shredded it and made a mopping cloth with it. Here are some of the pieces.'

Radisene was devastated. Somewhere at the back of his mind he began to wonder if things would ever go right for him again.

He decided to take a walk in the streets of Florida and breathe some fresh air. He saw beautiful women in the street. How sweet they seemed to be. It would be nice to strike up a conversation with one of them, which might develop into a friendship, which might develop into a relationship. But suddenly he was struck with stark terror. What if there was a Tampololo lurking inside the sweet exterior?

And why were the women staring at him so strangely and giggling? Was his fly open perhaps? He looked and to his consternation realized that he was still wearing his pyjamas. He hurried home.

As he went he heard people talking about him. A woman leaning over a fence said, 'It is because Tampololo left him. Men are useless. A woman leaves for one day, and he can't even dress himself.'

And her neighbour on the other side of the fence replied: 'Tampololo was bound to leave him one day. She is such a sweet woman. A kind woman. But look at him. It is all his fault that their relationship broke down. Men never appreciate a good woman until she is gone.'

Radisene had the urge to answer them. But that would only reinforce their notion that he had gone mad. Instead he muttered to himself, 'We live in an age when a woman can do no wrong. When things go badly in a relationship people automatically take her side. She is the innocent party. It's payback time for all the centuries of oppression women have suffered. A woman is no longer a human being with human flaws.'

He chuckled, remembering how Tampololo used to beat up Trooper Motsohi in Mafeteng. Then the women of Ha Ramokhele would say it served him right, because men had been abusing women for centuries.

Three uneventful days passed, the tedium broken only by his secretary who kept on phoning for her salary. 'How will I spend Christmas without money?' she kept on asking.

'Be patient,' he pleaded. 'I'll work something out.'

'But it's only four days before Christmas.'

'I told you I have problems. I am trying to sell my Mercedes.

He screamed and hollered and said that he was sorry and that he had actually come to apologise and make amends in whatever possible way. But the women were in no mood to listen to his pleas. Tampololo suggested, 'Let's cut the very thing that causes his wildness!' But the other women recoiled at the thought. They beat him senseless and stabbed him instead.

'He is in hospital at the camp right now.' said Father-of-the-Daughters. 'They want to transfer him to the big hospital in Maseru. They say he might not live.'

'Let's hope he doesn't die. Otherwise those women have had it. The prosecution will push for premeditated murder, and that's a capital offense.'

Father-of-the-Daughters did not understand what Radisene was talking about, because he said those words in English.

'How's my baby?' asked Radisene.

'She is fine. She is with one of my daughters.'

That evening they drove to Ha Samane.

I'll give you all your money … and money for notice too. Plea:
bear with me.'

He heard the secretary sniffle, and he hung up.

The next day he received a surprise visit from Father-of-the
Daughters. Radisene knew that something was wrong. A mountaii
man did not leave his family just before Christmas to pay a friendly visit to a discredited pseudo-son-in-law.

'Your hair is greying all of a sudden, son, and you have tooth-
marks on your cheek,' observed Father-of-the-Daughters.

'It is because of the problems of the world. How are Tampololo
and the baby?'

'Fine. The baby is fine. How are things with the government
these days?'

'A bit quiet. You know that the young king's rebel government
only lasted for two or three weeks. The world – especially the three
neighbouring presidents – persuaded him to restore Mokhehle's
government.'

'Yes, I know all that. It is old news.'

'Well, in return Mokhehle has agreed to consider returning the
king's father, Moshoeshoe the Second, to his rightful throne. So
now we are waiting to see what will develop from there. But you
didn't come here to talk about the problems of the government.
What has happened, father?'

'We need you to come to the village immediately. You are a
lawyer. You will know what to do.'

'But what is it, father?'

'Tampololo, Mother-of-Twins and Mother-of-the-Daughters ar
all in jail at the camp.'

Radisene got the story out of the old man in bits and piece
Trooper Motsohi had gone back to Ha Samane to apologize
Father-of-the-Daughters for what he had done to his wife. B
Father-of-the-Daughters was not home at the time. To his misfc
tune Trooper Motsohi found the three women sitting on the sto
peeling peaches for canning. As soon as they saw him they f
upon him, waving the knives they were using to peel the peach

15. Marwana Ants and Marie Biscuits

Some people of the village cultivated dagga. They planted it in the middle of the fields and surrounded it with maize so that the police would not see it. Expert cultivators of dagga were able to hide it so that even the sharp eyes of the police helicopters saw only maize when they hovered over the fields in search of the illegal plant.

They harvested the dagga in the middle of the night. Then they stuffed it into jute bags, loaded it onto the donkeys and took it to a prearranged spot, where traders from the lowlands paid a good price for each bag. They in turn sold it to Cape Town dealers who came in flashy cars.

Sometimes mounted police came to the village in search of cattle rustlers and horse thieves. If your neighbour hated you and had a grudge against you, he would whisper to the police about the dagga in your field. Depending on who they were, the police might demand a bribe from you and then leave your field alone. Sometimes, however, honest policemen came and burnt the whole field of dagga. Invariably the wind would blow the smoke towards the village, and everyone who breathed it would get stoned.

It was on one such day – on Christmas Day too, for the good men of the law did not rest even on the Lord's own birthday – that a dishevelled Radisene arrived in Ha Samane. He had left Father-of-the-Daughters sitting forlornly outside the prison gates at the camp. He had been sitting there for three days, hoping that the prison authorities would be merciful and release the women to spend Christmas at home. Radisene had taken him to lawyers, but they said nothing could be done about bail until the new year, since all the magistrates were already on holiday.

For the first two days Radisene sat with the old man, mainly because he could not think of anything better to do. As he sat there, contemplating his future, it struck him that the insurance company had given him a month's reprieve to wind up his business. He had almost a month to lodge at least one big claim ... maybe more. That would give him the money he needed to start a small business. Perhaps a café at Ha Samane. Or even a general dealer's store, depending on how much he got from the claim.

He decided that, no matter what it cost, he was going to drive back to the lowlands. He was going to lay his hands on at least one more good accident, even if he had to bribe and grovel. Without saying a word to Father-of-the-Daughters he stood up and left.

Father-of-the-Daughters remained sitting outside the prison gates. He vowed that he was going to squat there until they released the women.

When Radisene arrived at Ha Samane people were sitting around outside their houses, laughing and giggling. Old grandmothers and grandfathers were roaring with laughter. Peals of laughter came even from little children. Everywhere people were clutching their aching ribs and gasping for breath.

'What are you laughing at?' asked Radisene.

Instead of answering him they burst out in new gales of laughter. He was angry, for he thought they were laughing at his misfortunes. He had never imagined that their hatred for him was so deep. Was it because of what they claimed he had done to the grandmothers? He walked away, feeling a little giddy.

After all that laughter people of the village became very hungry. They ate pots and pots of food. Then they dozed off wherever they were sitting.

At that moment Dikosha was sitting in her rondavel playing with the darkness. The door and the windows were firmly closed, so the smoke of dagga had not affected her. She was the only person in the village who was still awake – except for Radisene who had arrived after the best of the smoke had already wafted away.

Dikosha had spent Christmas morning hearing confessions. These were busy times for confessions, for many of the men who worked in the mines were home for the holidays. Some men had come from towns in the lowlands. They all had such a strong urge to confess that they went to her house even before going to their wives and children.

Strangers came to confess too, such as the truck-drivers who delivered food at Staff Nurse Mary's clinic, or drove project and government vehicles. Of late they seemed to monopolize her services. She preferred them, because they came with strange and exotic confessions from far-away places. Often they spent the whole night confessing, whereas the locals confessed only for a few hours and then went back to their families with clear consciences.

Sorry My Darlie had taken his fair share of the smoke, and was dozing on Dikosha's stoep. His flies were stoned as well, and were taking a nap on the lower part of his supine body. Radisene almost tripped over him as he knocked at her door.

Dikosha knew who it was, and so she ignored the knock. Because she was a child of the head of the ancestors, she felt it in her bones that something terrible was going to happen to her.

'Open up, Dikosha! I am sick and tired of your nonsense!'

But she did not respond. She clutched tightly at the darkness, hoping it would protect her.

'Dikosha! Things are bad out here! Our mother is in jail! Open up! I am in trouble, Dikosha! I've got to talk with you!'

Still she did not open.

Radisene kicked the door and hurled his whole body against it. The door gave in with a splintery crack and he fell into the house on top of it. As light flooded into the room, Dikosha cowered away in fear. She was shaking life a leaf. 'What do you want with me, Radisene?' she asked in a quivering voice.

'Is that how you greet me after all these years?'

He stood up and took a look at her.

'You haven't grown old, Dikosha!' he gasped. 'And you are still wearing the red dress I bought you!'

'I told you it would last for the rest of my life.'

'I am going to take you away with me.'

'Take me where? Please, Radisene, leave me alone. I cannot go away from here. I have work to do.'

'You are coming with me, Dikosha. I have tolerated your non-sense for long enough. I don't care if you wail like a banshee. I am taking you with me.'

She could only repeat, 'Please, Radisene ... please ...' But when she saw that he was determined to have his way she begged that she be allowed at least to take Shana's sekgankula with her.

'You can't even play the damn thing!' shouted Radisene.

She clung to the instrument for dear life, as if it would protect her.

People of the village were still dozing when he forced her into the Range Rover. No one saw him driving away with her.

Dikosha was silent throughout the journey. Only her fingers were busy playing with the eggshell beads that she had been given by the people of the cave. Once he bought her food at a roadside café, but she refused to eat it. They arrived in Maseru the next day.

Radisene spent the whole of Boxing Day sniffing out accidents, with Dikosha beside him all the time. She did not speak. She did not make a single comment about the wonders of Maseru, although she had never been to the city before. She seemed not to see anything around her, nor to care for anything except her sekgankula, which she was holding tightly to herself.

He stopped at restaurants and bought himself fish and chips or a cup of coffee, so that he could ask the waitresses about accidents they might have heard about. And he stopped once at a petrol station in Ha Hoohlo, just across the road from Florida. The attendant, from whom he bought petrol almost every day, by way of making friendly conversation asked, 'Where are you going with your daughter ... or is it your granddaughter?'

Radisene looked at himself in the rear-view mirror. He had changed beyond recognition. His face was gaunt. He looked like a battered old man. His hair had gone completely white, and the perm made it look as if it belonged on the head of some malnourished old white man. He still permed his hair, even though the fashion had died out long ago.

As usual, the Christmas season provided a bumper crop of accidents. Buses, taxis, cars, trucks ... all were involved in an orgy of self-destruction. Many human beings died in the process. Because death was in abundance, Radisene knew that his competitors, now limited only to legitimate law firms, would concentrate on the easy money in the vicinity of Maseru and other lowland towns. It would be senseless for them to attend to accidents in far away districts such as Quthing or Qacha's Nek, when deaths in Maseru and near-by districts were plentiful. He decided that he would drive to Quthing. The chances were that he would find some clients there who had not been spoken for.

At a roadside stall on the road to Quthing he heard that there had been a really good accident on Christmas eve at the Seaka Bridge on the Senqu River. The Senqu divided the districts of Mohale's Hoek and Quthing. He immediately drove there.

Some boys playing in the river below the bridge told him that one of the men who had died in the accident was from Ketane Ha Nohana, deep in the mountains of Mohale's Hoek. It was most unlikely, Radisene thought, that any lawyer had gone there. They were all busy with easy-to-reach families in the lowlands. He drove to Ketane Ha Nohana. On the way there he kept on repeat-ing, 'I am doing this for us, Dikosha. I am doing this for us.' But Dikosha did not respond. She held even more tightly to her sek-gankula.

They arrived in the village late at night. It was easy to find the home of the dead man. There was a big tent in the yard, and people had gathered for a wake. They were singing hymns and dancing in the tent. From time to time a member of the congrega-tion stood up and preached on a passage from the Bible, or spoke about the good deeds of the deceased.

'You will be at home here, Dikosha,' said Radisene. 'They are dancing.'

But Dikosha did not dance. She cowered in some corner. Radisene joined the congregation, thumping on the emergency Bible that he carried in his car for such occasions. After a few people had preached and a few hymns had been sung, he took the floor.

'Hallelujah!' he shouted.

The congregation responded in unison, 'Amen!'

He repeated the hallelujahs three or four times, then said, 'Brothers and sisters, fathers and mothers, let us praise the Lord for his merciful ways ... Amen! Hallelujah! ... We are gathered here at this wake tonight to mourn for our brother who left us so unexpectedly. But we are gathered here also to praise the Lord. Amen!

'Our brother was taken from us by a stroke of misfortune. He was in a taxi on his way to see his family. He was from the mines, where he worked hard for them, digging gold from the bowels of the earth. Amen!'

Somebody whispered that their deceased brother had never worked in a gold mine in all his life. He worked at a coal mine in Natal. Radisene went on undeterred.

'Then all of a sudden the taxi collided with another vehicle, and unfortunately our brother here was one of those who lost their lives. Amen!'

The taxi did not collide with another vehicle, whispered the spoilsport. It hit the iron railings of the bridge and plunged into the river.

'I say to you children of this home: be consoled. The ways of the Lord are wonderful and bountiful. Do not cry, for our brother has gone to join his maker. Amen! Hallelujah! God wanted him by his side. In his infinite wisdom, he merely used the hand of that taxi-driver to take the life of our brother, so that he could join the Lord at his right-hand side.'

He took the third-party insurance forms from his pocket, and brandished them.

'But the Lord, my brothers and sisters, is both merciful and bountiful. He has not forgotten those who remain on earth – the widow and the children of our dead brother here. He has catered for them through what is known as third-party insurance. Amen! That is why I am here, my brothers and sisters – to see to it that this family is taken care of in its hour of need. I am the hand that the good Lord uses to alleviate your pain and suffering. Amen! Hallelujah!'

Then he sang the hymn 'Peace, Perfect Peace', and the congregation joined him and danced around, thumping their bibles. Throughout the night people sang, danced and preached.

In the morning Radisene asked to be taken to the mourning-room, to talk with the widow of the deceased. He asked Dikosha to come with him, but she chose to remain outside with her sekgankula. People looked at her curiously. They did not understand what a sekgankula was going at a funeral. Moreover, girls were not known to play the instrument.

The widow sat on a mattress in a rondavel that did not have any furniture. She had a shawl over her shoulders and her face was almost covered by a black doek. She was surrounded by four fat women who sat on a grass mat next to her. They were relatives who were accompanying her in the mourning.

'I came about the sadness that has befallen this house, mother,' said Radisene. The widow did not respond, so he went on, 'I came all the way from Maseru to be of assistance to you, mother.'

'What assistance, father?' asked one of the women.

'Your husband died a terrible death in a road accident. It is my work to know about these things. I help the nation to get compensation from the third-party insurance when God has taken their loved ones through motor-vehicle accidents.'

Another woman asked, 'How do you help them?'

'I show them how to claim and how much. It's usually many thousands of rands. You see I have the forms here. All you do is just sign here and leave everything to me. That is all. Just sign the form. If you do not know how to write, just put your thumbprint. I do all the work and you don't pay a cent for it.'

The widow finally spoke. She did not address herself to Radisene, but to one of the women. She said, 'Ask him why a stranger would want to help us without charging a cent for his services.'

'Because I am a good Samaritan, mother,' Radisene put in, 'and

I believe in the Bible. Why else would I come all the way from Maseru and drive on these dangerous mountain roads at night? The Bible says …'

'Never mind what the Bible says.' the widow interrupted him.

'Okay then, let us talk about the forms.'

'We are in mourning here, father,' said the widow. 'We do not want to talk about any forms.'

'I understand that,' said Radisene, becoming desperate, 'but it is very important for you to sign these forms.'

'It is important for you, not for me. I will not sign any forms. It is against my religious convictions to claim compensation from insurance companies.'

'That's ridiculous!' shouted Radisene. He saw his general dealer's store at Ha Samane slipping away. 'I have never heard of such religious beliefs before!'

'You must leave now, please,' said one of the fat women.

But Radisene was becoming hysterical. 'I will not leave until you sign these forms!' he shouted. 'Do you think I am going to waste my time and petrol coming all this way for nothing?'

A man came and dragged Radisene out, kicking his legs and struggling frantically to free himself. The man sent Radisene sprawling and said, 'You have no respect for the mourning-room. You are lucky that there is a death in this family. Otherwise I would be cracking your skull with my knobkerrie!'

Radisene stood up and looked for Dikosha. She was crouching next to the door of the mourning-room. He pulled her to her feet and dragged her up a hill behind the homestead. All the while he was screaming, 'That bloody widow is lying. How can she do this to me? How can she? How can she?'

'Where are you taking me?' asked Dikosha.

They climbed to the top of the hill. Radisene saw people coming and going at the mourning-room below, and his Range Rover parked on a path beyond the homestead, where, as far as he was concerned, it was going to remain for ever. They sat down on the rocks next to some chichi bushes. They did not move even when the red marwana ants rushed from their holes to nibble at their legs.

They sat in a limbo. Darkness fell. Clouds gathered.

'I want to go home, Radisene,' moaned Dikosha.

'Home!' Radisene laughed hysterically. 'Do you know where home is from here? Can you fly like a bird?'

'Take me back, please. I have confessions to hear.'

'Has it ever occurred to you that I also might have confessions to make?'

Dikosha was alarmed. 'No,' she whimpered, 'you can't confess to me. You are my brother. We are from the same womb.'

'Why did you refuse to see me for more than twenty years if I am your brother?' he asked. Then he added, with all the viciousness he could muster in his voice, 'No. You are not my sister. You merely visited my mother's womb. You are the child of the night dance!'

After this they were silent for many hours, until dawn came. Down in the valley people were beginning to make fires outside, preparing to cook for those who would be going to the fields to hoe. There were no holidays in the villages of the land. Even during the festive season the crops had to be tended. Just as the dead had to be buried.

The smoke of the chichi wood wafted to the top of the hill, and invaded Radisene's refuge. He remembered Nkgono. He remembered himself as a little boy. Early in the morning he used to smell the smoke of the chichi wood soaked in her dress. He knew that she was hovering over him where he slept on the floor, perhaps getting the enamel plates from the wall rack. He would open his eyes slowly and look at her cracked foot next to his head. He would look up her striped flannel petticoat, and be struck by the fear of going blind.

'Do you remember Nkgono, Dikosha?' asked Radisene, with nostalgia in his voice.

'I didn't kill her!' Dikosha clung to the stem of the sekgankula as if it were a cuddly teddy bear or a security blanket.

Radisene laughed. Thunder joined his laughter.

'What's going to become of us, Radisene?'

'I don't know. We'll sit here for ever; until the marwana ants finish us.'

Then it rained. A relentless downpour. It drenched them to the marrow of their bones. Radisene wondered whether somewhere in the camp of a distant mountain district it was raining on Father-of-the-Daughters also as he sat in his limbo outside the prison gates. Yes, maybe it was raining there too …

Those were the lazy days of summer. Grandma 'Maselina and Sorry My Darlie were in a lazy mood, in keeping with the weather. She decided that they should drink tea, for hot drinks cooled the body. They would drink from new cups, and eat the Marie biscuits that remained from Christmas.

She called Sorry My Darlie into the rondavel and showed him her treasures. Chief among them was an ox-plough. It had been bought for her by her son, Father-of-the-Daughters, when he worked in the mines many years ago … before he became Father-of-the-Daughters, for he was not yet married then. The plough still looked brand-new: it had never been used. She did not want it to get old. All her life she had used a makeshift hoe instead, which only scratched the surface of the ground.

She proudly showed him her crockery. She had bought it when she was still a young woman, when Father-of-the-Daughters was a boy looking after calves. It was stored away in a wooden crate. It too had never been used. 'These cups and plates are for visitors,' she used to say. But somehow the visitors who came were never worthy of the crockery. Once she had insulted a neighbour who was presumptuous enough to try and borrow the cups when she had a feast for the ancestors. 'But today we are going to drink tea in them,' Grandma 'Maselina told Sorry My Darlie. 'With lots and lots of condensed milk.'

They fussed around, boiling water on a Primus stove and making tea. They were like little children playing house.

Then they sat on a bench outside the rondavel and watched a

hen scratching the ground for her brood of chicks. Grandma 'Maselina threw crushed maize to them. They were soon joined by another hen and a cock, which furiously pecked at the maize.

These were Grandma 'Maselina's friends. They slept in the house with her. She said they were just like people. The two hens had fought over the cock, and the hen with the chicks had won. She was always with the cock now. Even when they slept behind the door they were together. The loser spent all her time looking after the chicks that were not even hers.

At dawn the cock would crow and wake Grandma 'Maselina up. It would crow incessantly, until the other cocks of the village responded. It was Grandma 'Maselina's cock that had the honour of waking up Ha Samane every morning.

Sorry My Darlie and Grandma 'Maselina sat quietly for some time, sipping their sweet tea and munching the biscuits. Then the doves descended from the sky and joined the hens at their meal.

'Drive those doves away,' cried Grandma 'Maselina. 'They will finish the food of my hens.'

'What can one do with doves?' asked Sorry My Darlie. 'Anyway, you feed these hens too much.'

'You are right. Let them be. These are the doves of God. Let them eat with my hens.'

'It is true, Grandma. Doves are angels.'